Praise for *Katana:*

"Starts with a bang and never lets up. Prepare yourself for a smart, sassy heroine, and seriously swoony romance... with a little butt-kicking thrown in for good measure. A cracking debut."

—Antony John, author of
the 2011 Schneider Family Book
award-winning *Five Flavors of Dumb*

永遠戦士

KATANA

COLE GIBSEN

flux™
Woodbury, Minnesota

First Edition
First Printing, 2012

Book design by Bob Gaul
Cover design by Adrienne Zimiga
Cover images: Woman © Nikolay Mikhalchenko/Shutterstock Images
Blossom © OriArtiste/Shutterstock Images

Flux, an imprint of Llewellyn Worldwide Ltd.

Library of Congress Cataloging-in-Publication Data
Gibsen, Cole.
Katana / Cole Gibsen.—1st ed.
p. cm.
Summary: When seventeen-year-old Rileigh Martin discovers she may be harboring the spirit of Senshi, a samurai, she is torn between continuing as an ordinary, shoe-loving girl and embracing the warrior inside, with help from a handsome martial arts instructor, Kim.
ISBN 978-0-7387-3040-0
[1. Samurai—Fiction. 2. Martial arts—Fiction. 3. Supernatural—Fiction. 4. Reincarnation—Fiction. 5. Love—Fiction.] I. Title.
PZ7.G339266Kat 2012
[Fic]—dc23

2011035526

Flux
Llewellyn Worldwide Ltd.
2143 Wooddale Drive
Woodbury, MN 55125-2989
www.fluxnow.com

Printed in the United States of America

To Josh,
Who lent me his faith when
I ran out of my own.

1

I stepped outside the department store and felt something squish against my heel where concrete should have been. “Oh no.”

“What’s wrong?” My best friend Quentin shoved the last bit of a soft pretzel into his mouth and passed through the automatic doors, joining me under the mall’s awning. The St. Louis summer night enveloped us like a towel pulled too soon from the dryer, causing beads of sweat to form along my forehead and plaster stray hairs along my cheeks in blond lines.

“You tell me.” Balancing the large box I held, I closed my eyes and lifted my foot. “How bad is it?”

Quentin sucked in a sharp breath, rattling the chain hanging from his pocket. “A big ol’ wad of bubblicious bad.”

Opening my eyes, I dared a look. Sure enough, a line

of gum stretched from my new DC skate shoe to the sidewalk. "Craptastic! These shoes cost seventy dollars." I scraped the bottom of my sneaker against the edge of the sidewalk, but it did little more than turn the pink wad of gum into a black wad of gum. "Maybe I have time to run back inside and grab some napkins?"

As if in answer, the night security guard locked the door behind us.

Groaning, I shifted my grip on the box. "This stupid toaster is ruining my life!"

"I don't think the toaster has it out for you," Quentin said, batting a moth away from his face. "It could be karma. Or it could be your own guilty conscious for trying to kill your mom via a credit card statement." He nodded to the chrome, digital, top-of-the-line monstrosity I'd chosen for my cousin's wedding. "Seriously, two hundred dollars for a toaster? Was that thing even on the gift registry?"

"It's chrome, Q. *Chrome.* How could we show our faces at the wedding with some pathetic stainless steel toaster in hand? People would talk."

He laughed. "*Uh-huh.* Denial isn't just a river in Egypt, you know."

I looked at him and huffed. "Seriously, Dr. Q? Can you lay off the head shrinking just for tonight?"

He shrugged. "I'll try and contain myself."

After several more attempts to scrape the lump off of my heel, I gave up. "Good. Our last day as juniors—we should be celebrating with the rest of our class, not hanging outside the mall while I destroy the cutest pair of skate shoes in existence."

"Relax," Quentin said. "You know the party doesn't *officially* start until we arrive." He looped his arm through mine and we made our way along the sidewalk. We fell into step behind an elderly couple who had been in the checkout line ahead of us.

"Yeah? You wanna know what *does* start?" I said. "Your stupid sister putting the moves on that hot transfer student Whitley Noble because I'm not there to stop her."

Angry heat rushed through my veins as I recalled our earlier run-in with Quentin's twin sister Carly. She had stood fluffing her chocolate-colored hair and puckering freshly glossed lips in the mirror at Clinique's display counter when Quentin and I rounded the corner.

"Rileigh and Q!" she'd said. "Can't wait to see you at the party tonight. If you run late, I'll make sure to tell Whitley '*Hi*' for you." Then she planted two sticky kisses on either side of our faces before dashing off, leaving Quentin and me scrambling for makeup remover and cotton balls.

"Don't worry about Carly." Quentin's voice dissolved the memory. "I don't know what her disorder is, but I'm sure it's hard to pronounce."

Laughing, I shifted the bulky appliance against my hip.

Quentin glanced at the leather cuff on his wrist that was also a watch. "There is one problem, though. By now, the wine coolers have started to work their magic on Carly and her friends. If we don't get there soon, we're not going to witness—and more importantly, make fun of—all of their bad choices. I'll bet you five bucks they're dancing on the tables by eleven."

"You're on! I'm giving them until ten-thirty." I reached into my pocket and engaged my skinny jeans in a game of tug-of-war until I finally pulled the car keys free. Quentin sped into a trot and dragged me behind like a three-legged mule. I struggled to keep up, giggling each time I had to stop to adjust the toaster that slipped lower in my grip with each step.

Hearing our commotion, the older couple in front of us shot us the stink eye as they walked on. The woman was so focused on perfecting her pinched-eye glare that she bumped into a man as he hurried around the corner of the department store.

"Oh!" She clasped her hands as she stepped to the side. "I'm terribly sorry."

I didn't realize that I slowed my pace to stare at the stranger until Quentin huffed impatiently. Something about this man triggered a silent alarm in my head, like when I walked past the alligators at the zoo and felt their hungry eyes upon me; only this time there was no protective glass.

The stranger frowned. He was a little man with tanned skin and dirty brown hair that hung loosely over his face. His long pointy nose and bucked teeth reminded me of a weasel. He mumbled something I couldn't hear from where I stood.

The elderly man straightened and the woman took a step backward.

"Come on, Ri-Ri." Quentin tugged my arm.

Weasel screamed, "I said give me your purse!"

Fear tore the breath from my throat in a gasp and Quentin went rigid at my side, his fingers digging deep into my arm.

With a shaking hand, the woman tried to slip her purse off her shoulder, but Weasel snatched it before she was through. The white strap tightened around her wrist and she was jerked forward.

We watched, not daring to breathe, as she fell to the ground.

Cursing, Weasel tugged on the purse again, and this time the thin leather strap broke, freeing the old woman. Weasel tucked his prize under his arm and ran down the sidewalk in our direction.

I could feel my arm bruising under Quentin's iron grip as we stood paralyzed. I begged my legs to move, my lungs to breathe, but my body wouldn't listen.

Weasel drew closer.

Realizing that our chance to run had passed, I hugged the toaster against my body and closed my eyes. The soft thud of the mugger's footsteps tied themselves to the beating of my heart until they were a single pulse that locked my jaw tighter with each beat. Quentin pulled me against him so close it seemed I could smell his fear, a bitter scent that lay just below his Polo cologne.

The footsteps were in front of us, yet there was no pause in his stride. Would he run right past us? Or was he going to attack us, too?

Curled around each other, we waited to find out.

A second passed.

Followed by another.

When nothing happened, I cracked open an eye and found Weasel lying on the sidewalk next to me, his face a combination of bewilderment and fury. The purse he had stolen lay neatly on top of the toaster box in my arms. Before I could move, he scrambled to his feet and ran empty-handed out into the parking lot.

I remained frozen, too confused to move. What had happened in the few seconds while I had my eyes closed?

"Ri-Ri?"

I turned to Quentin, who now stood a good two feet away from me. The blood had drained from his face, leaving his skin the same color as his bleached hair. His mouth flapped with questions that wouldn't form. He looked like a possessed nutcracker.

I heard a soft shuffle behind me and turned away from my best friend to find the elderly man helping the woman up off the sidewalk. As she brushed gravel from her sweater, I noticed that her wrist was purple and swollen.

I plucked the purse from the top of the toaster box and walked over to the couple on shaky legs. I held the purse out to her. "Here." My voice was barely a whisper.

The woman's eyes welled with tears as she grabbed on to the broken strap. "Oh, dear." She pressed her lips into a thin line. "Please don't think that I'm not grateful, but that was a foolish thing for you to do. What were you thinking, going after a man like that?"

I shook my head. "What are you talking about?"

The man put an aged hand on my shoulder. "Maybe 'going after' isn't the right way to phrase it. But we saw you trip him. I know you were just trying to help, but you could have been hurt."

That wasn't possible. I remembered standing perfectly still with my eyes closed. I couldn't have tripped the mugger without knowing I did. I shook my head harder. "No, you're wrong. The mugger must have tripped and somehow I caught your purse." My mind raced to make sense of it. "Maybe because it's not very well lit here, you got confused." I looked to Quentin for support.

He shrugged a shoulder. "Maybe . . . "

"Now wait just a minute." The old man held his hands up in surrender. "We're not trying to upset you, honey. We're just worried, that's all. We need to report this, so why don't you two wait with us until we can get the police out here."

"Wait? In the dark, empty parking lot?" I laughed, a high-pitched, nervous sound. "I'm sorry, but there's no way I'm just going to stand here and wait for that guy to come back." Even as I spoke, the shadows around me seemed to grow bigger and darker. I shivered, and it felt like my skin wanted to slide itself free from my body. "Besides . . . I—I don't feel right."

"Are you hurt?" Quentin asked.

"No." But I wasn't okay, either. I tried to find the words to tell him what was wrong, but I didn't know how to explain. A strange feeling pressed against me—like static in the air before a thunderstorm. It was a familiar feeling, almost *déjà vu.* I tried to place it, but the more I reached, the faster it sank into the recess of my mind.

Swallowing took more effort than it should have. "Q, I'm out." I shot him a questioning glance as I began my backward retreat. "You with me?"

The old man said, "I don't think you should go anywhere just yet."

I refused to look at him. "Q?"

Quentin glanced from me to the old couple and back to me. He huffed. "Let's go."

Without waiting for him to catch up, I turned and ran as fast as I could, which wasn't that fast considering the jeans I wore were meant to show the curves of my legs, not allow them to bend. By the time I rounded the second corner of the mall, my arms burned from carrying the toaster, but I spotted my blue Ford Fiesta. Relief deflated the tension that had ballooned inside of me. I'd never thought I'd see the day when I couldn't get away from the mall fast enough.

When I reached my car, Quentin skidded to a panting halt at my side. "If the toaster relay was an Olympic sport, you'd get the gold."

I ignored him as I sorted the keys in my hand, looking for the one that would open the door.

"Ri-Ri?" Concern wrapped around his words, making them thick like syrup. "Maybe we should hold off on the party. It couldn't hurt to talk to the police."

Was he crazy? "Actually it would hurt quite a bit if that guy came back and murdered us while we waited."

Quentin opened his mouth to reply, but was interrupted by a soft chuckling.

"What's this—you're talking about me?"

We wheeled around in the direction of the voice. From the side of a rusted conversion van, out stepped Weasel.

2

No one ever said that life was fair.

Maybe if I'd had more time, I could have figured myself out. But now, with my potential death a parking spot away, I realized I was nothing more than a jagged puzzle piece in a world of smooth edges. I had no place, no purpose. If Quentin died, his death would be a tragedy. I knew he'd make a great therapist someday, and the world would suffer from the loss. But me… I tried to think how my death would affect anything and came up blank. My list of aspirations ended just past getting more air on the ramps at the skate park and graduating high school.

Weasel took a step forward. I dropped the toaster and thought my heart might join the box on the warm asphalt. Blood rushed through my head, beating against my temples and drawing beads of sweat onto my forehead. I licked my dry lips.

"Rileigh, get behind me." Quentin pushed me roughly against my car and stepped in front of me. He stared at Weasel. "Listen up, you can have my wallet." He pulled it out of his back pocket, unclipped the chain, and threw it on the ground at Weasel's feet. "Now get the hell out of here."

Weasel folded his arms as a smirk spread across his face. "Whaddya know, the queer's got balls."

Quentin stiffened, but said nothing.

I peeked around his shoulder. "You got his wallet, now go away. Go away, or I'll . . . " I cringed inwardly as I left the unfinished sentence floating in the air. Or I'll what? Throw a gigantic toaster at you? The man in front of me was not a piece of bread.

Weasel chuckled again and walked toward us.

"Don't come any closer," Quentin said, his voice wavering.

"Like this?" Weasel kept walking until he was directly in front of Quentin.

Quentin took a step back with his arms held wide, plastering me against the driver's side window. "What do you want?"

"Payback." Weasel balled a fist into Quentin's shirt collar and yanked him forward.

Quentin thrust out his arm and wedged it against Weasel's chest—but it didn't pry him far enough apart. Weasel's other arm reached back, his fist quivering in the air for just a second before striking out and connecting with Quentin's temple. Quentin spun like a drunken ballerina in an awkward circle before he crumpled to the ground.

I finished a scream I hadn't realized I began and dropped to help my unmoving friend.

"Shut up!" Weasel grabbed me by the back of my tank top and threw me against my car. The fiberglass popped inward from my hip and I tumbled to the ground in a heap.

Weasel smiled, exposing long, gray teeth. "She's alone," he called over his shoulder.

Two men emerged from behind the same van and joined Weasel. They looked alike—their skin was the same caramel color and their hair the same ash brown. Their eyes hung back in their skulls, casting dark shadows underneath. They had to be brothers. The younger one, who looked my age, seemed afraid.

My hair fluttered from a breeze that swirled around me. It seemed to rise from the very spot where I sat. I shivered as I inched my way back to my feet, using my fingers against the car door to guide me.

A very tiny voice in my head, one that I didn't even know existed, spoke up for the first time: *The young one will go down with the least resistance.* It was barely a whisper, like a mother hushing a crying baby. The words brushed across my mind like icy fingertips and raised the hair on the back of my neck.

Fantastic. As if the night weren't bad enough, now I was hearing voices inside my head. The car keys that I'd managed to hang on to until this moment slipped from my hand and fell on top of the toaster. The soft pretzel rolling in my stomach felt like it would soon join them.

The older thug—possibly in his late twenties—snarled at me. His features were harder than his brother's, with scowl lines etched deep into his skin. "Stupid kid," he said. "Whaddya think? You're gonna stop a snatch and save the day?" He took another angry step toward me. "I think you're going to pay for not minding your own business."

My legs trembled and I tried to work up another scream, but my voice caught in my throat like a knotted balloon.

"Now wait just a minute," Weasel said, stepping in front of him. "There are plenty of ways to teach her a lesson, and I'm more interested in the ways that are fun for us."

Younger brother's eyes bulged while his older brother smiled.

A whimper escaped my throat. I sucked my bottom lip into my mouth to keep the flood of other pathetic sounds from falling out. I was dangerously close to spilling the warm tears collecting in my eyes when the breeze returned, lifting my hair and swirling through my fingers. *For that last remark, we hurt Weasel first.*

What? Hurt Weasel? That didn't make any sense. But then again, it was a voice in my head that said it, so why should it make sense? I rubbed two fingers against my temple.

"Um, guys … "

I looked up, surprised to find it was the younger brother who had spoken.

"I think we should go. Somebody might show up and … I think there's something wrong with her." He whispered the last part, as if worried it might upset me.

"Nah." Weasel pushed the younger brother back. "We're not going anywhere."

His smile made my skin crawl. I couldn't decide which I wanted to do more—pass out or throw up.

Weasel cocked his head to the side. "Don't you worry, baby doll. You just might like it."

This couldn't be happening. Surely there was a security guard patrolling the lot nearby who could put a stop to this. I took a deep breath, ready for the scream I'd been waiting for to finally come out.

But instead, I opened my mouth and said, "You're right. I am going to like this." My eyes flew wide and I took a step back. I hadn't meant to say anything. I sucked in another breath and tried screaming again; only, like before, words replaced my cry. "It's been a long time, and I've been itching for a good fight." Wide-eyed, I clamped both hands over my mouth before I could say more.

Weasel's mouth dropped open.

"See," the younger brother whispered. "I told you something's wrong with her."

"She's screwing with us," the older brother said, but his eyes danced nervously between me and Weasel. "She thinks she's a badass."

Me? Badass? That word and I didn't even exist on

the same planet. Skateboarding aside, I was obsessed with strawberry lip gloss and adding to my stuffed animal collection, and my idea of manual labor was washing the dishes by hand when the dishwasher was broken. Badass … I would have found it funny if I wasn't so terrified.

Weasel snorted. "You think you're a badass?"

I wanted to shake my head, but my neck refused to cooperate. I could only stare back.

"Sure she does," the older brother said with a frown. "Look at her just staring at us like that."

Weasel spit on the ground next to my shoe, which I'm sure had been his target. "So Little-Miss-Barbie-Badass, you're itching for a fight, and I'm itching for something else. Let's see if we can help each other out." He moved toward me.

My stomach lurched and I felt sure that throwing up had won the battle over passing out. He was almost upon me, mere inches separating his cigarette-stained fingers from my bare arm, when it happened.

A tight pressure squeezed the inside of my chest, like firm hands holding a struggling rabbit. It enveloped my heart and forced it to return to its regular beat. Next, like silk sliding beneath my skin, I felt myself being tried on like a suit. I stretched my arms, flexed my fingers, and rocked back on my heels, only it wasn't me doing those things.

I braced myself for the wave of terror that was sure

to wash over me, but it never came. Instead, a smile that didn't belong to me pulled at my lips.

"Rich!" the younger brother warned, but it was too late.

I dodged to the side, just beyond the reach of Rich's grasping hand. As he moved past me, I hooked my right arm around his outstretched limb, pulling it behind his back and bending him over. Before I could stop myself I struck his extended elbow with my left hand, shattering the bone.

He screamed and dropped to the ground, landing on the toaster. He rolled off the crumpled box, cursing me as he cradled his forearm that dangled in unnatural angles.

Oh, gross. From far away, I felt the stirrings of nausea, but just as quickly a warm pressure wrapped around my stomach and the feeling left. I couldn't be certain, but I was pretty sure I was still smiling.

The older brother, his face drained of color, jumped back from the groaning man. He looked up at me with red veins webbed across his protruding eyes. "You're gonna die!" he screamed. Flecks of spit foamed at the corners of his mouth. He reached in his back pocket and pulled out a large switchblade, releasing the blade from the hilt with a click. From deep within the cotton comfort of my brain, I thought I should be concerned about this latest development, but my possessed body didn't flinch.

I saw one of my eyes—large, blue, and serene—reflected in the blade as it fell toward my face. I wondered if everyone felt so at peace right before they died. I closed my eyes and waited for ... I wasn't sure exactly. I hoped it wouldn't hurt.

"Donnie, don't!" the younger brother cried.

I braced myself for the bite of metal, but it never came. Instead, a small wind brushed along my cheek, and I opened my eyes in time to see Donnie's blade miss my face by inches. "You're going to have to be faster than that," I heard my voice taunt.

Donnie cried out, his pulse pounding in his temples. His second strike was a wide-open arc that I ducked with time to spare. "Faster still," my voice teased. I felt my smile grow wider.

Donnie screamed again and charged at me with three rapid stabs.

I ducked to the left. "You missed." And again to the right. "Missed again." The third swing went wide and I spun behind his outreached arm, turned back, and kicked.

I heard a sound like a twig being snapped in two and saw Donnie's blade fly through the air. He was too busy holding his hand to his chest and screaming to notice. More broken bones, and still I felt nothing. For someone who couldn't watch a scary movie without throwing a pillow over her face, I thought I should feel something—horror, fear, disgust—*anything.* My smile twitched.

Careful, the voice whispered inside my head, *the battlefield is no place to lose focus.*

Since when is the mall parking lot a battlefield?

The battlefield is the ground under your enemy's feet, the voice answered.

"Donnie, let's just go," the younger brother pleaded. "She's not worth it."

Donnie snorted in agreement, but his eyes never left my face. The fingers of his good hand slowly curled into a fist.

"Don't." The younger brother's voice cracked.

Donnie nodded his head dismissively at his brother and lunged forward.

The silk that enveloped my body lengthened until it brushed from my fingers to my toes. Time seemed to move in slow motion as I spun to the side of Donnie's fist. I turned to face the back of his body.

Donnie stumbled back around. I dropped to the ground and swept my leg around and through his. He looked confused in the instant when his feet were off the ground, right before his head made a sickening crack against the pavement.

I turned back to face the younger brother, casually flipping my hair over my shoulder as I did. The smile was still in place, but I could taste the beginnings of bile on the back of my tongue.

The younger brother pulled out his own knife, but he didn't handle it nearly as well as his brother. His hand trembled, making the weapon look more like a flopping fish than an instrument of death. "Please," he whispered.

My body stepped forward.

The blood drained from his face, leaving his skin the color of ash. He stepped back. "I don't want to fight you."

"And I didn't want to fight you three," I replied, and

this time the words were my own. "I *wanted* to go to a party tonight and *finally* hook up with this boy I like. It was the end-of-the-school-year party; the entire junior class was invited. It was pretty much my last chance to see this guy until fall." I balled my hands into fists. "Guess we're both out of luck tonight." My nails dug into my palm, sending twinges of pain up my arm. It was wonderful to feel again.

The little brother took another step back. "But it wasn't my idea," he said. "Rich was mad because you messed up his snatch-and-grab. He said he wanted to scare you."

The smile fell from my face. "How would you like *me* to scare *you?*" I took another step closer.

He took two steps back. "You already do," he whispered.

"Good." I stomped at the ground in front of me, and the younger brother dropped his knife and jumped so high I thought for a moment he might pop out of his skin. He twisted in midair and started running in the opposite direction the moment his feet hit the ground.

I turned to check on Quentin, but the voice in my head stopped me. *We must not let our enemy escape,* the voice whispered. *He can't be allowed to harm again.*

I sighed. What was I supposed to do? I was a little over five feet and he had a head start. There was no way I could catch up.

We don't have to, the voice answered. I felt the silk stretch out and brush the inside of my fingertips. Before I knew it, I was bent over and picking up the younger brother's discarded knife. My thumb closed the blade into the metal hilt. My right leg stepped back and my arm rose over my head. I shut my eyes, threw, and didn't open them until after I heard the thud. When I did, the younger brother lay unconscious four parking rows over.

It was done. I should have felt relieved, but the ropes of anxiety twisted tighter around my chest until I thought my ribs would break from the pressure. Now that I was done with the outward threat, the battle had moved inside of me. My muscles strained against the unnatural presence, my breath locked inside my lungs until, inch by painful inch, the warm silk beneath my skin unraveled, leaving my blood cold in its wake. Despite the warm night air, I began to shiver, the trembling growing more violent with each second until I was sure I was having a seizure.

"Rileigh?"

From far away I heard Quentin talking to me, but I couldn't respond. My throat convulsed, and as much as I gasped, I couldn't suck enough air down. I didn't even realize I was on the ground until I saw Quentin leaning over me.

Darkness seeped along the edge of my vision, and I gave in to the weight pulling at my consciousness. I heard the wail of emergency vehicles, but drifted away even as their red and blue lights tumbled and twirled against the black behind my eyelids. I hung there, clinging to the place that teetered between awake and unconscious, before landing somewhere with no colors and sirens, only the comfort of thick, dark silence.

3

Japan, 1493

Senshi jolted upright from her sleeping mat, her startled gasp rousing the man next to her.

Yoshido, accustomed to her premonitions, awoke in an instant and grasped beside him for his sword. "How long do we have?"

"The enemy is almost here," she replied.

He cursed softly as he tied his long black hair into a knot on top of his head. When he finished, he asked, "Are you ready?"

She nodded, biting the insides of her cheeks so her emotions wouldn't betray her. Yoshido had once commented on her inability to smile. He didn't know that it was because she was always biting, trying to swallow the dangerous fear that continued to break her guarded surface.

And there was reason to fear with Japan currently at war with itself. Every land-hungry Shogun was sending his armies to take over the villages of peaceful rulers like Senshi and Yoshido's Lord Toyotomi. As a samurai, Senshi had sworn an oath of blood that she would not let that happen, even if the cost meant her life.

Yoshido stood in the doorway and peered out into the night, the moonlight casting harsh shadows against his angled face. Despite the calm silence, the threat of violence thickened the air like fog. "We should separate. I will go find Zeami, and together we will protect Lord Toyotomi. I need you to go warn the other samurai."

"Of course," Senshi answered. Zeami and Yoshido had trained together since boyhood. Together they were an unstoppable force.

"Good. I urge you to locate the twins first. I worry about tonight; I feel a great evil lurking about."

Senshi understood. The twins were the youngest and had the least battle experience. Yoshido was the leader of their samurai army, and she knew he felt great responsibility for his soldiers.

Senshi moved past him to grab her own sword, but he snatched her by the wrist and pulled her roughly against him. "Senshi, I—"

"No, Yoshido," she interrupted him, pressing her cheek against his chest. Why must he do this before every battle? He would tell her how much he loved her, and how he always would. He would tell her his love would never die, even if this was the battle that ended his life, an outcome she could not fathom.

She placed a finger against his lips. "We have no time for talk. Tonight we fight, just like any other night. And then later, when our lord is safe and our village secure, we will return to each other and all will be well."

Smiling, he gently tilted her chin up toward him and kissed her parted lips. "All will be well," he repeated.

She nodded, reluctant to let him go. He gently pushed her back, giving her one last smile before turning for the door.

Senshi bit down on her cheeks. She knew she had precious minutes left to warn the other samurai, but for the first time, she hesitated. She found herself rooted in place watching Yoshido run, and when the night swallowed the last of him, her heart broke, and she could barely breathe under the weight of despair.

She knew then that she just kissed the man she loved for the last time.

4

"How are we feeling, Rileigh?" A stranger's voice cut through my dream, shattering it like the pieces of a mosaic.

"No!" I opened my eyes and reached for the fleeting image, my heart already aching with a loss I didn't understand. Instead of seeing the black-haired Japanese warrior, I was blinded by a bright light at a very close range.

Jerking back, a man in green scrubs clicked off a pen light and stuffed it into his shirt pocket. "Sorry about that. I should have given you a chance to get adjusted."

I tried to grumble in agreement, but my throat was so dry I could only manage a cough. Once the annoying spots left my field of vision, I tried to figure out where I was. Dusty blinds had been slanted enough to allow thin purple strips of predawn sky to decorate the plain white walls and hospital equipment that lay asleep in the corner.

But that couldn't be right. The last thing I remembered was leaving Macy's with Quentin and the toaster. After that … I wasn't sure.

"You are a very lucky young lady."

I glared at the man leaning over me. He was in his thirties, with brown, curly hair cut short. He looked more like the lead singer in a boy band than a doctor.

"Three men," he continued. "That's quite a feat."

"What are you talking about?" I asked, struggling to form words around the grit in my throat.

Before he could answer, a red-haired nurse with bangs curled so high they defied gravity skidded to a halt just inside my room. Her eyes widened and she smiled. "Dr. Wendell, I didn't know you worked the pediatric wing."

He cleared his throat. "Normally I don't, but I took a special interest in this case." When she didn't move, he narrowed his eyes. "Will there be anything else?"

She took a step back. "No, I, uh … " She looked at me. "I'll check back with you later, sweetie." She turned on her heels and strode from the room.

"Now," Dr. Wendell raised a single eyebrow, "am I to understand you are suffering from memory loss?"

I tried to shrug, but it hurt to move my shoulders. "I remember buying a toaster."

"Which I'm afraid didn't fare as well as you."

I followed his gaze to a gray vinyl chair positioned next to my bed and gasped when I took in the torn box taking up most of the seat. Through the hole I could see my own frightened eyes multiplied by the dent gouged into the chrome.

I curled my fingers around the plastic bedrail to quiet the tremors that shook my body. Images came back to me: Weasel's twisted grin, a knife flashing under the parking lot lights, and the bodies of my attackers hitting the ground. "No. It's impossible." I shook my head, hoping to mute the sound of breaking bones that played on a continuous loop inside my throbbing head.

"Rileigh?" Dr. Wendell leaned in closer and peered into my eyes. "Are you all right?"

My mind raced to make sense of it. There was no way I could have fought off three men by myself. I probed my scalp, my fingers searching for a bump or any sign that I'd hit my head. I couldn't find anything.

"Rileigh?"

I snapped my head up and gave him a seething look. "Of course I'm not okay! Three men tried to kill me last night!" And that's when it hit me—I wasn't the only one attacked. The image of Quentin's face-pirouette seemed to appear from behind a velvet curtain inside my mind. I curled my fingers into my bedsheet as I relived the moment. "Oh my God. Q!" I threw the blanket off of me, but Dr. Wendell placed a hand against my shoulder before I could swing my legs off the mattress. I tried to shake him off. "I have to find him!"

"Your friend is fine—just a little bump on the head." He released my shoulder and patted my hand once, but I snatched it away before he could do it again. "Easy." He took a step back and held his hands in the air. "I'm only trying to help."

I sat back against the pillow. Whether it was intuition, or a side effect from the attack, I was suddenly very aware of the fact that I was in a strange room, alone, with a man who had a "special interest" in my case. Whatever that meant. "You can help by not touching me."

He frowned. "Well, that's going to make an exam difficult." When I didn't answer, he shrugged and reached for my chart. "Okay then. Other than being a little disorientated, how do you feel physically?"

"Are you kidding me with this? You went to med school, right? I was attacked, I'm in the hospital—can't you draw your own conclusions?"

Dr. Wendell coughed into his hand in a failed effort to hide an amused smile. "Sure, I could draw my own conclusions, but that's how malpractice suits are started. I like not getting sued, Rileigh." He moved the toaster from the chair to the floor and sat down. "You don't have to answer my questions now. I can sit here and wait until you're feeling more communicative." He reached for the TV remote clipped to my bed and flipped through several channels. "Look here, Springer."

I ground my teeth together as the title sequence played. I leaned over, ripped the remote from his hand, and turned the TV off just as a toothless man wandered onstage to discuss his secret farm romance. As if I wasn't traumatized enough. "You win." I sighed. "There was this time in junior high when Q's mom made JELL-O shots for her Pampered Chef party and we ate ten before we realized they had alcohol in them. I feel like I did the morning after that happened."

"Mm-hmm," he murmured as he jotted notes down. "That's perfectly normal."

I glared at him as he stood and returned the chart to the foot of my bed. "Normal for who?" I paused to cough. "Reality-show skanks?"

He tucked his pen into his shirt pocket. "The after-effects of shock can feel like a bad hangover. I imagine you're experiencing a headache? Maybe some nausea?"

I pulled the blanket up and closed my eyes. He wasn't kidding. The throbbing in my temples was so powerful, I would swear at any moment the force would push my eyeballs from my skull.

"Can I at least check your pulse?"

I cracked my eyes. "If you make it quick."

He placed two tan fingers on my wrist and counted the beats of my pulse under his breath. "Your vitals are great."

"Then why are you still touching me?"

He let go with a chuckle.

From the hallway I could hear a rapid clacking of high heels as if someone were trying to attempt Morse code via Prada. I groaned. It had to be Debbie. She was the only woman I knew who ran as if her legs were plastic-wrapped together from her thighs to her ankles.

Debbie burst into the room and I tried to sink deeper into the bed to avoid the whirlwind of Oscar de la Renta clothing and Chanel perfume that made up my mother.

She pulled her phone several inches away from her face and said, "My poor baby, you look like hell. I'm going to take care of this. I'm going to hire the best lawyer and—" She flinched and brought the phone back to her ear. "No, no, Marcy. I wasn't talking to you. How would I know what you look like right now?" With a groan she plugged her free ear with her finger and twisted away from me and the slack-mouthed doctor. "It's swimsuit season. If you're that hungry, go suck on a Tic Tac!"

"That's your mother?" Dr. Wendell whispered.

"Debbie Martin; agent extraordinaire," I answered, pinching the bridge of my nose between two fingers.

"Good to know." The doctor, with his eyes never leaving my mother, straightened his scrubs. "Rileigh, would you like me to send in the nurse with something to relieve the pain?"

"Oh, do you have a cure for mothers?"

"I'm sorry?" Dr. Wendell asked.

"I *said*, 'That'd be great.'" I flashed an innocent smile. "I had a headache, but all of a sudden it's so much worse."

Debbie closed her phone with a snap and turned back toward me, wrapping perfectly manicured fingers around my bedrail. From this close, I could see the dark circles around her eyes that concealer failed to hide. "Rileigh, baby." She sighed and her body deflated like a busted water bra. "I want you to know I came as soon as I could. I grabbed the first flight out of LAX."

"It's cool, Mom. You're busy. I get that." And I did. Debbie had done some modeling in her youth, making the transition from print ads to runways at sixteen. But like Debbie always said, fame is fleeting. At seventeen, she found herself preggo with yours truly. With her career over she could have faded into obscurity. Instead, she returned home, finished her degree, and started her own talent agency. She barely scraped a living until she discovered a four-year-old-girl in a McDonalds PlayPlace who went on to become the hottest child actor in Hollywood. I haven't seen my mother for more than a couple of days at a time since.

Debbie opened her mouth, but the words died on her tongue as she turned to Dr. Wendell. "How is my little girl, doctor … ?"

He smiled. "It's Wendell. And your daughter is doing exceptionally well. But, as you can imagine, she's going to need plenty of rest." After a pause, he continued, "In fact, rather than disturb Rileigh further, why don't we continue this conversation in the hall?"

Debbie's acrylic nails clicked softly as they slid away from the rail. "I don't know if that's a good idea. I just got here. I'm sure Rileigh needs her mother right now—"

"Trust me." Dr. Wendell gave a reassuring nod. "Rileigh needs her rest."

If I didn't know better, I'd swear Dr. Wendell winked at me, like he was doing me a favor or something. It didn't earn him any points. I didn't want or need his help.

Debbie frowned, never taking her eyes off my face. "Will you be okay by yourself?"

It was a ridiculous question. Before Nana got sick and

died the previous year, she stayed at the house with me when Debbie went out of town. But now, every couple of days it was me alone with a drawer full of takeout menus. "I'll be fine."

Debbie nodded, though she didn't look convinced.

"You must be exhausted, Mrs. Martin," Dr. Wendell said. "If you like I can show you where you can grab a cup of coffee."

"It's Ms.," Debbie answered automatically.

I thought I saw the trace of a smile on the doctor's lips. "My apologies, Ms. Martin." He held his arm out and gestured for the door. "After you."

Debbie hesitated, studying my face. I closed my eyes, faking exhaustion, until I heard the shuffle of rubber soles move past my bed, followed by the snaps of Debbie's heels.

It wasn't more than five minutes until someone rapped lightly on the door frame. I opened my eyes to discover the red-haired nurse standing in the doorway. "Are you feeling up to a visitor?"

"Do you know who?" I pulled my hair over my shoulder and combed my fingers through the knots.

The nurse shook her head. "He says he's a friend."

Quentin! I smiled and nodded, sending the nurse away. Despite what I'd told Debbie, I wasn't ready to be alone. Without someone to distract me I would be forced to face the memories of last night. It didn't make sense. I should be dead.

My fingers trembled as I pulled apart a tangle of hair. The longer I sat alone in bed, the harder the shadows of last night's memories pressed against me with needle-like claws. The snap of a bone. An agonized cry. A voice of calm detachment directing my next move.

"No." I pressed my palms against my temples, begging the images from last night to stop playing like a horror movie marathon inside my head. I heard the pad of swift footsteps down the hall. Relief drowned the scream that threatened to rip from my throat.

But the relief was short lived. The stranger that strode into my hospital room was definitely not a friend.

5

The Asian guy who entered looked to be only a few years older than me. He wore a blue T-shirt that couldn't hide the solid frame beneath it, and his black hair looked gelled in place strand by strand. "Rileigh Martin?" he asked.

"Yes?" My skin prickled. I stopped combing my hair and threw it behind my shoulder.

His eyes swept over me as if sizing me up. He frowned.

I pulled the thin blanket higher around my chest. "And you are—?"

Before he could answer, Quentin burst through the door like his shoes were on fire. He rushed up to my bedside and flung himself across my lap. "My poor, poor Ri-Ri," he sobbed.

The stranger took a surprised step backward, glancing at me with wide eyes.

I sighed and rubbed the roaring ache under my temples with my fingers. Quentin and I had been friends for so long, I had grown used to his theatrics. Only this time his timing sucked.

Quentin's shoulders heaved and I squirmed under the growing wet spot in the blanket where his tears fell.

"Q," I whispered, nudging his shoulder with my hand.

"I'm a failure as a friend!" he wailed into my lap.

"Q!" I growled between clenched teeth. When he still didn't move, I pinched the skin underneath his ribs.

"Ow!" Quentin scowled at me as he pushed himself off. "What was that for?"

I cleared my throat and rolled my eyes in the stranger's direction.

"Oh!" Finally realizing we weren't alone, Quentin dabbed his swollen eyes with a tissue he pulled out of his pocket and looked the new guy up and down. "Oh," he repeated, showing off his chemically brilliant smile.

The stranger frowned. "There's been a mistake—you're not who I'm looking for. I'm sorry for the disruption."

Quentin batted his lashes. "Going so soon?"

The stranger left without answering.

Quentin turned to me with an open mouth. "Who was that?"

I shrugged. "Some freak. I've been attracting them all morning. I think it's this sexy hospital gown." I tugged on the putrid green smock tied around my neck.

"I always heard a full moon will bring out the freaks."

I swatted at him.

He laughed. "But seriously, that was one gorgeous freak."

"Q," I groaned. "Did you forget your Ritalin today? Focus."

He shook his head, jumped up onto the side of my bed, and lay down next to me. "You're right." He put his arm around my shoulder and I snuggled happily against him. "But that guy just came to visit you, huh? I thought I was your only hot guy friend." He swept a hand through his freshly styled hair. Only Quentin could track down hair wax in a hospital.

I laughed at him. "You *are* my only hot guy friend." I lifted my head and kissed his cheek. "I'm so glad you're okay." Aside from a little purpling on his left temple, Quentin looked like his normal self.

"Yeah." Quentin nodded, his tone serious. "About that … I feel awful about what happened … leaving you on your own … not that you *needed* my help. I was interviewed by the police … "

I moaned and buried my head against his chest.

"Ri-Ri, there was this footage on the news … the mall surveillance video … it was fuzzy, but it looked like you went all Chuck Norris on three different guys." He shrugged his shoulders, as if unable to find the right words for what he wanted to say next.

"On the news?" I could feel the blood drain from my face. There was now physical evidence of the one event in my life that I hoped to put behind me. Which meant, of course, that all of my friends knew about it and would want a first-hand account. But how could I explain to others something I didn't understand myself?

"What happened after I was knocked out?" Quentin asked.

I sighed and let my head fall against the pillow, at the same time wishing for the floor to open up and swallow me whole. "I wish I knew. It's hard to remember. I was scared and—" I didn't know how to explain the voice in my head without sounding like a crazy person.

"I think it has something to do with adrenaline," Quentin said.

Adrenaline. That made perfect sense. I'd heard stories on the news about men lifting cars off people when pumped up by adrenaline. Maybe the voice in my head had something to do with that as well.

"I've read articles about it," Quentin continued. "People can do incredible things in stressful situations. One time when I was on vacation, I accidentally sat on my Fendi sunglasses. I actually had to go into one of those souvenir shops and buy some cheap plastic shades." He shuddered. "Can you imagine? Without adrenaline, I never would have made it."

I laughed until the hard knot of fear, confusion, and anxiety that was lodged inside my ribs broke free and I began to sob. Quentin didn't say a word; he just squeezed me against his chest until I went limp with exhaustion.

"My parents were here earlier," he said. "They brought me my car. Wanna go home?"

I could only nod.

"I called Debbie when you were in the ambulance. Did she find a flight in?"

"Here and gone," I answered.

Quentin nodded. He'd been my friend long enough to know the only way to get Debbie to stay in one place was to Super Glue the floor of a Starbucks. "All right, sweets." He kissed the top of my head and gently pried me off of his chest. "I'll text Debbie and let her know I'm taking you home. Then I'm going to go see what we need to do to get you outta here."

Quentin's dad was a plastic surgeon, so Quentin knew his way around a hospital. He left my room and returned moments later followed by the red-haired nurse and two uniformed police officers. It turned out that all I needed to do was give the police an official statement and have Debbie sign the discharge papers. Debbie's signature was not a problem. With the occupants in the room focused on me, it was nothing for Quentin to quickly forge Debbie's name on the release papers. He'd perfected the signature signing the many report cards and permission slips that Debbie hadn't gotten around to. The police statement concerned me, for the simple fact that I still couldn't process what really had happened last night. My pulse raced as I recounted the night's events. I left out the part about sensing danger and hearing voices. I felt a little guilty, but I couldn't think of a way to explain without sounding like a nutcase. I could just imagine it:

"Hey officer, it wasn't me beating up those men. I was possessed by a voice inside my head."

The first officer would put his pad away and cast a sideways glance at his partner. "Okay, sweetheart, you just relax while I get the doctor. He's going to give you something to make you sleepy, and then you're going to go away for a while. By the way, what size straitjacket do you wear?"

Not for me. Luckily, I didn't have to worry. The officers seemed to think the whole thing was hilarious. They cracked jokes about having me join the squad while they half-heartedly jotted down my answers to their questions. They informed me that all three men had been placed into police custody after being treated for their injuries. And despite the muggers' claims, between the mall surveillance video and the elderly couple's statement, what I did to the men could only be construed as self-defense.

I snorted. Who did they think I was? Some sort of psycho who hid in parking lots looking for groups of innocent men to beat up? *Right.*

As they continued their joking, Quentin politely butted in to ask again when I would be able to leave. Only then did they realize that I wasn't taking the situation as lightly as they were. After clumsily putting away their notepads, they said I was free to go. They turned to leave, but not before the older of the two officers, the one with a thick gray mustache even though his hair was brown, touched me lightly on the arm.

"I got a girl your age at home." He leaned so close that I could smell the spearmint gum in his mouth. "I've seen lots of things ... and ... well ... " The words he didn't say buzzed in the air like flies around roadkill. He scratched his chin. "Let's just say, there are some very bad people in the world. Promise you'll be careful?"

I tried not to shrink under his gaze, his eyes locked on mine, challenging me to tell him anything but the truth. "Uh, sure. I'll be careful." When he didn't immediately move I added, "I promise."

The cop studied my face for another moment before nodding once. "Good." He glanced at Quentin, adding, "Take care, you two," before following his partner out the door.

"That was weird," Quentin muttered from the doorway after the cop was out of earshot.

"I know, right?" I hugged my arms across my chest to ward off the chill that had settled inside my bones. "I mean, why was he so worried about me being careful? They caught the bad guys. What else is there to worry about?" I didn't need to tell him about the voice in my head. As far as I was concerned that was a one-time thing, the effect of adrenaline.

"Exactly," he said. "Those guys are safely locked away. Though, I guess it couldn't hurt if we were a little more cautious." He shrugged. "We could buy some pepper spray or get one of those alarm apps for our cell phones."

I nodded, even though the idea of having to carry around pepper spray made my stomach twist. Obviously, I understood that it was better to be safe than sorry, but every time I looked at the little canister dangling from my key chain I would be reminded of Weasel, the way he'd licked his lips before—no. It was best not to think about it, to just let it drift away like a bad dream.

"Ri-Ri, you're shivering." The nearness of Quentin's voice startled me; I was so lost in my thoughts I hadn't noticed him move. He grabbed my jeans and socks from the bedside table and tossed them to me. "Take these. You must be freezing." He motioned to the hospital gown.

"Thanks." I slid my feet out from under the blanket and slipped them inside last night's asphalt-stained pants.

After I pulled my socks on, Quentin handed me my shoes. "Better?"

"So much," I lied, hoping he didn't notice my fingers shaking as I tied the laces. The last thing I needed was for Quentin to know my trembling had nothing to do with the cold.

6

Seated in a wheelchair outside the hospital, I watched clouds made from cotton candy tumble and change shape as I waited for Quentin to get his car from the lot. It was like the sky itself dared me to be unhappy on such a beautiful day.

I covered my eyes and sank lower in the chair.

Behind you!

I was so stunned by the appearance of the voice in my head that I didn't realize I'd twisted in my wheelchair and grabbed the wrist of my assailant until he was on his knees before me.

Only it wasn't an assailant.

An acne-scarred hospital orderly stared at me in wide-eyed shock from the armlock I'd placed him in. He took several ragged breaths before managing to say, "You forgot your meds."

"Oh, God." I released my grip on his wrist.

The young man fell back and scrambled away from me like a crab. Once he'd put some distance between us he cautiously stood up, rubbing the elbow I'd bent at a gross angle. He released his breath in a hiss. "What are you? Some sort of martial arts expert?"

Good question. If only I knew the answer. "You shouldn't sneak up on people like that!"

He narrowed his eyes. "I'll remember that. And maybe you should take a couple of these." He tossed a pill bottle at me, which I caught in one hand. "They'll help you relax... so you don't break someone's arm or something."

A wave of nausea rolled through me. I'd almost snapped his wrist, just like I'd done to Weasel last night. Only this guy had done nothing wrong. What was going on with me? Was I becoming dangerous to be around?

"Get some rest," the orderly said, his eyes still wide. He walked backward into the hospital, staring at me the whole way.

"Impressive," a new voice announced.

I whirled around in my chair to find the Asian guy who'd visited my room earlier standing next to me with his arms folded.

I glared at him. "What do you want now?"

His chocolate eyes bore into my own. "It appears I was wrong about you."

After studying him for a moment, I realized it was a good thing Debbie wasn't here. She would have signed him on as a model in a second. The brooding types always sold the most underwear. "What's that supposed to mean?"

"It means I can help you." His English was clipped and tight, as if each word he spoke might be the end of his sentence. He pulled a business card out of his pocket and handed it to me: Black's School of Martial Arts. The name Kim Gimhae was neatly written across the bottom in pencil.

I turned the card over in my hand. "What's this for?"

"So you can call me and we can discuss this."

I frowned. "Discuss what?"

Kim leaned toward me, and I detected the scent of sandalwood—warm and earthy. He kept his eyes focused on the parking lot and lowered his voice to a whisper. "The doctors told you that you went into shock, right? The police probably said that adrenaline helped you fend off your attackers." His eyes flicked to mine and he shrugged. "You can believe them if you want." He lowered his voice further, so it was little more than a hiss. "Did you hear whispers in your head last night, Rileigh?"

My chest convulsed as fear squeezed my heart into pulp. Impossible. How could he know about the voice? Who was this guy?

Before I could ask, Kim straightened. "Now that it has begun, people will be looking for you—dangerous people." He eyes swept over the parked cars and I couldn't help but follow his gaze, half expecting someone to come charging at us as we spoke. Instead, a woman got out of her car gathering a balloon bouquet behind her.

"If she charges us," I whispered, "just dive behind that rose bush over there. The balloons won't stand a chance."

Kim frowned at me. "You should take your safety a little more seriously."

"So everyone keeps telling me," I mumbled.

He went back to scanning the parked cars. "It is only a matter of time before they find you. I can help. Call me when you're ready."

I shoved the card in my pocket, making a mental note to toss it into the nearest trash can the moment he was out of sight. "And how will I know when I know when *I'm ready*?" I made air quotes with my fingers.

He looked at me, the intensity in his eyes melting the sarcastic grin from my face. "You'll be ready when you realize just how much trouble you are in."

7

My nerves were frayed worse than my favorite pair of American Eagle destroyed-wash jeans. It was bad enough that I was attacked at the mall and spent the night in the hospital, but now I had some freaky Asian guy telling me that he knew the truth about the voice inside my head?

I was quiet when I'd climbed into Quentin's Mini Cooper. I'd even turned on the radio ear-bleedingly loud to discourage talking. But when he pulled out of the hospital parking lot a knot in my chest loosened. And the farther away we drove the more it unwound until, for the first time since before the attack, I could breathe. In fact, once we'd turned onto the interstate I felt a teensy bit embarrassed I'd allowed that Kim guy to get to me. After all, I *had* met him in a hospital. He could have been a patient himself. Maybe he had a head injury, or more likely, escaped from the mental ward. Both possibilities were more realistic than a group of dangerous people coming after me just because I had a rush of adrenaline.

We arrived at my house in South City at ten in the morning, which was nothing short of a miracle. The trip that should have taken forty-five minutes took twenty. The day Quentin got his driver's license I learned he could bend the laws of space and time with his driving. I'm not sure how, exactly, because I usually kept my eyes hidden behind my fingers. Today was no different, and when I heard the familiar sound of my chipped driveway crunching beneath the tires, I dropped my hands.

Quentin casually flipped the sun visor back into place. Warp speed was nothing new to him.

After my pulse slowed from a gallop to a trot I asked, "Wanna hang for a bit?" When Quentin had sent Debbie a text to let her know we were leaving, she texted him back to say she'd pick up my car at the mall and then had to make a quick stop at the office before coming home. Debbie's and my version of quick were very different and I didn't really feel like being alone at the moment.

He turned to me and smiled. "Sure thing."

"Can you grab the toaster?"

Quentin turned to the beaten box in the backseat. "What is it with you and this thing? You don't really want to give it to your cousin, do you? It's probably broken."

Just like me. I knew last night had done something to me, something that wasn't as obvious as the dents in the toaster. I could feel the strangeness of my own change fluttering inside of me with each breath. "Just bring it inside," I snapped.

Quentin held his hands up in surrender. "Sorry I said anything."

I knew I should apologize, but I was afraid that if I opened my mouth the sob building in the back of my throat would break free. Instead, I bit my trembling lip and climbed out of the car, crossing the small yard to the front door of my house. I was home. The nightmare was over.

Be vigilant. We are being watched.

I fisted my hand inches away from the storm door handle as spiders with ice-crusted legs crawled down my spine. I wanted so badly to believe the voice sweeping through my head during the attack was the result of stress. But now, inches away from my home, it called to me again. What did it mean? *Who* was watching?

Reflexively, I turned on the porch stoop to see if I could spot a threat. The street was empty. Several months ago I helped Quentin research a paper on paranoid schizophrenia and I ran through the symptoms in my head. Hearing voices? Check. Obsessively anxious? Check. Unreasonably suspicious? Check.

The bones in my legs melted to mush one by one. I couldn't go crazy. The damage to my reputation would be horrible and just *forget* about scoring a date to senior prom. I clung to the door handle to keep from melting into a quivering puddle.

Quentin frowned as he walked up beside me. "Are you feeling okay?"

I chose my words carefully. "I'm so tired I could pass out right here." Which wasn't technically lying, but that didn't stop a wave of guilt from washing over me.

"Totally understandable." He whipped out the key that Debbie had given him last year after I'd locked myself out of the house three times in a row. He pushed the door open. "Let's get you in the house, then. Nothing takes the welcome out of a welcome mat like an unconscious girl on the porch."

I allowed him to usher me inside and collapsed onto the couch with a blanket. Quentin brought me Shawnee, my stuffed black Labrador, and continued to scuttle around my house straightening things, as he always did when he came over. I tried to sleep, but my racing mind refused to shut down. Frustrated, I turned on the TV in the hopes that it would distract me, but I couldn't stop thinking about the voice whispering in my head. What did it mean? Was I losing my mind or was it something else altogether? And more importantly, was there a way to get rid of it?

I tried to come up with answers, but found none. In fact, the more I thought about it, the more my head ached. Exhausted, and with a promise to figure it all out later, I wandered into the bathroom and popped two of the pills from the bottle the orderly had given me at the hospital.

Next, I pulled my favorite sweatpants from the hamper—the ones with a star printed on the hip—and after a quick change, made my way back to the couch. I wasn't sure if it was the stress of the previous night, the medication, or a combination of both, but sleep did not come easily.

As I dreamed, I found myself in a place I almost remembered, slipping from the arms of a man with a face I could not see. I gripped him tighter as our entwined fingers, slick with sweat, slid apart, leaving me completely alone in a black room.

Out of the darkness I heard him scream.

8

"It's not too late, you know."

Against my better judgment, I cracked my eyelids open.

Debbie stood before me in a form-fitting strapless pink dress. A wide fuchsia belt cinched her thin waist.

"You can't be serious." I groaned as I pulled myself up into a sitting position. My body ached from spending the morning sprawled on our extremely expensive yet extremely uncomfortable couch. When the pills began taking effect, Quentin had offered to lead me to my room, but I'd been too lazy to venture off. And, boy, was I feeling the consequences.

Debbie frowned, jutting her bottom lip out in what I knew to be a well-practiced pout from her modeling days. "I don't like the idea of you staying here alone. Besides, it's family. They're going to want to see you."

I shook my head. "Forget it, Mom. There's no way I'm going to a wedding today. I feel awful."

Her face softened. "Are you alright?"

"I'm kind of achy, but I'll live. I think I need to spend the day in bed. Where's Q?"

"He said something about needing to check in at home, but said he'd be back around dinnertime." Debbie looked thoughtful for a moment before she opened her sequined clutch and pulled out a small pink cell phone. "I better call Jason, just to make sure you'll be okay on your own."

I pulled the afghan over my shoulders. "Who's Jason?"

She flushed crimson. "Oh, um, I mean Dr. Wendell."

All traces of grogginess were gone. "You have his home phone number?"

"Cell phone, actually." Debbie avoided my gaze as she dialed the number and walked out of the room.

I remained frozen. Just what had happened between Debbie and the doctor during coffee that they were now so close? From my spot on the couch, I couldn't make out more than a word of two of her conversation. But then she laughed, the noise setting off a chord of unease that rippled across my shoulders.

Moments later I heard the snap of a cell phone shutting and Debbie was back in the living room. "He says you should stay in bed and rest."

I rolled my eyes. "That's the expert medical advice? Good thing you called him. I was just about to go run a marathon."

Debbie gasped. "Rileigh Hope Martin! I understand you don't feel well, but that is no reason for you to take on such a nasty attitude. I'm just trying to look out for you."

I sighed. "You're right. I'm sorry."

She nodded, satisfied. "Apology accepted. Now, I have my cell phone on me so if you need anything, you know to call me, right?"

"Got it." She didn't need to know that she was number two on my speed dial behind Quentin.

"Good. I want you to get plenty of rest today, and don't wait up for me. I'll probably be out late."

No surprise there. After she left, I settled in as best I could into the stiff-as-a-board cushion and flipped the TV on to a Degrassi marathon. Exhaustion crept over me like a heavy blanket, and slowly I gave in to my drooping eyelids.

I wasn't sure how long I'd been asleep, but it felt like only minutes when the doorbell chime woke me.

I didn't bother to open my eyes. "Mom, I already told you I'm not going!"

Debbie didn't answer.

I opened my eyes and glanced at the clock on the DVD player; it was almost five. I'd been asleep for two hours.

There were several sharp raps against the front door.

Heaving a sigh, I lifted myself off the couch. As I drew closer to the door, I heard a muffled voice from the other side.

"One sec," I called out, pulling my afghan tighter around my shoulders. I flipped the deadbolt, but stopped myself before I turned the knob. Hadn't last night taught me anything? I dropped my hand and backed away from the door. "Who's there?"

A male voice answered. "Whitley Noble."

My heart did a backflip against my ribs. Whitley Noble? *The* Whitley Noble? The new student I'd spent the last semester lusting after was at my door? I reached for the knob, but stopped short when I caught a glance at myself in the hallway mirror. My hair had matted itself in a clump where I lay against the couch, sticking out at odd angles. I squealed in horror.

"Are you okay?" Whitley called from the other side of the door. The doorknob twisted under my fingers.

Panicked, I rammed the opening door shut with my shoulder and latched the deadbolt. "I'll be right with you!" I called. Whitley Noble was on my porch and I looked like I'd stuck my hand in a light socket! I ran into my bedroom and frantically pulled a brush through my hair, not caring that I felt like I was ripping half of it out. Once I had it tied back into a sleek ponytail, I started to leave my room when I remembered that my sweatpants were wearing thin in the back seam. Since I didn't want Whitley to know the color of my underwear, I ran to my closet and pulled out a clean pair of jeans, purple tank top, and black flip-flops. After I dressed, I grabbed my shiniest lip gloss from my vanity and slathered it on as I ran back to the door. I did a final check in the mirror before taking a deep breath and opening the door.

Whitley raised his eyebrows in amusement. He was

strikingly handsome, with an angled chin and razor-edged cheeks, like an Abercrombie ad brought to life. Which was weird, because the guys I typically went for were the grungy skater types. Whitley had more of that "I play polo and go yachting on the weekends" look. But, and I don't know how he did it, he made it work without coming off as a jerk.

My heart spun in my chest, as if it were the wheel of a gerbil hopped up on Pixy Stix. What was Whitley doing here? It wasn't like we'd ever talked before. But that didn't matter. He was here now and this was my moment to make an impression. To show him what a smart and savvy girl I was. I opened my mouth but, apparently, the smart and savvy was out of the office. "Huh-eye." I winced internally. Good thing awkward and stupid were more than happy to fill in. Why didn't I just tell him, "Colors are pretty." Or, "I like cake." It was all I could do to keep from bashing my head against the wall.

Luckily, Whitley didn't seem to notice my lack of socialization skills. He answered me with a boyish grin. "Hi."

The dimples! I swallowed hard and barely managed to suppress a shudder of appreciation. I'd studied the dimples from afar during what Quentin called my "Whitley Watching Safaris" and often wondered what it would be like to be on the receiving end of such a smile. I now knew the effect was knee-weakening.

"So—" Whitley swept a hand through his shoulder-length blond hair and shifted his weight from foot to foot.

“So?” I stared into his eyes. From this close, I could see that they were two shades of blue. Just like the ocean grew darker the deeper you waded, I knew if I wasn’t careful, I could fall in and sink.

“Um, can I come in?”

I snapped out of my trance. “Oh my God, I’m sorry. Yeah, come in.” I moved out of his way and fought the urge to smack my own forehead as he stepped inside. After I closed the door, I motioned him to the couch and positioned myself across from him on the loveseat. Putting some distance between us seemed like a good idea. I hoped it would lessen the effect he had on me so I wouldn’t embarrass myself further.

He cleared his throat and fidgeted with his green T-shirt. “I felt really bad when I heard what happened to you.”

My heart sank. The attack wasn’t a topic I wanted to discuss.

He seemed to sense my hesitation. “You don’t have to talk about it or anything. I just wanted to make sure you were okay.”

I was at a loss for words. Whitley Noble not only knew who I was, but he cared about my well-being? It seemed too good to be true. Subtly, I reached down and pinched my thigh. The sharp pain assured me I was awake.

“I almost forgot!” Whitley’s face brightened as he reached for his back pocket. “I brought you something.” His smile faltered when he withdrew a wilted arrangement of daisies and carnations. Several yellow petals drifted lazily to his lap. His face reddened as he brushed them away with his hand. "They looked better earlier this morning. I tried to bring them to the hospital, but you'd already left."

I took the pathetic arrangement, ignoring the petals that continued to fall. "I think they're beautiful."

Whitley smiled and relaxed back against the couch.

"It's also very sweet of you to check on me."

He shrugged. "It's nothing. Before I found out what happened to you, I was really disappointed when you didn't show up at the party last night."

I swayed slightly, woozy from the extra heat burning up my neck and into my cheeks. "Really?"

"Yeah. You see, I was going to ask you something."

I leaned forward. "What?"

He opened his mouth just as my phone on the coffee table lit up and played my favorite dance mix. I groaned inwardly and scooped it up.

He sighed. "To be continued?"

"Give me one minute." I stood up. "Don't go anywhere, promise?"

"Promise." He gave me another sizzling smile.

The voice, like a winter breeze, blew through my mind.

He wants something.

Startled, the phone slipped from my grip and I juggled it from hand to hand before I steadied myself. *Please,* I silently begged the voice. Not now. Not with Whitley here.

"You okay?" Whitley asked, leaning forward.

Realizing I'd forgotten to breathe, I inhaled sharply.

"Almost tripped on the rug." I forced a chuckle. "Sometimes I can be such a klutz." I wanted to scream.

His forehead pinched into lines of concern. "Uh, are you going to answer that?" He inclined his head to the still-singing phone in my hand.

Great. I hear one little voice in my head and my composure goes to hell. "Right! Phone!" I repeated, still laughing. I held my finger up to him and spun around before pressing the talk button. "Hello?"

"Rileigh?"

The voice was unfamiliar. "Who is this?"

"Kim Gimhae. I talked with you at the hospital. Are you well?"

I mentally groaned—it was the mental patient with the business card. I held my hand over the receiver and mouthed the words *one minute* to Whitley before walking the short distance into the kitchen and propping myself against the counter.

"Stalker much?" I hissed into the phone.

"I'm sorry?"

"I haven't even been home a full day and you're calling me? How did you get my number? No wait, better yet, *why* are you calling me? I was supposed to call you when I was ready. Remember that?"

If I didn't know better, I would swear I heard the guy smile. "I do. I just thought it wise to check on you. Your experience could attract some unwanted attention."

Like annoying phone calls? I started to tell him, but the voice interrupted.

He is not to be trusted.

I shivered against the tremors brought on by ghostly fingers tickling along my spine. He who? If the voice was so bent on ruining my life, the least it could do was specify.

Kim caught my hesitation. "You are not alone."

Pulse still racing, I scrambled to grab the phone as it slipped—yet again—through my fingers. "No."

"Then do not say more. It's not safe."

An icy jolt shuddered through my heart. Having Kim voice my fear out loud only made it more real—I wasn't safe. The realization wrapped around me, tightening to the point of suffocation. "What's going on?" I whispered.

"It's imperative that we meet," Kim answered. "Then I will be able to answer all of your questions … as well as my own."

Meet Kim? Not likely. He could be the one the voice warned me about. "Sure thing," I answered in my best syrupy tone. "My appointment with the ax murderer was cancelled so I can pencil you in."

"Good," he answered without a trace of irony. The boy obviously had no clue what sarcasm was. "Tomorrow evening, my dojo, seven o'clock. The address is on the card I gave you."

I leaned my forehead against the wall. There was no way I was going to his dojo, but if it got him off the phone I was happy to lie. "I'll be there."

"Tomorrow then." I heard a click as he disconnected.

I felt cold from the inside out and was only vaguely

aware of my trip back into the living room, where I plopped back onto the loveseat.

"You look a little pale." Whitley's voice startled me as it brought me back to the here and now. "Are you feeling alright?"

I gave him a weak smile. "Fine."

"Boyfriend giving you a hard time?" He tucked his chin and raised his eyebrows, like he was trying to look cute. It worked.

I laughed despite myself. "No."

"'No' because he's not giving you a hard time? Or 'no' because you don't have a boyfriend?"

"Does it matter?"

He lowered his eyes, the humor gone from his face. "I'm afraid I wasn't totally honest with you. I'm not here just to check on you. I have a hidden agenda."

My chest tightened. The voice was right again! He *did* want something. And I was dumb enough to let him in the house. Stupid dimples!

He cleared his throat. "What are you doing tomorrow night?"

I blinked. I'd been waiting to hear those words for so long that my mind refused to make sense of their meaning. "Are you asking me out?"

He flushed. "Am I out of line? Is it too soon with you getting out of the hospital? I wanted to ask you last night and ... well ... you know. It's just that I haven't been able to stop thinking about you."

It took me several tries before my mouth was able to form words. "Are you serious?"

"Absolutely." His smile wavered when I didn't respond. "Did I make you mad?" He held his hands in front of him in surrender. "Please don't kick my ass."

That did it. A laugh erupted from my throat before I could smother it with my hands.

He leaned back, satisfied. "Tomorrow night then?"

YES! YES! YES! I wanted to jump up and do a happy dance on the loveseat, but then I remembered my part-time job and my mood deflated. "I'm busy tomorrow."

"Since when?" a new voice asked.

I turned to find Quentin leaning against the door, legs crossed, balancing a pizza box on his palm. I narrowed my eyes at him. How long had he been standing there? "I work a double shift at the salon."

"Salon?" Whitley asked.

Quentin pounced on the couch next to Whitley. "We both have summer jobs shampooing hair at *Today's Reflections.* We're trying to earn our parents' love and approval by showing them how responsible we are by paying for our senior trip to Cancun ourselves."

"I see," Whitley said.

Quentin shrugged. "But that's beside the point. How does Tuesday work for you?"

I stood up. "Q, that's not—"

"Tuesday works," Whitley interrupted. "Is six okay?"

Quentin frowned. "Hmmm. If I remember the schedule correctly, Rileigh works that day, too." He tilted his head. "Tell you what, I'll cover her last hour. You could take her out to dinner at seven."

"Excuse me," I said.

Whitley shrugged. "I was thinking more casual. Coffee?"

I stamped my foot. "Now wait just a minute."

Quentin nodded. "Coffee's good. Pick her up at eight."

I could feel my cheeks burn. "You know, people, I *am* in the room."

Quentin leaned over without looking at me and patted my arm. "Of course you are, sweetie."

Whitley stood up. "Eight o'clock." He turned and smiled at me. "It's a date." Before I could answer, he darted out the door, closing it behind him.

"You're welcome," Quentin stated smugly, getting up to sit next to me on the couch.

"Oh, I'm not about to thank you," I snapped, snatching the pizza slice he was about to bite into. "Honestly, Q, I was doing just fine on my own."

Quentin laughed and quickly smothered it behind his hands. "Oh, Ri-Ri." He stuck out his lip and patted my hand. "You're serious, aren't you? That's adorable."

I glared at him as I chewed. It was all I could do to keep from slapping the perfect cleft off his chin.

He laughed again. "Rileigh, I'm your best friend—"

"I think you mean *were* my best friend," I muttered.

He rolled his eyes as he pulled out another slice from the box. "I've witnessed you make too many mistakes in the love department. I couldn't let you spend your entire summer massaging old-lady scalps for dollar tips. Especially when someone as delicious as Whitley is at stake."

"If you weren't so busy butting in, you would have seen that things were going pretty well."

"When's the last time you've been on a date?"

It had been more than six months, but I didn't want to voice what he already knew. Instead, I angrily tore a chunk out of the pizza, averting my gaze from him as I chewed.

"That's what I thought," Quentin answered. "Not to mention your last couple of attempts at love were ... " He rolled his eyes, searching for the right word. "Disastrous." He shrugged and happily devoured his pizza.

"Thanks for your concern, but you're forgetting that I'm the first girl at the skate park to land an Ollie Impossible. Remember last summer when I fell off the half-pipe and broke my wrist? I didn't cry, *did I?* And who punched John Wringer in the face for calling you a queer?"

Quentin stopped chewing. "Me."

"Yeah, well, I totally would have if you hadn't done it first. My point is, I'm more capable than you give me credit for. I think can handle something as basic as my own love life."

He sputtered, nearly choking on his food. "Really? How do you explain the last guy?"

"Tom? We just didn't have enough in common."

"I'll say." He slapped his knee. "You'll go to any college that's close to a beach. He's applying to Harvard. You like skating and scary movies. He likes country music and making out with other girls. Yep, you're right—not enough in common."

"Aaron was a good guy," I countered.

"True, and you two crazy kids might have made it if he wasn't already in love."

"Aaron didn't cheat on me!"

"I was talking about his Camaro."

He had me there. I crossed my arms. "What about Tony?"

"Girl, I had a better shot of living happily ever after with Tony than you."

"Really? You know, I always wondered."

"Hmphf," Quentin muttered with a full mouth.

I shook my head. "But that's not the point."

Quentin huffed. "Then what is?"

"I can't have you managing my dates for me, because when it comes down to it—I'm going on them alone." My eyes flew wide as the realization hit. I dropped my half-eaten crust in my lap and gripped Quentin's shoulders, shaking him slightly. "Oh my God. I'm going on a date with Whitley Noble—alone. This is bad! I'm going to screw it up, I'm going to—"

"Ri-Ri!" He grabbed my cheeks, smooshing them painfully between his fingers. "Stop! You're freaking out."

I could only nod.

He sighed and released his grip on my face. "There's only one way to get your mind off everything." He looked at his watch. "If we leave now we can get a couple of hours in before the sun goes down."

"Skate park!" I leapt off the sofa and clapped my hands. "Great idea! Let me grab my board!" I raced to my room and snatched my beaten and chipped board from under my bed. The pink paint—once the same color as my helmet—was now faded and chipped from constant ramp abuse. There was even a blood stain, long dried a rusty brown, in one of the cracks.

Humming to myself, I kicked aside the dirty T-shirts on my floor in the hopes of uncovering my knee pads. A trip to the skate park was exactly what I needed. There was something reassuring in the adrenaline rush that came from balancing on one hand, the world upside down, and nothing between your feet but sky. I couldn't explain it (and I tried a million times to Debbie, who insisted that I "act more like a girl"), but a thundering pulse and a heightened sense of danger had always been comforting, familiar even. Quentin called me an adrenaline junkie. Maybe I was. And if so, maybe a good rush was exactly what I needed to snap back into the old, not-hearing-voices, pre-attack Rileigh.

"Ready?" Quentin asked as I rolled into the living room.

"Skate park!" I shouted, kicking my board into my hand and leaping out the door.

He followed, locking the door to my house as I climbed into his car. Seconds later he was in the driver's seat, turning the key. "Listen ... I want to say I'm sorry. You're right, you know. I shouldn't have interfered. You were doing fine on your own."

I frowned. “I was?”

“Absolutely. You’re just going out for coffee. It’s not like you’re getting married or anything.” He twisted in his seat so he could back out of my driveway. “Honestly Ri-Ri, what’s the worst that could happen?”

I’m sure Quentin didn’t mean to phrase his question so ominously, but that didn’t stop the hard lump from forming inside my throat. The worst that could happen? I had a date with Whitley that I was sure to botch. I was hearing voices and fighting off bad guys with skills I shouldn’t have. This Kim guy said he had answers, but at what price? When you looked at the whole picture, the possibilities were endless.

9

The next day at the salon, I busied myself with shampoos, answering the phone, and sweeping hair in hopes that it would distract me from the insanity that was now my life. Unfortunately, the stylists' curious stares and muffled whispers amplified my feeling that I was, indeed, a walking freak show. And it only got worse.

An hour before I was scheduled to get off, I was halfway through organizing the shelves when a tap on the shoulder startled me into dropping a stack of towels on the floor. Before I could stop myself I whirled around in a crouch and raised my arms in front of me in defense.

Quentin threw his hands up in surprise and took a step back. "I was going to ask if you wanted to grab a Frappuccino, but now I'm thinking you should lay off the caffeine." His face softened. "Still on edge?"

"What? No!" I dropped my arms and studied a spot on

the ceiling. My cheeks burned. "I'm fine. Better than fine, actually. You just need to learn not to sneak up on people. It's rude."

"Uh-huh."

"Seriously. You need to wear a bell or something." Squatting down, I could feel his gaze on the back of my neck as I retrieved the towels. I sighed. This was so Quentin. One little life trauma and he has to talk about feelings and uncover buried emotions. So not for me. "Can we just … you know … not?"

He ignored the question and instead picked up a towel. "Let me help."

I was pretty sure he wasn't referring to the towels. "I don't really want to talk about it."

"I've noticed."

I stopped stacking towels and looked at him. "Are you upset with me?"

He sighed. "Not upset, Ri-Ri, just worried."

I wrinkled my nose at him. "There's nothing to worry about, I'm fine." Hoping to discourage further conversation, I turned my attention back to the remaining towels on the floor. "As far as my date with Whitley goes, I was thinking about wearing my black skirt—the one with the chain dangling from the hip. What do you think?"

Quentin placed a hand on my shoulder. "Rileigh, we were attacked."

I snapped my head up. "You think I don't realize that? *Hello.* I had a front row seat!"

"Realizing and accepting are not the same thing."

"What's that supposed to mean?" I shrugged his hand off my shoulder.

"I'm worried because you act like nothing happened. And I know I haven't helped. At the time, I thought setting you up on a date and taking you to the skate park was a good distraction. But now, I'm not so sure distractions are what you need."

I laughed angrily. "So, Dr. Q, what do I need? A good cry under my covers?"

He tilted his head thoughtfully. "Maybe."

"Is that how you dealt?"

"No. I don't think I can deal with this without some help. I'm thinking about seeing a certified therapist."

I opened my mouth, but the heated words died on the tip of my tongue. I looked away from my friend's worried gaze and sat down on the floor next to him. "Don't take this from me, Q. I need to be angry."

Quentin linked his fingers through mine. "Why?"

I remembered the feeling of silk as it slid through my body, and the crunch of breaking bones, and I shuddered. "Because ... " I searched for the right words. I knew the anger was important. It overwhelmed the terror that threatened to devour me. Even now I could feel a chord of fear biting into my heart like jagged teeth. "I just want to forget it happened, you know? But I can't, because there's all this other crap that I have to deal with."

"I've had nightmares every night."

I looked up, surprised. "Me too." But I was willing to

bet that Quentin didn't dream about long-haired Asian men screaming in the dark. Then again…

Quentin gave my hand a squeeze, a subtle reminder that I was connected to another human being and not as alone as I felt.

"Q, I—I think I'm in trouble." The words I'd been thinking for the last two days became a solid, almost touchable, thing the moment they left my tongue. Soft tremors wracked my body.

"It'll be all right," he whispered.

Then, before I could chicken out, I spit out the words as fast as I could. "I heard a voice—not mine—and I freaked and lost control. Then yesterday, when I got home, that Kim guy from the hospital called—something about answers and his dojo. Then I heard the voice again, but first—"

"Rileigh!" Quentin gave my shoulders a quick shake.

I blinked. "I'm rambling, aren't I?"

He nodded.

"Can I start over?"

"Please."

I opened my mouth to try again just as Jeannine, the salon owner, stuck her head through the heavy maroon curtain that blocked the sink room from the rest of the salon.

"Rileigh, you have a visitor."

"Visitor?" Quentin asked.

"Beats me." I shrugged.

Quentin helped me up and together we walked out into the lobby.

Jeannine inclined her head toward the door. "He said he'd wait outside."

"He?" Quentin gave me a wink before helping me untie my smock. "I guess we'll have to continue our talk later—without the *distractions*."

I nodded, glad that my confession would wait. After handing him my apron, I turned and walked outside. I spotted Whitley sitting on a bench in front of the deli. My throat went dry. He was even more gorgeous today, with the sun's rays making his loose hair hang from his head like threads of gold.

"Rileigh!" He smiled and motioned me over.

My heart pounded harder with each step I took until I was directly in front of him and I thought my rib cage might burst. "Why are you here?" I immediately regretted my choice of words.

His smile melted. "Are you upset?"

"No. That's not—I didn't—" I hung my head and sat down next to him. His arm extended along the back of the bench and grazed my shoulders. It felt nice. "I'm sorry. I've had a crazy day, and you just surprised me."

His smile returned. "I *wanted* to surprise you. I remember you said you worked a double shift today, so I thought I might be able to snag you on a break and take you to get something to eat."

Of course he did. It turns out Whitley was not only gorgeous, he was surprisingly sweet. So it was just my luck that after a semester of pining over him he'd show an interest in me at the same time I started hearing voices in my head.

"So how about it?" He grinned.

I said nothing. Even the dimples couldn't cheer me up today. He continued to smile, forcing me to look away. If only he knew what I already did—our relationship was doomed. I was pretty sure most guys put "crazy" last on the list of qualities they look for in girls.

"Rileigh? Is something wrong?"

Not something—*everything.* Reluctantly, I turned to face him. "Whitley, I'm sorry. It's so sweet of you to think of me like this. It's just that … I already took my break. In fact, I better get back inside before I get into trouble."

"I see." He didn't bother to hide the disappointment in his voice. "In that case, I better not keep you." He stood up and walked into the parking lot.

I pressed my lips together to keep from calling him back. It would only complicate things.

But as he reached the first line of cars, he stopped anyway and turned back to face me. "I have to ask you something."

I stood up from the bench and waited.

His face remained blank. "Do you feel it too?"

I frowned. "What do you mean?"

His cheeks burned red and he ducked his head. His hair spilled across his face, forming a barrier between us. He hid like a ten-year-old who had just given his crush a dandelion and my heart melted a little, allowing warm stickiness to trickle down and heat my insides.

Whitley cleared his throat before continuing. "I feel like there could be something between us worth exploring."

Something between *us*—as in Rileigh and Whitley? The mere thought made me feel weightless, and I gripped the back of the bench to keep from floating away.

He tucked the curtain of hair behind his ear and looked at me. "Maybe I'm over-obsessing, but you didn't technically agree to go out with me." He held his hand up before I could protest. "What I'm trying to say is that I feel something when I'm with you. I just want to know if you feel it too."

I thought about the way my stomach fell into my knees when I first caught sight of him leaning against the bench. Was that the feeling he was referring to?

Whitley crossed the asphalt with quick strides until only inches separated us. "I'm drawn to you, Rileigh. I don't know what it is—but I'd like to find out." He lifted my hand and rubbed his thumb across my knuckles, bringing goose bumps along my arm. "Do you feel it?"

I opened my mouth to answer, but snapped it shut when I felt the girlish scream of delight thick on my tongue. After several more PAC-MAN impressions, I gave up and remained silent.

Whitley smiled and it was nothing short of dazzling. "Can I take that as a 'yes'?"

I could only nod.

"Cool. Then we're still on for tomorrow night?"

I nodded again.

"I'm glad we had this talk." He gave my hand a squeeze before releasing it. "I'll see you tomorrow, and don't even think about backing out." He gave me a playfully menacing look. "I know where you live."

10

Jeannine rapped on the wall of the storage closet where I stood taking inventory of hair dye. “You look like hell, honey. I know it’s early, but go home.”

It took a moment for her words to register. As long as I’d been working at the salon, Jeannine had never let anyone go home early. Before she could change her mind I flung off my smock and scrambled for my car keys. I made a dash for the door, not even pausing with a snarky comeback when one of the stylists said something about me looking so haggard she could use my face as an anti-theft device.

A whole night all to myself! I thought of the many things I could do as I made the short drive home: reality show marathon, repaint my chipped nails, or even a nap! What wouldn’t make the list: obsessing over the attack and the voice in my head. This night was a chance to get my head on straight and forget about all the drama that had recently infected my life. I wasn't about to waste it.

After pulling into my driveway, I practically bounced the entire way from my car to the front porch.

Use caution. All is not as it seems.

The reappearance of the voice caught me off guard, causing my foot to catch on the first step. My arms pinwheeled, grasping for a hold as I stumbled forward. Luckily, my fingers found the door handle before I did a face plant in Debbie's pedestal of long-dead marigolds beside the door. As I pulled myself back to my feet I loosened the storm door just enough that a folded sheet of yellow legal paper floated free from the crevice where it had been tucked.

I couldn't explain it, but I had the sudden urge to go back to the car and drive away. I shook my head. It was just a piece of paper. That didn't stop my breath from catching in my throat as I reached down and allowed my fingers to hover over the note, too afraid to actually touch it.

Five seconds passed with my breath held and fingers dangling centimeters away. Fifteen. Thirty. Nothing happened. "Rileigh, you really are a mental case," I whispered as I snatched the paper. Despite the typical hot and humid St. Louis summer day, the notebook paper felt cool in my hand. I fought against the urge to tear it into a million pieces as my shaking fingers pulled the folds open, revealing the scratchy handwriting inside:

I know your secret.

I ran a fingertip along the edge of the paper and jerked it back when it sliced into my skin. A small bead of blood formed on the cut and I wiped it away on my shirt. Each biting throb was proof that I wasn't going crazy—delusions didn't draw blood.

Still, I had no explanation for the note or the message it carried. The only secret I kept was padded and enhanced my chest by one whole cup size. Unless …

Kim.

The answer hit me like an overturned pot of boiling water straight to the stomach. I crumpled the paper up and shoved it into my pocket as I stormed inside my house. It made perfect sense. That jerk thought he could scare me. A little insurance on his part to make sure that I went running to his dojo.

It was the last straw.

My body shook as I yanked a tank top from a hanger in my closet and slipped it over my head. I kicked off the black ballet flats I had to wear for work and laced up my Adidas running shoes. Kim had messed with the wrong girl. He was probably counting on the fact that I'd show up afraid and crying, begging him to help me. Maybe that's how he got his kicks. Maybe he staked out the hospital for vulnerable girls, hoping to seduce them by scaring them and then rushing in as the hero. The more I thought about it, the angrier I got. Well, he was in for a big surprise. I was going to his dojo tonight, but not to ask for his help. I was going to tell him to leave me the hell alone … or else.

The only problem? I didn't know what the "or else" was. I brushed the thought away as I rushed out the door. I could figure that out along the way.

11

I was still seething after I'd entered Kim's address into my phone's GPS and climbed into my car, but the second I buckled my seat belt and turned the ignition, my confidence wavered. By the time I'd reached the highway my hands were shaking so badly I had to tighten my grip on the wheel to keep from swerving.

Was I crazy? What if this Kim guy turned out to be a psycho? I glanced at the phone in my cup holder, fingers itching to call Q—at the very least to let him know where I was going—but I didn't. I didn't need to drag anyone else into my mess.

I considered turning my car around. I wanted nothing more than to forget this whole thing ever happened and move on with my life, but somehow I knew it wouldn't be that easy. The threatening note proved that Kim wasn't going to leave me alone. If I wanted this to end, I was going to have to confront him in person.

Thirty minutes later I crossed the Jefferson Barracks Bridge that connected Missouri to Illinois and found myself in a town called Waterloo. I drove by several corn fields and a weathered-down shack that, given the neon beer signs, was apparently a bar.

"I'm in hillbilly hell," I mumbled.

But soon enough, the fields gave way to housing developments and I realized this was one of those secret Midwestern treasures that the big-city dwellers devoured in search of a simpler life. Give it another couple of years and it was sure to have its own super shopping center.

I located the dojo easily. It was right off the main drag, a simple stand-alone metal building with a brick apartment complex on one side and a lumberyard on the other. As I parked the Fiesta, I noticed several cars scattered around the parking lot. Interesting. Kim wasn't alone.

The metallic taste of fear rose up the back of my throat as I got out of my car. I managed to swallow it by the time I reached the building's glass doors. An Asian girl roughly the same age as me frowned from behind a glass counter as I entered the reception area. Long black hair spilled over her shoulders, nearly hiding the image of a golden dragon on her red T-shirt. She folded her hands neatly on top of a stack of receipts, rubbing her thumb over her index finger.

"We're closed," she said coolly.

I didn't realize I had squeezed my hands into fists until

I felt the bite of my nails against my palm. "I'm looking for Kim Gimhae. He's expecting me."

Her almond eyes narrowed into dangerous slits. "I wasn't aware he had any private lessons tonight."

Kim appeared in the doorway directly behind her. "Sumi, that's not your concern."

"Oh, Kim!" Sumi's back snapped straight as her eyes widened in surprise. She shuffled the papers in front of her and spun to face him, her icy expression melting into lines of pleasant appeasement. "I'm sorry, Kim. I didn't know she had an appointment."

He crossed his arms and leaned against the door frame. His eyes glittered, the black pupils matching the color of his loose-fitting pants. My eyes drifted up to the hard lines of his bare chest.

Kim smiled at me, but I wasn't sure if it was in greeting or from noticing my staring. With burning cheeks, I pretended to study the Bruce Lee poster next to him with exaggerated interest. *He's a jerk, Rileigh,* I reminded myself. *He preys on innocent girls.* But then, I wondered, with abs like that, why would he have to?

Kim took the papers in front of Sumi and slid them inside a nearby folder. "Sumi, leave these for tomorrow." He placed the folder under the counter. "Why don't you take off early?"

"But," she said, lowering her thick lashes, "I was hoping to train with you tonight. My test is in a few weeks, and I want to be ready."

He set a hand on her shoulder and something flashed

over her face. Adoration—or something more? It happened so fast it was hard to tell. "You'll be fine," he assured her. "You're the highest-ranking brown belt and my best student. You'll have no problem earning your black belt."

She beamed.

"However, I have business to attend to tonight. It's time for you to leave."

"I don't understand. The others—"

"Sumi." Kim's smile disappeared. "I am not asking you."

Her face wilted like a week-old rose. She snatched her car keys from the counter and marched toward the door I was still blocking. The anger that radiated from her prickled my skin as she stopped in front of me, scowling, as if sizing me up for a fight.

I wasn't sure what her problem with me was, but I wasn't in the mood for any more drama. With my hands held up, I moved to the side.

She still managed to bump my shoulder on the way out.

"Nice girl," I said as soon as she was through the door. "Very wise of you to have her as your receptionist—a real 'people person,' that one."

Kim laughed. "Sorry about that. Sumi has difficulty affording lessons, so I allow her to organize my class lists in exchange for training. She's a good student, but can be a bit… abrasive."

"Uh-huh," I answered, rubbing my shoulder.

He laughed again, but this time there was a ring of familiarity in it that inspired a chill under my skin. There was something about that laugh, a clue of sorts, lying under the blanket of my subconscious. But that couldn't be. I narrowed my eyes, comparing his image to the memories of people I'd met at events like football games and parties. Other than the hospital, nothing came to mind. So I asked, "Have we met before? I mean, before the hospital. Your laugh … " I couldn't put my finger on the weird feeling of *déjà vu*.

He raised a single eyebrow.

I shook my head. "No, that's silly."

He tilted his head. "You know, you do look like someone who just woke up."

"What?" I smoothed my hands along the sides of my pulled-back hair. Maybe the rolled-down windows had done more damage than I thought. "I've been up all day."

The corners of his lips curled down in an amused upside-down smile. "That's not what I was talking about."

I quit fussing with my hair. "Then what *are* you talking about?"

"Follow me if you want to find out." He swept his hand in front of him as a gesture for me to walk through the door.

I shook my head. "Uh-uh. There's no way I'm following you into that room."

Kim cocked an eyebrow.

"I don't know you. I don't know what you want or why you won't leave me alone. In fact, the only reason I came here tonight is to tell you to stop bothering me. No more phone calls and no more notes."

"Notes?" All traces of amusement left Kim's face. "What notes?"

I groaned. "Puh-lease. Like you don't know. The one that said 'I know your secret.'" I wiggled my fingers in the air to exaggerate the eerie effect I knew he was hoping for.

"Rileigh, I didn't leave you a note." Kim's voice was full of concern, with a hint of fear. He must take acting lessons.

"Whatever. Just know that if you don't leave me alone, as of this second, I'm going to ... file for a restraining order." Brilliant. I mentally patted myself on the back.

Kim seemed to think about this for a moment. Finally, he said, "You want me to leave you alone?"

Seriously, did this guy ride the short bus? "I just told you that."

"Fine. Then I have a proposition for you. Come with me into the training room. I only want to show you something. It won't take long. After that, you can leave and I'll never bother you again."

I eyed him skeptically. It sounded too good to be true. A couple of minutes and I would never have to deal with him again? "What's the catch?"

"No catch," he said. "Do we have a deal?"

I could sacrifice a couple of minutes if it meant never having to be bothered by Kim again. "Deal."

He smiled and disappeared through the door without waiting for me to follow.

So this was it. The key to being left alone and getting my life back was a room away. I trembled in anticipation—or was it fear? It was getting harder to tell the difference.

All I had to do was walk through that door. The door with who-knows-what on the other side. I turned and looked longingly at the glass door through which I had entered the building.

Two doors. Two choices. Two outcomes. I turned away from the exit, pushed my shoulders back, and stepped into the unknown.

12

I wrinkled my nose at the smell of rubber that permeated the room. A solid wall of floor-to-ceiling mirrors projected my wide-eyed wariness back at me as I cautiously stepped onto the giant jigsaw puzzle of blue and black mats that covered the dojo floor. Four punching bags hung from the ceiling along the left-side wall of the large room, and several more bags clustered in the far corner on floor stands. Two of the floor-stand bags had the shape of actual men from the waist up, with scowls molded onto their rubber faces. I found it funny that a designer would go through the trouble of making a punching bag appear menacing.

Above the bags, a wooden shelf stuffed with trophies of various sizes looked like a miniature city crammed with golden towers. I was about to take a closer look at their engravings when a glint of metal reflecting in the mirror captured my attention.

Kim stood across the room staring at various sharp weapons mounted against the wall.

My throat went dry. I didn't like where this was going. "So this is your dojo?"

He kept his focus on the weapons. "For two years now."

"But you look so young."

He turned to me and smiled. "I am currently eighteen years old."

"*Currently?* That's an odd way of putting it."

He gave a soft laugh and returned his focus to the weapons. There were more than a dozen of them, in all different shapes and sizes. Some I recognized from the martial arts action flicks Quentin and I watched, and others, with wicked sloping angles, looked like the blades of demons. Kim stopped in front of a small, slightly curved blade about the length of my arm. He reached for the wrapped black handle, but stopped short, allowing his hand to linger inches above it, fingers still. He closed his eyes and seemed to be physically straining against—what? I had no idea, and my tongue was too thick to ask. After what felt like an eternity, he snatched it from its resting place, nodded his head in approval, and turned to me. "Please forgive me for this. There is no other way."

My heart knocked painfully against my chest, drawing the blood from my body and leaving me shivering. "Excuse me?"

"Have you even seen one of these before?" he asked,

gesturing with his head to the slightly curved sword still in his hands.

I shook my head while taking a step backward. "Is this what you wanted to show me?"

"It's okay. You don't need to be afraid," Kim said. He swung the sword in a circle in front of him, then drew the blade back so that he presented the sword to me hilt first. "Here. Take it."

"If you think I'm all impressed by your pointy-object collection, you're seriously mistaken." I recoiled from it as if it could bite. I thought Kim and I had a deal—now I wasn't so sure. Had I made a fatal mistake in coming here? Too many scenarios from Nana's beloved crime dramas flashed through my mind. Being alone with a crazy guy and his sword was never a good thing.

He took another step forward, urging me with his eyes.

I took another step back. "We had a deal. You wanted to show me something. I've seen the sword, and now I'll be going."

Kim shook his head. "You haven't seen what I want to show you yet. By the way, this *sword*," he inclined his head toward the weapon, "is a katana. Japanese samurai used them in battle."

My nerves were so fried, they bordered on crispy. "Okay, that's great. I appreciate the history lesson, Kim. But I'm really not comfortable with what's going on. This was a mistake. The whole thing is a mistake." I spun on my heels, but wound up almost smashing my face against his chest. Startled, I took a step back. "How did you move so fast?"

He didn't bother to hide his amusement as he thrust the blade toward me. "Take it," he repeated.

I hesitated, slowly bringing my fingers up to hover over the blade. I didn't want to touch it, but I figured if this guy was nuts, it was probably better that the blade was in my possession. Self Defense 101: A weapon is always better than no weapon when dealing with crazies.

Carefully, I wrapped my fingers around the handle, bracing myself in the event he decided to snatch it back. Instead, he stood as still as a statue, moving only to suck in a breath as I lifted the sword from his open palm. I cast him a nervous glance, waiting for him to do something, but his gaze remained locked on the katana. Figuring I was safe for the moment, I turned my attention to the sword in my hand. Strangely, it felt familiar: the weight in my hand, the texture of the wrapped handle, even the size of the hilt. I knew I'd held one before; I just couldn't remember when.

"Does it feel familiar to you?"

The precise timing of his question left me too stunned to answer. This whole situation began to have an unreal feel to it, like walking the line between a dream and the darkness that surrounds it.

"I understand how much this is to take in." His eyes softened, and for a minute he seemed sincere. "You are confused. Your world has been thrown off balance, and you are having conflicting thoughts and feelings about things you were once so sure about. You don't know who you can trust, including yourself."

Once again, he'd put my thoughts into words. "How—How do you know these things?"

He laughed. "You are not the first to experience the awakening."

"The wha—" I tightened my grip on the sword.

"The awakening," he repeated matter-of-factly. "Walking through the shadows of your past life."

I choked down a laugh. Past lives—he couldn't be serious.

As if sensing my disbelief, he almost grabbed my arm, but stopped short before actually touching me. He let his hand linger in the air above my arm so I could feel the heat radiating from his open palm. He balled his hand into a fist and dropped it down at his side. My skin tingled where his fingers no longer hovered.

"Why wouldn't you consider the possibility that you were a fighter in a previous life? Rileigh, it was those forgotten skills that resurfaced when you were attacked."

I was going to answer him when the familiar wind stirred through my head, raising the hairs along the back of my neck.

They're waiting. Behind the door.

My laughter came out a pitch higher than normal. I quickly choked it down and shook my head furiously, as if I could somehow shake the voice loose from my skull.

Kim frowned. "Rileigh ... are you well?"

I stopped shaking and smoothed my ruffled hair back with my hands. "You're wrong. It was adrenaline that helped me that night. That's all."

"Oh, adrenaline. I see." He turned his body away from me, watching me from over his shoulder. "Is that what you really think?"

I wanted to tell him that yes, that's exactly what I thought, but I didn't have the time. He spun around so quickly that he was nothing but a blur of color. I saw his kick form just as fast and knew that his intended target was my head. I closed my eyes—my first instinct—giving myself no time to make any other move.

Waiting for my nose to be bashed in, I was startled when a slight breeze tickled past my cheek.

Cracking my eyelids open, I found Kim towering over me wearing a smug smile. I felt slightly dizzy and it took me a minute to figure out why he loomed so far above me —somehow I'd ended up crouched on the floor, with one hand defending my face and the other bracing the katana out in front of me. I dropped the sword like it was on fire.

He laughed. "Did adrenaline help you do that?"

I barely heard him over the blood pounding in my head. I couldn't believe he'd tried to kick me, regardless of whatever point he was trying to prove. What if he'd been wrong? I'd have been knocked out cold. Hot flames of anger licked along my insides. I embraced it, allowing it to burn away the fear and insecurity still inside me. I'd had enough. "Listen, buddy, I may not know what's going on here, but the next time you try to kick me, remember one thing." I picked the sword up and stood up to face him. "I'm the one with the sword, and apparently I know how to use it." I wasn't sure I really believed that, but this guy was entirely too cocky.

He laughed again, a deep-throated hearty sound that reverberated throughout my body, melting my anger. That, more than anything else, scared me.

"Well," he said when he could speak again, "that's what I intend to find out."

"Yeah, how's that?" Even if I wasn't angry, I could still act the part.

He turned away from me and headed toward a door to the side of the mounted weapons. He opened it a crack, turned his back to me, and said, "It's time."

I had a moment to wonder who he was talking to before three figures, dressed in what looked like head-to-toe white pajamas, stalked through the door. The scarves wrapped around their heads hid their faces, but it was more than obvious from the intensity in their eyes that they weren't here for a slumber party.

I licked my suddenly dry lips as trickle of sweat ran down the length of my spine.

Their eyes weighed me as they made their slow, steady approach. They didn't stop until I was placed in the middle of a very dangerous circle. Moving in sync, they reached behind them and drew out their own katanas. The tips of the blades flashed in the light of the overhead fluorescent bulbs. Scared as I was, I couldn't help but appreciate the beauty of their movements—how each move held enough grace to make even the most practiced ballerina jealous.

One of the figures raised his sword over his shoulder,

and my own terrified eyes were reflected back at me from the blade. "Oh no, no, no." I held a single hand in front of me.

The three figures took a collective step closer.

My heart dug into my chest like a jagged stone. This was crazy! I wasn't supposed to die this way—diced to pieces by ninjas. It sounded ridiculous just thinking it in my head. "Kim," I pleaded, "I don't know what you think is going on, but it's not true. I'm not a reincarnated warrior. I just got lucky before. I can't fight. Don't let them do this!"

His face was an expressionless mask. "There is no other way." He bowed his head. "Kill her."

13

The first attacker lunged for me, screaming, with his blade held high over his head. As he got close, the cold silk from the attack outside the parking lot returned. It unraveled from within, stretching to my fingers and toes. It pushed open my lungs, allowed me to breathe, and froze my fear into a solid lump that fell and shattered against the hard pit of my stomach. As it had in the mall parking lot, a calm focus flooded through me and pushed the confusion from my mind.

This one is inexperienced with a blade, the voice whispered. *It won't take much to bring him down.*

I felt the unfamiliar smile return to my lips—this was going to be fun. I dodged the outstretched blade inches before my skin was to be torn apart by sharpened metal. Spinning behind the first attacker, I ducked low to the ground, kicked my leg, and swept his feet out from under him. He landed on his back and groaned.

The next attacker circled me, his eyes darting nervously back and forth between me and his fallen comrade. His body was rigid as he waited for an opportunity to move in.

This one is looking for a hole in our defense. We mustn't give him one.

"Sounds good to me," I whispered.

The attacker hesitated.

I straightened my stance. "Yeah that's right, I'm talking to myself! What of it?"

He peeked over his shoulder at Kim, who motioned him back to me with a nod. We circled each other, back and forth, staring, each waiting for the other to make the first strike. Eventually, his muscles shuddered with strain and he dropped into a crouch.

He's going to make his move.

I swung the blade out in front of me in a defensive stance, ready and waiting. He paused as uncertainty flashed behind his eyes. Was he changing his mind?

She's coming from behind.

I sensed the girl behind me before I saw her. It was an odd feeling, to know a person's movements without seeing them, just like when I felt Whitley listening in on my phone conversation. I didn't have time to be freaked out by the new sensation—

I needed to move. I spun and dodged her blade, which missed my shoulder in its downward arc. She was faster than the first attacker and twisted to face me before I was able to dart away. With another yell, she swung her katana high, exactly as I anticipated. I raised my blade to protect my face and decided that if she insisted on aiming for my head, I didn't want her holding a blade.

Our swords met, sliding with a hiss before I flung her back with a hard shove. She stumbled, but caught herself. She yelled and pushed forward again, aiming for my throat. She lashed out, but this time I sidestepped the blow. As she fell into the space I'd deserted, I planted a knee in her stomach.

She cried out, doubling over as she hugged her sides. I grabbed her by the arm, positioned my body along her side, and used her own weight to flip her over on her back. She cried out again and dropped her katana when she hit the floor.

I plucked her blade from the ground so that I now held one in each hand. Swinging them before me, I turned my attention to the remaining attacker. The man turned and glanced nervously at Kim, who was too busy smiling at me to notice.

"I thought you couldn't fight?" Kim said.

"When I'm done with this guy here," I said, licking my lips, "why don't you come over here and find out?" I crossed the two blades in front my body.

I was ready.

The standing man—left with no other options—dropped his shoulders and charged. As he hugged his sword against his body, I brought my arms inward to meet his blow and pushed out the moment I heard the hiss of metal sliding down metal.

His initial grace lost, he scrambled backward, almost tripping in the process. I let him get about twenty feet from me before I lunged. His eyes—I noted with pleasure—bulged from his head as I advanced. Bringing my blades back tight against my body, I dove between his legs, snaring his right knee with my foot as I rolled through.

He tumbled down, but rolled over and hopped to his feet in one fluid motion.

No problem. My mind, already a step ahead, instructed me what to do and where to move. I could barely keep up with my own actions—kick, dodge, roll. I wasn't in control, so I just sat back and enjoyed the ride.

But the ride was a long one. I wasn't certain how long I'd been fighting. It couldn't have been more than ten minutes, but it felt like hours. How long could this guy keep attacking me? How long could I fend him off? Another kick. Another sword strike. Both missed their target. I was vaguely aware of a slow burning creeping through my muscles. I was tiring. It wouldn't be much longer.

My attacker was tiring too. He moved slower, sloppier. His kick went wide and I used that moment to launch my own kick between his shoulder blades as he swung past. He sailed past me and landed, gasping for breath, on the mats. I lowered my arms, twisted my blades downward, and trapped his sword in a steel grip. With another twist, I swung my arms to the right and tore his katana from his grasp, flinging it across the room.

"We're finished here," Kim said from across the room.

Oh, but *I* wasn't finished. Not even close.

I stood over my fallen enemy, both swords quivered in a high arc above my head. Finishing a yell that I hadn't even realized I'd begun, I brought the two blades crashing down.

"Senshi, NO!" Kim's yell brought me back, but not soon enough.

I closed my eyes just as the girl attacker cried out. In that instant, the world froze so that nothing existed but me, the dark, and the girl's scream echoing through my ears. What had I done? A pounding pressure built in the back of my skull until a massive migraine consumed my whole head.

"It's okay. I'm okay!" It was a male voice.

I opened my eyes cautiously, blinking against the light that amplified the pounding in my head. The remaining attacker was still on the floor, untouched. His head lay between the two blades I had planted mere inches from his ears.

He sat up slowly, pulling down the scarf that covered his face and exposing a lopsided grin. "That was amazing!" He laughed, stood, and patted my shoulder. He was short for a teenager, only a couple inches taller than me. He pushed back his white hood, exposing wavy auburn hair. "Incredibly scary, but still amazing!"

Moments ago, this guy was trying to kill me—now he was smiling and patting me on the back? I didn't understand, but didn't feel well enough to talk. I hated not being in control of my body, and the last move was just a little too close for comfort. No, amazing was not the word I would use. Terrifying, horrifying, gut-wrenching—those were much better choices.

Suddenly I was hit by a headache so intense that my vision blurred. Each pulsing throb became more terrible than the last, until I was sprawled on the floor, unsure of how I got there.

Kim appeared before me. His fingers almost brushed my cheek. Again he caught himself, stopping short before we touched. He turned and spoke to the others, but I couldn't make it out. I was too far away.

My vision swam in a kaleidoscope of multicolored triangles that tumbled and merged, forming new triangles that fell into the same tumbling pattern. Inch by inch, darkness crept along the edges of my beautiful hallucination, like ink seeping into a rag. Tighter and tighter, until—for the second time—I fell into darkness.

14

Japan, 1493

Staring at the pool of blood outside Lord Toyotomi's door, Senshi struggled to swallow the bile that pushed up her throat. She drew a sharp breath while sliding her katana free from her obi. There was so much blood—too much for anyone to—no, she couldn't think that.

As decorum required, she announced herself before entering Toyotomi's room.

"Help us!" a female called back. The despair in her voice tugged on Senshi's heart and pulled her into the room as fast as her feet could carry her.

Just as she feared, she was too late. Two house maids huddled together on Toyotomi's sleeping mat. The first, a girl in her early teens, rocked back and forth. Her vacant eyes looked at Senshi, but stared through unseeing. She had raked her nails down her cheeks, leaving tear-diluted bloody trails down her face and throat. The second, an elderly woman, cradled an unmoving Toyotomi in her lap, whispering words of comfort while stroking his long, white hair.

Right away Senshi spotted the arrow protruding from Toyotomi's chest. "No," she whispered. It couldn't be. She approached cautiously, not believing her eyes. Toyotomi had saved her from the pleasure district when she was a young girl. He took her into his estate, and, despite the outcries of most of the other samurai, started her training. Senshi kneeled beside him, hesitant to touch him and confirm the worst.

As if sensing her presence, Toyotomi smiled. "Senshi. I knew ... you would come." His face, normally the color of the herbal tea he was so fond of, was now ash gray. With great effort, he placed a trembling hand on her knee.

That single touch shattered her. She threw herself onto his lap, clutching the fabric of his robes as if her grip alone could keep his spirit rooted on earth. "My lord, I have failed you."

He chuckled without sound. "No," he whispered, his chest straining to give sound to his words. "Never fail ... not you ... my greatest honor."

"What?" She lifted her head, exposing the long trails of tears that ran down both cheeks.

"Senshi ... I saw ... great things. You ... did not disappoint."

"But I—"

Toyotomi lifted a single finger. "Do not ... argue ... dying man."

Senshi bowed her head. "Forgive me."

Toyotomi closed his eyes and smiled, but his peace was short-lived as a coughing fit tore through him. When at last he was through, he waved his hand dismissively. "Nothing ... forgive. Now go ... help others." He tried to take another deep breath, but instead coughed up flecks of blood.

Senshi shook her head as she clasped her hands around his. "You need help."

He closed his eyes, sucking in a thick, wet breath. "No ... Yoshido and others need you ... Go to them." He looked up at her with eyes she had never seen before: young and bright. The next moment he was gone.

Senshi shuddered as the wind of death blew through the room. Her insides convulsed with pain, but she could not allow herself to crumble. A warrior could not break in battle. She clenched her jaw so hard that her teeth ground together. Pain shot along her mouth. She welcomed the distraction. With a deep breath, she turned away from the hysterical house maids and followed the sounds of battle deeper into the mansion.

15

I felt like I was jammed inside a washing machine going through the heavily soiled cycle. Back and forth my world shifted and spun, shaking me so violently that when I finally opened my eyes, I knew I was going to have to make a run for the nearest toilet. I tried to pull myself off the dojo floor before it was too late.

"Whoa, maybe that's not such a good idea. You should probably take it easy for a bit."

I looked up at the girl kneeling beside me, recognizing the brown hair that haloed her head in an I-just-stuck-my-finger-in-a-light-socket kinda way. "You're Michelle Walters, from my biology class." I should have been surprised to see someone from my school, but getting attacked (again) and passing out (again) dulled my reactions. I felt pretty sure that Justin Timberlake could walk through the door at this point, propose marriage, and I wouldn't bat an eye.

Her eyes widened. "You know my name? I've seen you around school and all, but we've never hung out. You hang out with the skaters, right? I didn't think—"

"A little help?" I interrupted as I pushed up on my elbows. Though she'd lost the scarf, Michelle still wore the white pajamas marking her as one of the three attackers. My mind was so full of questions that it felt dangerously close to exploding, but then again, so did my stomach, and that took priority.

"Oh, sure." Michelle placed a small, delicate hand on the back of my arm. "I'm sorry, sometimes I ramble when I'm nervous. Do you ever do that?" She snorted and shook her head. "Of course not. What a stupid question, right? I bet—"

"Michelle!" I flinched as my own raised voice beat the back of my eye sockets.

She snapped her jaw shut and made a motion as if sliding a zipper closed over her lips.

"Look," I clamped a hand against my forehead. "I didn't mean to yell at you, but my head is killing me and I have to puke."

"Oh jeez, I forgot about that part." She reached down and pulled me to my feet. She led me to the bathroom, careful not to let me fall on my gelatin legs.

When the bowl was within reach, I tumbled to my knees and wrapped my arms around the cold tank. Everything I had eaten since this morning came back with a vengeance. My beloved toaster pastries and I were now mortal enemies.

If Michelle felt any anger toward me for the whole knee-in-the-gut thing, she didn't let it show. For the next five minutes, she pulled my ponytail behind my shoulders and politely flushed the toilet in between my heaving. Even as I reached the point where my stomach was empty but the heaving wouldn't stop, she placed her hand on my forehead to keep me from falling in, as I barely had the strength to sit up.

"Thank God that's finally over," she said when I relaxed my cheek against the plastic seat, too tired to care what might have been there before. She stood up and brushed her pants before pulling several paper towels from the dispenser on the wall. She wet them in the sink and kneeled down beside me, pressing them against the back of my neck. It was bliss.

Several minutes later, when the pulsing in my skull quieted down, I lifted my head, which felt like it weighed fifty pounds, and locked my watery eyes with hers. "Why are you being so nice to me?"

She looked confused. "Why wouldn't I be?"

"Um, maybe because you tried to kill me?"

Her laugh was explosive. "Kill you? Are you crazy?"

Apparently. I dug my fingers into my temples, partly to numb the new round of throbbing and partly to keep from strangling Michelle. "I heard Kim tell you to kill me."

"Oh that." She rolled her eyes. "He wasn't serious. It was only a test."

She had my attention now. I pushed myself away from the toilet and turned to face her, but not before spitting one last time. "A test? What for?"

She stiffened, her brown eyes growing large. "I couldn't—Kim wouldn't—it's just not my place." She stood, but I grabbed her leg before she could escape.

"Then whose place is it? Kim's? Because all he's done so far is lie to me." I gave her my most exasperated look, which wasn't too difficult considering how I felt. "Come on, Michelle, I need to know what's going on."

She bit her lip and looked longingly over her shoulder at the door. "He really didn't tell you?"

I rolled my eyes and folded my arms.

She whined softly, settling down on the brown ceramic tile beside me. "I don't know, Rileigh, I'm not the best at explaining things and this is going to be hard enough for you to understand. I remember when I went through it. Kim tried to explain it to me and I was like, 'Whoa!' and then—"

"Michelle," I growled her name through clenched teeth.

"Right. Sorry." She took a deep breath. "This is going to sound crazy. Really, really crazy. But I swear it's the truth."

That wasn't a promising beginning, her telling me to be prepared for crazy and not taking into account everything that I had been through. If that was normal to her, I didn't know that I could handle her definition of crazy.

She studied the ceiling. "How do I start?" She chewed on her lip for a minute before bringing her gaze back to me. "Okay, the four of us: Kim, me, and the two other guys you sparred, Braden and Drew... we have all known each other for a very long time."

I braced my hands behind me and leaned back. My vision was still blurry. "How long?"

"Five hundred years."

I rested my head against the wall and sighed. I had come here tonight looking for a way to rid myself of the crazy ruining my nice, normal life. I was given a sword, lied to, and forced to defend myself against three armed attackers. And did I get the answers and help that I wanted? No, I got *more* crazy. I sighed again.

"I know how it sounds," Michelle continued. "When Kim saw you on the news last week, he recognized something in the way you fought. You reminded him of someone he knew and it got us all excited. You see, we've been looking for this person for quite a while." She turned her attention to the soap dispenser hanging over my head.

"And?" I prompted.

"We believe you are the one we have been looking for," Kim answered as he stepped into the small bathroom, this time wearing a T-shirt and tennis shoes with his black pants. Either he had been listening outside the door or he had great timing.

I had too many questions to count, but the bile in the back of my throat kept them from forming on my tongue. Instead, I stood on wobbling legs, ignoring Michelle's offered hand, and rinsed my mouth out at the sink. I finished by splashing cold water on my face. The icy sting assured me I was not dreaming.

I turned to face Kim first. "Is that why you called me Senshi?"

He nodded but added nothing.

Michelle huffed and gave Kim an exasperated look. "Senshi was one of us—a samurai."

He exhaled sharply, slumping his shoulders in defeat. "Yes. You remind me of her. The way you fight, and other things ... " I watched his eyes dull as his memories pulled him inside himself. "Please forgive me for calling you that; I was just caught up in the moment. We won't know anything for sure unless you transcend."

Before I could ask what that meant, Michelle climbed to her feet. "Rileigh, why don't you join us in the break room? I'll make a pot of coffee, and we can sit. It'll be a lot more comfortable than discussing things here."

I leaned against the sink for support. Of course they wanted me to follow them into another room. Because it worked out so well for me last time. "I'm not going anywhere with you guys. I've already been lied to once. How do I know you're not going to lure me into another *test*? Maybe you want to put me in a plane and then have the pilot bail to see if I know how to fly. Or how about giving me a bomb? Maybe I'll know how to diffuse it!"

Michelle nervously traced a scuff mark on the floor with her toe, but Kim fought off a smile that played along the edges of his mouth.

I couldn't believe his nerve. "You think this is funny?"

Before he could answer, the door to the bathroom swung in and the boy whose head I'd almost impaled walked in, followed by another guy with a waist-length blond braid that swung behind his back like a rope.

"Is everything all right?" the blond guy asked. He looked just shy of the seven-foot mark, towering above us and making me suddenly aware that I was in a small, windowless bathroom with the only exit blocked. "We heard shouting."

Michelle answered him. "Rileigh's still ... adjusting." She turned to me and gestured over her shoulder. "Rileigh, this is Drew."

The blond giant nodded and gave a weak smile.

"And I'm Braden." The second guy gave me a lopsided grin as he reached across the room and offered his hand.

I folded my arms across my chest and glared at him.

Braden's smile withered. "Um, right." He pulled his hand back and used it to sweep the auburn waves from his face, which immediately fell back over his eyes.

Kim clasped his hands and stared at the ceiling. "I'm sorry that you feel betrayed, Rileigh. I wouldn't have tricked you unless it was absolutely necessary. You had to believe you were in danger to trigger an awakening."

I hugged myself tighter. "I don't understand."

Kim settled his gaze on me and I fought the urge to flinch under its weight. "Many of us in this world, if not all, have lived before in various times and places. Most live their multiple lives without this realization. Their minds are closed, enabling them to only see what is, not what was. The awakening begins when pieces of your past collide with your present. *Your* past warrior was first awakened by the danger you felt in the mall parking lot."

The walls of the bathroom seemed closer than they had moments ago. I sucked in a deep breath to calm myself, but the room felt too small, like there wasn't enough air. "Let me see if I have this straight—you guys think I'm your reincarnated warrior-friend."

"Not just a warrior. A *samurai,*" Braden corrected.

"Whatever," I snapped. "So you invite me here and attack me in the hopes of drawing the spirit out? Does that sound about right?"

The four of them nodded, as if happy I'd figured it out.

I threw my hands in the air. "Are you insane?"

They stopped nodding. Michelle's lips parted in surprise, but no sound came out.

"That's the stupidest thing I've ever heard!" My hands began to tremble and I gripped the sink behind me to keep them steady.

Kim closed his eyes and breathed deeply. "I understand that you skate. But you've never done martial arts. Am I correct?"

I nodded, not liking the fact that he obviously knew so much about me.

"Tell me," he said, "when you fought, first those three men in the parking lot and now here in the dojo, were you not calm? Did the fighting not come naturally to you? Almost like you were possessed?"

I nodded again, but slower this time.

Kim continued. "Then what other explanation is there?"

My knees wobbled. If what Kim said was true and this was a situation that would require more than a prescription of anti-psychotics, then I was in a world of trouble. "Let's just say for a moment, hypothetically, that you're right—that there's a ... samurai living inside me, whispering in my head, and taking over my body. Okay, fine. Now let's move on to what really matters—how do I get rid of it?"

"You can't." Kim stepped forward, but halted when I shrank against the sink. "Once an awakening is triggered, there's no way to stop it."

"You're wrong!" He had to be. I had senior year to look forward to, with skate competitions, prom, and graduation. I couldn't let a dead spirit take all of that away from me—at least not without a fight. "I'll find a way to get rid of it. And if you won't help me, I'll figure out a way to do it on my own!" I blinked back the tears stinging my eyes.

Kim ducked his head and lowered his voice as if he were coaxing a frightened animal out of a corner. "I'm afraid that's impossible. Because of the test I've put you through, you've proven that buried inside of you is a powerful warrior. That's going to make you a target for some very bad people."

"Like you guys?" I asked.

Kim seemed at a loss for words, so Michelle spoke up. "We would never hurt you, Rileigh. We're only trying to help."

I almost laughed. I'd had enough of their help for one night. "You want to help me? You can start by leaving me the hell alone!"

The four of them stared at me in stunned silence.

I marched up to Drew, who stood wide-eyed and frozen in front of the door. "Move!"

"Rileigh, give us another chance," Michelle begged. "If you'd just let us explain ... "

I shook my head. I needed to get out of here. I felt myself coming apart at the seams, and I wouldn't let them see me break.

Kim ushered Drew to the corner of the room and pulled the bathroom door open, motioning me to it with a sweep of his arm. "Let her go if that's what she wants."

I stared at Kim. Was it going to be that easy?

"We can't just let her walk out the door," Braden argued. "She's in no state to be going anywhere."

Kim turned on him, snarling. "I said, let her go."

It was too much. I was on sensory overload. My body felt like it held a Ferris wheel with anger, confusion, and fear spinning round and round, each taking their turn at the top. I couldn't focus enough to organize my thoughts, so I did the first thing that came to mind.

I ran.

16

Reincarnation? Samurai? The whole thing was crazy.

I turned on the radio in the hopes that the music would distract me from the thoughts swirling around my head. It didn't. I kept thinking about what Kim had said—how it would be impossible to rid myself of the spirit. He was wrong. If there was a samurai warrior inside of me, then I would find a way to get rid of it.

But first I had to make sure I really was possessed. My fighting skills could still be the result of an adrenaline rush from the unexpected attacks. I wanted to know what would happen if I put myself in danger on purpose.

I thought back to the tired-looking bar nestled between cornfields. When I saw the blinking florescent lights advertising different types of beer from behind smoke-stained windows, I turned off the road and pulled into the gravel lot. There were more than a dozen motorcycles lined up out front. I parked next to them and killed my engine.

My hands gripped the steering wheel so hard my knuckles turned white. "Are you crazy, Rileigh Martin?" I whispered. I guess I was about to find out.

I took a deep breath and exited my car. The key to this experiment was staying calm. If I became scared and triggered an adrenaline rush I'd learn nothing.

Two men dressed in leather vests and black bandanas stood outside the bar smoking cigarettes. They eyed me curiously as I walked past. The first dropped his cigarette to the sidewalk and ground it out with a metal-tipped boot. "Are you lost, darlin'?"

It took me several tries before I could answer. "No. I—uh—I'm looking for someone."

The man had the name "Dino" embroidered on his vest right under the image of a snake hanging out of an eyeless skull. He gave me the once-over. "Sure you're looking in the right place?"

I fought the urge to give up on my experiment and make a run for it. But I had to know. There was no going back. I swallowed hard. "This is the spot."

He nodded and held the door out for me, gesturing me in with a sweep of his arm. A haze of smoke and AC/DC's *Back in Black* lay beyond.

Immediately the weight of a dozen pairs of eyes pressed against me. *No going back,* I reminded myself. The bartender, a man with yellow skin and more lines on his face than a digital barcode, stopped pouring a drink and leaned against the bar. "What gives, Dino?"

He shrugged. "Says she's looking for someone. Are they here, doll face?"

I pretended to scan the room before I shook my head. This was poor planning on my part. How was I supposed to prove whether or not I was possessed? Pick a fight? The idea was so ridiculous I almost laughed.

Dino cocked his head. "You all right?"

If he only knew. I leaned heavily against a barstool, my knees suddenly weak and my throat dry. "This was a mistake," I answered. "Would it be all right if I got a drink of water before I go?"

The bartender frowned.

"Just give her a drink, eh, Teddy?" Dino said. "Then she'll be on her way." He looked at me. "Right?"

"Absolutely."

Dino nodded at me before walking across the room and joining two men at a pool table. The bar patrons turned back to their beers.

"Here." The bartended dropped a chipped plastic glass in front of me with enough force that water sloshed over the side. "Drink up, then you're out of here."

I climbed the wooden bar stool and took a giant gulp from the glass. That seemed to satisfy the bartender, who went back to pouring beers.

The bar top was sticky and I was careful to keep my arms off it as I sipped my water. My experiment had been a bust. I hadn't proved anything other than bikers are a lot nicer than I'd assumed. Or so I thought until I felt the lumbering presence behind me.

"Here I am."

I spun the stool around to find a guy in his late twenties with red-rimmed eyes. I set my glass on the bar. "I'm sorry?"

He hiccupped and the movement dropped his bandana across his eyes. With greasy fingers he pulled it back up. "You said you were looking for someone. Well, here I am."

A cool breeze floated through me even though the door to the bar remained closed. I jerked straight up in my seat. No! It couldn't be! This guy was a loser, too drunk to be a threat, yet ribbons of satin uncoiled beneath my skin anyway. I had my answer; whatever was going on with me, adrenaline had nothing to do with it.

I gripped the edge of the stool. Maybe I could fight it off? I clenched my teeth and tightened my hold, but the effort proved pointless. A tingling numbness sucked me deep inside myself, holding me captive in my own body.

"So how 'bout it, sweet thang?" The biker teetered to the side, but righted himself with a hand on the counter. "Wanna ride on my bike? It's got a *big* engine."

"No, thanks," I said. "I'll pass." If he turned away everything would be fine. I could go home and pretend this whole thing never happened.

But he didn't budge.

On the inside I screamed. On the outside my mouth

twitched. If this guy hadn't been such an idiot I might have felt sorry for him.

The threat of conflict filled the room like humidity in a sauna, pressing, making it hard to breathe. Sensing the tension, the bar patrons twisted in their stools, searching for the source. The bartender stopped wiping the counter and threw his rag down. "Oh, sweet Jesus," he muttered. "Dino, get your boy."

Dino froze mid-shot and placed his pool stick on the table. "Jesse, she's jail-bait. Leave her alone."

Jesse ignored him. "Come on, baby. Don't be that way. I don't like a tease." He lifted a hand. What he intended to do with that hand I'd never know, because in the blink of an eye I'd struck the soft flesh under his jaw with my palm. Jesse's eyes rolled into the back of his head seconds before his body collapsed to the floor.

The entire bar rose to their feet, looking at each other as if waiting for someone else to decide what to do.

The bartender broke the spell by throwing his rag over the bar, where it landed on top of the groaning heap that was Jesse. "Mary, mother of all that is holy, somebody get him out of here. And you." He glared at me. "Get. Out. Now!"

I flexed my jaw side to side and tested my voice. "S-s-sure thing." All systems were in working order. The spirit was gone and had left me another mess to clean up. I slid off the stool and made my way, backward, toward the door.

"Hey!" A woman wearing leather pants and a leather

vest with nothing underneath stepped forward. "She can't get away with that!"

I froze. So close.

She set her beer down on the bar. "Jesse may be a dumb-ass, but he's pack. Ain't nobody treat a pack member like that and get away with it."

Most of the women grumbled in agreement while the men merely looked amused.

"Marlene," the bartender growled. "I don't want any trouble in here."

Marlene sneered. "Then we take it outside."

The experiment had gone too far. While I hadn't been afraid of Jesse, the same couldn't be said about the half-dozen women staring at me with death in their eyes. I didn't know what my limits were and didn't feel like finding out.

Marlene lunged for me and, for the second time in just a few hours, I turned and ran.

17

I darted into the parking lot with Marlene on my heels. A fist wound its way into the back of my shirt and pulled me backward. A yelp escaped my mouth before I could smother it.

Marlene jerked my face inches from her. "You are in for a world of hurt." Her breath smelled like onion rings and cigarettes.

I struggled against her hold like a puppy caught by its scruff. Where was the voice now?

Marlene laughed at my pathetic attempt to escape before throwing me down on the ground. Pain exploded from my elbows where gravel embedded itself in my skin.

Behind Marlene, six more women exited the bar, only they were more like rhinos in leather and braids than women. A few laughed while the rest just looked pissed.

Marlene tossed her head back, her braided hair swinging like a whip. "You're young. I bet you like games."

I shook my head.

Marlene laughed. "Well, that's too bad because we're going to play a game called 'Pickle Jar.' The rules are like this: I'm going to take your neck and see how many twists it takes until your head pops off." She cracked her knuckles and I couldn't help noticing the thick silver rings on each finger.

It took me several tries before I could swallow. Why couldn't I think before I acted? If I hadn't been so upset with Kim and so desperate to prove him wrong, I might be at home enjoying a hot cup of cocoa and an episode of *The Real World* instead of waiting to get my face pummeled in.

Marlene jumped on top of me, startling me from my thoughts. My head was thrust against the concrete upon impact. Before the stars could clear from my vision her forearm pressed into my throat, cutting off my air supply.

It was then I felt the cool sliding sensation under my skin.

"About time you got here," I gasped.

Marlene frowned and let up on her grip. "What?"

Instead of answering, my mouth curled into a smile. I braced my weight on my elbows and swung my legs up, snatching Marlene's thick braid between my feet. With as much force as I could muster, I brought my feet down, pulling Marlene away by the hair and releasing her grip on my neck. She toppled over backward.

Wide-eyed, she climbed to her knees and launched

herself at me. But I was ready. I curled my legs against my chest and kicked out the moment she collided against me. She spun in the air once before landing on the asphalt, sliding on her face before coming to a halt.

Marlene had her back to me when she stood up, but the hisses and winces from the rhino women let me know that she didn't look good. I didn't waste time. I scrambled inside my car and locked the doors.

"You think it's gonna be that easy?" Marlene yelled from outside the driver's side window. I gasped when I saw her face reflected under the bar's lone streetlight. Small pieces of gravel clung to the bloody ribbons that were all that was left of her right cheek.

Marlene whirled around and snatched a bottle of beer from the hands of the woman standing behind her. Spinning back, she brought it down on my side mirror, wrenching it off my car. She swung again, this time shattering the bottle across my hood and eliciting a scream from my lips.

My car! The image of the moon looked like a broken puzzle reflected in the fresh dent on the hood. The Fiesta had been a sixteenth birthday present from my Nana, the last gift she'd ever given me.

The rhino women surrounded my car and pressed their hands against the sides. My screams couldn't be heard over the groaning metal as they rocked my car back and forth. With each passing second they gathered more momentum and my car came closer to tipping over. I felt like a hamster in a plastic ball rolled around by a group of sadistic cats.

My only hope was escape. I clung to the steering wheel, grasping for the keys that dangled from the ignition just out of reach. I tried again. And again. The keys continued to bob from my grasp with each shake of my car until finally I'd circled my hand around them. Unfortunately, the next shake caused me to rip them from the ignition—that's when it happened.

The moment the keys fell into my lap, something exploded inside my chest. I gasped. The pressure grew fast, rolling and pushing against my skin like an animal trying to claw its way out.

So caught up in my pain, I barely noticed when a bottle smacked against the passenger window, leaving behind a spider web of cracked glass. Time was running out. I needed to move, but couldn't think past the ripping inside my chest. So much pain. Was I having a heart attack?

There was another crack, this time next to my head. Glass, like chunks of ice, rained down on me. I knew I should run, fight, do *something*—but all I could think about was the force crushing my ribs until I thought my heart would burst through, falling heavy and wet onto my lap.

Marlene shouted something and my car stopped shaking. This was it. I was either going to die from a heart attack or Marlene and the rhino women would pull me from the car and finish me off. The pain was unbearable. Either way I wanted it over.

Marlene grinned as she leaned through my window. "Ready to play nice?"

I closed my eyes and whimpered. Each second I felt myself stretched further as the animal inside me clawed its way through bone and muscle, until, finally, it burst through my skin, spilled out my pores, and ripped the scream from my throat.

The pain was gone.

I opened my eyes, afraid I would find my skin shredded into a bloody mess. But what I saw was something else entirely. Like a stone thrown in a pond, there was a ripple of… air? Energy? Whatever it was, it spilled forward, invisible except for the slight distortion in the air it projected as it grew. The ring left my car and hit Marlene and the others, tossing them to the ground like dandelions popped from their stems, before melting into the night.

Like it had never existed.

"This isn't real," I murmured. Chest heaving, I rested my forehead against the steering wheel. I felt like the bones had been pulled from my body, leaving me a pile of shivering goo. "I'm dreaming. This is a nightmare."

But the groans of the women drifting through my shattered window proved that they were, in fact, very real.

I pressed my hands against my chest to steady my heaving gasps. It didn't make sense. One minute I'd been screaming in agony and the next I'd been pain-free with the rhino women on their backs, littered among the cigarette butts. Did this have to do with the possession or was it something else all together?

A movement off to the side pulled me from my thoughts. A burly woman with a sleeve of skull tattoos was slowly pushing herself up from the gravel. With strength I didn't know I had, I sat back against my seat and started my car.

Time to go.

Later that night, as I lay in bed, my thoughts raced around in my mind like cars in the Indy 500. Round and round they sped, each coming just close enough for me to try and grasp onto it before another would fly in and take the lead. After my encounter with the bikers, I was willing to believe I was possessed. But what could I do about it? Could I really believe Kim when he'd said there was no way to get rid of the spirit, or was it just another deception? He'd lied to me once; who's to say he wouldn't lie again? He'd also said I could be the target for "very bad people." Were these people really dangerous and were they the ones who left the note on my door? I pushed the thought from my mind. I had enough to deal with.

Kim promised to protect you.

I clamped my hands against my ears. "Shut up! Shut up! Shut up!" I screamed at the inner voice. I couldn't even trust myself. Was I in a fight for my body? What if *I* became the one trapped inside my head?

Unable to lie still any longer, I threw the covers off my legs and stomped into the living room. Debbie's keys were still missing from the hook by the door, so I could only assume she was at an event schmoozing with clients.

Happy to be alone, I turned on the TV in the hopes of distracting myself from my thoughts. I flipped through the recorded shows until I found the latest episode of *Built To Shred.* As I watched the host lead a crew in turning a ravine, a fallen tree, and several sheets of plywood into a makeshift half-pipe, I was reminded how my love affair with skating began. I'd been eight years old and climbing the jungle gym at the park when a group of skaters showed up and began freestyling in the basketball court.

I remembered watching them, mesmerized, not only by their tricks but also by how they interacted. There was something about the way they laughed and slapped each other on the backs, like they were more than just friends. It was almost like they were a family. And I don't know why, but I wanted to belong too. Because, even at eight, I knew I was different from the girls gathered around me. Princesses and tea parties? They just didn't do it for me.

So I ditched my dolls for a skateboard and traded dance recitals for road rash. It took several years, but I managed to prove myself as a skater. I had friends. I had respect. I had exactly what I'd wanted all those years ago.

Or at least I did before the voice showed up.

I turned the TV off and leaned my head back against the couch, content to sit alone in the darkness. Although I wasn't *really* alone—I'd proved that with my little biker-bar adventure. And if Kim was right, I wouldn't be alone ever again. If only I knew why. Of all the girls in the world, why possess me? If I could figure that out, maybe I could figure out how to get rid of it.

"What do you want?" I asked the shadows on the ceiling.

As if in answer, my hair fluttered around my face, stirred by a breeze that shouldn't exist in a room with closed windows.

18

Japan, 1493

Senshi spotted several fallen ninja scattered among the bodies of dead servants and samurai. She should have known the dishonorable assassins-for-hire had a part in this. Now the real question surfaced: Who was the benefactor? She upped her pace to a jog as she mulled it over. It didn't really matter. Whoever he was, his head would come off as easily as anyone else's.

Senshi darted around a corner and came to an abrupt halt in front of the door leading out into the gardens. Outside, from within a black cloud of ninja smoke magic, she could hear men shouting and the clashes of metal on metal. Smoke entered the hallway through the door, reaching for her like tentacles.

The smoke didn't concern her. When she had been accepted into Toyotomi's household, he had recognized her rare ability to manipulate ki energy and worked with her to master the gift. It was one of the reasons Toyotomi insisted that she train as a samurai, despite the outrage over her gender.

She drew her energy inward in calm focus, holding her katana in front of her as she stepped out into the gardens. Senshi's skin prickled as the energy built to painful levels within her. Something was different. She was unable to filter her grief from her concentration. For the first time, her power took on an edge of instability as it mixed with her emotional pain. She gasped, fighting to hold on to the little control her emotions left her. Then she let go.

Senshi's power exploded from her body with tornado-like force. She could hear the muffled screams of men from within the spinning curtain of smoke, but the winds picked up as more of her spiritual energy left her body. Soon she could hear nothing but the roar of power beating against her ears. Squinting her eyes against the sting of the wind and her own whipping hair, she could barely see the blurred figures of ninja as they fell over and ran for cover.

One ninja held his ground, moving slowly forward one step at a time with his sword held out. Sensing his approach, Senshi turned her attention to him and the wind pulsing from her quickly subdued him. He toppled over and went scrambling away on his hands and knees, abandoning his weapon among the dead samurai littering the ground.

When Senshi succeeded in ridding the yard of the last of the smoke magic, she faced the difficult task of harnessing her power. Screaming, she threw her arms wide, swallowing the whirlwind down. It fought against being contained like a swarm of bees in a jar too small to hold them. When she succeeded in closing the ki off, she crumpled to her knees. There was no sound. For one terrifying moment she thought the roaring winds had left her deaf. Then she heard one set of hands clapping together. Looking up, she saw the man who had betrayed Lord Toyotomi and the entire village.

He was a brother samurai.

19

The soft shuffling of footsteps pulled me from my dream with a gasp. The voice in my head wasn't far behind.

INTRUDER!

I sat up in my bed and looked around my bedroom. The pale-blue glow of the moon filtering through my window provided me just enough light to see. I was alone.

I relaxed back against my pillow as the icy grip of fear relaxed its hold on my chest. "Stupid Rileigh," I grumbled. I was allowing my paranoia to get the better of me. The night's events had freaked me out to the point that I was imagining things. Of course there was no intruder. The voice I'd heard was probably leftover from a nightmare.

I pulled the blanket tighter but continued to shiver. With a sigh, I pushed the covers back and crossed my room to close the window, stopping short before I reached it. The pane, which I liked to keep cracked a couple of inches while I slept, was wide open.

My heart beat in a frantic rhythm. Did I leave my window open? I'd been so freaked out after the incident in the living room, maybe I forgot to close it...

The sound of a twig snapping outside pulled me from my thoughts. I rushed to the window and leaned my head out, looking in both directions. Nothing moved and the only noise came from the chirping cicadas. I laughed quietly and slid the window down. Inches before the pane met the sill, I heard another snap and saw a shadow slip around the front of the house.

Panic bubbled like a fountain through my body.

Remain calm.

I shook my head and took a step back. "Easy for you to say." The words came out a whimper.

"Rileigh?"

I spun so fast toward my door that I tripped over my feet and landed in a heap on the floor.

Debbie stood in my doorway, clutching her silk robe closed at the neck. Lines of concern pressed into her brow. "What are you doing? All your moving around woke me up."

"Mom!" I scrambled to my feet and rushed over to her, gripping her shoulders. "Call 9-1-1!"

Debbie's eyes widened and she dropped her hand to her side. "What?"

I took a deep breath and tried again. "Someone's sneaking around our house. You need to call the police."

Her mouth gaped open. Debbie could eat a casting director for breakfast. She could handle contract negotiations in her sleep. But now, for the first time in my memory, she looked like a frightened child.

"Mom!" I shook her. "Go!"

"I … uh … okay." She continued to nod as I followed her down the hall and into the living room. She grabbed her purse from the coffee table and rummaged through it with shaking hands.

While she searched, I looked out each window. The front yard stood vacant and well-lit, thanks to the streetlamps. I studied the unchanging scene for several minutes. Not a single car drove by.

Debbie threw her purse on the floor. "My phone's not in there," she whispered, her voice wavering. "Do you think it's safe for me to go back to my bedroom and check my jeans?"

I sighed. "I'm pretty sure."

After Debbie ran from the room, I walked over to the side window and surveyed the small path of grass separating our house from our neighbors. What if the police didn't find anything? What if there was nothing to find? Maybe I was now hearing things outside of my head as well as in it. I pushed away from the window just as a knock sounded at the door.

Debbie shrieked from behind me and dug a handful of half-inch-long French-tip nails into my arm.

"Mom!" I turned to dislodge her hand and came face-to-face with a gleaming butcher knife. "Wha—" I ripped my arm from her grasp and rubbed the burning trail her nails left behind. "Are you crazy?"

She continued to shriek with her eyes closed, waving the knife blindly in front of her like a miniature flag on the Fourth of July. I had to duck to avoid the cleaver shaking in her hand.

"Oh for the love of… " I ducked again. "Mom! Knock it off!" As she began a second circle rotation, I made a fist and hit the inside of her wrist as hard as I could. The knife flew across the room and sank into the front door.

"Ow!" Debbie frowned at me as she rubbed her wrist. "Why on earth would you do a thing like that?"

"You can't be serious."

"Debbie? Rileigh?" The voice was familiar, but I couldn't quite place it. "Are you guys okay?"

Debbie pressed her hands against her heaving chest. "Oh, thank God!" She pushed past me and threw the door open. "Jason!"

As Debbie pulled Dr. Wendell inside our house, my skin prickled as if wanting to free itself from my bones. What was he doing here, and at such a late hour?

"What's going on in here?" He looked younger out of his scrubs, in running pants and a T-shirt. "I heard screaming." Debbie closed the door and his eyes widened at the cleaver piercing the wood. "Are you all right?"

"We are *now*." Debbie combed her fingers through her hair. "Thank goodness you're here."

I took a step forward and narrowed my eyes. "But

that's the thing—why are you here? How do you even know where we live?"

"Rileigh!" Debbie scolded. "Don't be rude."

"Come on!" I thrust my hand toward the clock. "It's two in the morning! He didn't just happen to be in the neighborhood and decide that it would be a good time to check up on a patient."

He looked appalled. "Of course not."

"So what are you doing here?"

He retrieved Debbie's purse from where she had thrown it on the floor. "My pager." He stuck his hand in and pulled out the small black device. "Your mom and I went on a date tonight. While we were out I asked her to keep my pager in her purse and I forgot about it."

"You're dating?" I heard the words, spoke them out loud, but they still didn't make sense. Debbie didn't date—she didn't have time for it. And if she needed an escort to a social event—Dr. Wendell was cute, but a far cry from the cologne models she usually draped across her arm like jewelry. "Since when?"

Debbie picked invisible lint off of her robe. "I asked Jason to be my guest at your cousin's wedding. Then tonight I got caught up in audition schedules so Jason took me out for a quick bite." She smiled at him. "Which was very sweet, by the way."

Sweet? An uneasy tremor crawled along my spine. I couldn't remember the last time Debbie had spent two days in a row with me, let alone some guy she'd just met. Something didn't feel right. I turned to Dr. Wendell. "Okay, so you and Mom got dinner and you forgot your pager. You couldn't get it in the morning?"

Debbie stamped her foot. "Rileigh Hope, that's enough. I won't tolerate your attitude."

"She's fine." Dr. Wendell held his arm out to silence her. "Rileigh has been through so much. Increased paranoia and distrust is to be expected, and completely normal. But this," he glanced behind him at the butcher knife, "concerns me a bit."

"Rileigh thought she heard someone sneaking around the house," Debbie said.

Dr. Wendell turned to me. "Are you sure you weren't dreaming? There was no one snooping around while I was outside."

I snorted. "How about we wait and let the police make that call."

"The police aren't coming," Debbie said.

I looked at her, fighting to keep my face calm. "Why not?"

"I never went to get my phone," she answered. "I thought it would be better if I got a weapon."

I smacked my hand against my forehead. "Haven't you ever watched a horror movie? Don't you know what happens to the people who run to the kitchen for a knife instead of calling the police?"

Debbie rolled her eyes. "This is life, Rileigh, not a movie." She leaned into Dr. Wendell and whispered, "She's always been a little dramatic. I have no idea where she gets it."

I almost choked.

Dr. Wendell walked to the couch and sat down, patting the cushion beside him. "Rileigh, why don't you sit?"

I crossed my arms. "I'd rather not."

Debbie skirted past me and took my rejected seat.

He shrugged. "Okay. I'm not going to make you."

"I'd love to see you try," I grumbled.

He leaned forward. "What was that?"

"I said, 'I'm so tired I could die.' Can the talk wait? I have to work tomorrow. I know my mom does, too." I motioned to the front door with my eyes.

"I completely understand. But I would like to do something for you if you don't mind—let me sleep on your couch."

I opened my mouth to argue, but Debbie shot me a warning glance that melted the words on my tongue.

"I'm sure Rileigh would love it if you stayed, Jason," Debbie crooned, but her eyes continued to project daggers at me.

Dr. Wendell smiled. "Great. If someone is sneaking around, maybe they'll think twice about bothering you if they know there's a man in the house."

"Jason, you are so sweet for worrying about us." Debbie patted his knee before she stood up. "Let me get you some blankets from the linen closet."

I watched open-mouthed as Debbie made her way past me. Never in my entire life had she ever invited a man to sleep over, and now the first guy she'd be smitten with was the one guy who gave me negative vibes? I knew if I had to stand in the presence of his smug smile for one more second I was going to lose it. After Debbie disappeared down the hall, I turned to make my getaway.

"Rileigh?" Dr. Wendell called.

Crap. I froze.

"If you're having trouble with anxiety, I could prescribe you something."

"Oh really?" I laughed quietly as I moved to face him. "How about a new life? Can I get that in a capsule? Or does it have to be applied topically?"

He frowned.

"That's what I thought." Before he could answer I spun on my heels and marched down the hallway into my room.

Chewing on my thumbnail, I sat down on my bed and tried to pinpoint what it was about Dr. Wendell that gave me the heebie-jeebies. Was it merely a coincidence that he'd showed up shortly after I spotted someone sneaking around the house? Or was what he said true? Was stress getting the better of me?

When I couldn't bite my nail any shorter I switched to my other hand. In any case, Dr. Wendell was in my house, directly down the hall. I didn't know how I was supposed to sleep with him here, but I had to try. My shift at the salon began in less than seven hours.

With a sigh, I got out of bed and locked my door for the very first time.

20

When I entered the salon the next morning, Quentin stopped sweeping hair and dropped the broom on the floor.

"Oh my God!" He ran up to me and put his hands on either side of my face. "Ri-Ri, what is wrong with you? Jeannine sent you home yesterday because you looked bad and you come in today looking even worse."

I tried to tilt my head, but he was squeezing it like a vise. "I didn't sleep very well last night. Mom had a *friend* sleep over and I couldn't get comfortable with him in the house." The dojo attack, bar fight, and crazy dreams didn't help much, either. But it wasn't like I could tell Quentin about all that. How could I expect anyone to believe me when I myself could barely believe those things happened?

He tsked. "Well, you look just awful."

"Thank you."

He released my face and tugged me back to a stylist chair. "Brie, I'm using your station!"

Brie, the salon's resident Goth girl, nodded to him from behind the retail counter as she painted her nails an emerald blue color.

"Sit," Quentin ordered.

I groaned. When the alarm went off this morning, I had only slept for four hours. I didn't waste more than five minutes in the bathroom getting ready because I knew there was little chance of improving my haggard appearance. "Not today, Q. I'd really rather just get to work." I tried to move past him, but he sidestepped along with me.

"Nonsense." He gripped my shoulders and shoved me down into Brie's chair. "There's always time for a makeover. Besides, there's no one to shampoo just yet. I've already called dibs on Mrs. Cooper over there."

Plump Mrs. Cooper sat a few chairs over, getting her rolled hair doused with perm solution while she thumbed through a worn romance novel.

I pointed a finger at Quentin's reflection in the mirror. "You snake!" He knew just as well as I did that Mrs. Cooper was one of the few women that tipped five dollars after a shampoo.

Quentin grinned back. "You snooze, you lose. Anyway, I'm sure you'll be busy in a minute." His eyes gleamed.

"Maybe I should just check to see if the stylists need anything first." I tried to stand, but he pushed me back down and buttoned a smock around my neck. I craned my head to see around the corner of the partitioning wall that divided the salon in half, but all I could make out were several women sitting under the dryers, paging through wrinkled magazines.

"I'll let you know when someone needs you." He twisted my hair into several loops and pinned them to the top of my head.

"Alright." Reluctantly, I leaned back into Brie's chair.

"Why are you so crabby, anyway? I'd be doing backflips if I had a date tonight with Mr. McHottie!" He unraveled a lock of my hair and clamped it between the ceramic plates of a flat iron.

"What are you talking—?" But before I could finish my sentence the realization hit me harder than a six pack of Red Bull. My date with Whitley was tonight! I slumped deep into the chair. For as long as I'd dreamed of this moment, there was no way I could go now. First of all, I looked like hell. Second, until I got rid of the spirit living inside of me, I couldn't risk triggering another awakening. What if I dropped a spoon on the ground, the barista brought me another one, and the spirit misinterpreted the action as a threat and punched him in the face? What would Whitley think of me then? I groaned and buried my face in my hands.

Quentin snapped the flat iron together, drawing my attention to him. "Uh, no. I don't think so." He placed his free hand on his hip.

"What?" I spread my fingers apart enough to peek through.

He pulled another lock of my hair free from a pin

with a sharp tug. "I know that look. You're thinking about canceling, and I am not going to let you do that. You've been lusting after this guy from the moment he showed up at school."

I dropped my hands and folded my arms under my smock. "Look, Q, I have a lot going on right now. I don't think this is the best time for me to date."

"Then when will be, Rileigh?" Uh-oh, he used my real name. "When you're seventy and living alone with thirty cats? You think there'll be anyone left then?" He tugged on another lock of hair. "You have to get past your relationship issues, Ri-Ri. I know you're scared, but you're also not happy."

"I am too happy," I snapped. "And I do not have relationship issues."

Quentin snorted, rubbing pomade between his palms and smoothing down the hair around my part. "You harbor a great deal of resentment toward you mother because she spends more time with her clients than you."

I stiffened against the vinyl cushion.

Quentin smiled, apparently pleased to have hit the nerve and made his point. "And," he continued, "that's why you keep going out with all the wrong guys—because even though they're losers, they still give you the attention you crave from your mother. You don't know how to pick a decent guy because you don't know what to look for. It didn't help that your daddy didn't stick around to see you born—you probably have some guilt and abandonment issues associated with that. It's a simple case of self-sabotage." He wiped his hands on a towel and pulled Brie's makeup case out from under her station counter. "Brie, can I use your MAC?"

Brie shrugged without looking up. "Don't use up all the black."

I angrily snatched the cleansing cloth Quentin offered me and wiped off my hastily applied morning makeup. "Thank you very much, Dr. Q, for the diagnosis."

While I sat fuming, Quentin dabbed fresh concealer onto a makeup brush and covered the dark circles under my eyes. When he finished, he put the brush back on the counter and stuck a finger under my chin. "You know I love you, right?"

I nodded. I did know, and that's why his words hurt so much. They were true. He never hid his feelings from me because he trusted our friendship enough to know that even if I didn't like what he had to say, I would still listen. That's what friends did. What they *didn't* do was hide things from each other. Guilt curled around me like a python flexing its coils.

"Don't wiggle," Quentin scolded, reaching for an eye shadow palette.

Maybe he was right about the abandonment issues. Maybe that's why I didn't tell him what was going on right away, because I was afraid he wouldn't understand. It was unfair of me not to have faith in him. I needed to tell him the truth. "Um, Q?" I closed my eyes long enough for him to apply a smoky gray shadow.

"Hmmm?"

"I need to tell you something."

"Okay," he said, reaching for an eyeliner pencil.

"I don't want you to think I'm crazy," I started.

"Oh, girl," he laughed, "it's way too late for that."

I smiled. "Very funny."

"Whatever it is, you know you can tell me, right?" He stopped applying mascara and stared into my eyes. "No matter what."

I took a deep breath, struggling to hold the weight of his stare. "Do you believe in past lives?"

He laughed out loud. "How long have I been telling everyone that I'm a woman trapped in a man's body?" he announced to the salon, eliciting a few giggles from the waiting area.

"Shh!" I ducked my head and motioned around the room with my eyes. "Q, I'm serious. I know you're trying to be funny, but do you really think that maybe in a previous life you could have been a woman?"

He paused to consider it. "I guess it could be possible."

"That's what I'm trying to tell you, you see—" But before I could finish, Hillary, one of the veteran stylists, emerged from the other half of the salon. "Rileigh, I've got a client in the sink room ready for a shampoo."

I started to rise, but was pulled right back down by Quentin.

"Wait!" he ordered. He cupped my chin with his hand and applied a heavy, grape-scented gloss. "Perfect. Okay, now you're ready." He ripped off the smock in one fluid movement.

I twisted in the chair to meet his gaze. "I guess we'll talk later."

"Sure thing, Ri-Ri." He smiled devilishly. "That is, if you are still speaking to me."

"Speaking to you?" I let him pull me to my feet, noticing the nervous glances he kept making toward the partitioning wall. "What did you do?" I hissed over my shoulder.

He inclined his head toward the sink room, failing to repress a delighted squeal. "I think you're needed back there." He giggled.

With a heavy sense of dread, I walked past the four stylist stations and stopped in front of the sink-room curtain. Sighing, I parted it and looked inside.

Kim Gimhae gave me a small wave from the last chair, farthest from the door.

I spun on my heels to face Quentin, but he was conveniently at the reception counter checking someone in. "Please have a seat, Mrs. Walker. Your stylist will be with you in a moment." He waggled his eyebrows at me as he spoke.

Cursing Quentin under my breath, I stepped inside and let the curtain fall behind me.

Kim cleared his throat. "I am sorry to surprise you at work."

My new level of stress cracked the barrier inside of me that kept the hysteria at bay. A high-pitched laugh escaped from my throat, followed by a series of giggles.

Kim looked nervously around the room. "Is something funny?"

"Yes," I said between giggles. "First it was Whitley, then Dr. Wendell, now you."

"I don't understand."

I pulled a tissue from a box on the shelf above the sink and dabbed at the tears in my eyes. "It's just that my life has spun so out of control, there's no telling who will show up next!" I had a mental image of walking out of the sink room and seeing Elvis under a dryer. I laughed harder.

Concern flooded Kim's eyes.

I cleared my throat and tossed the tissue in the trash. "Surprise visits seem to be a theme in my life right now."

"Rileigh, are you okay?"

"No big deal," I told him as I pulled a clean towel from the shelf next to the door. He wore a plain white cotton T-shirt, with athletic shorts and white tennis shoes. My eyes lingered on the hard lines of muscle that rose beneath his shirt as he breathed. Forcing my gaze away, I snatched the smock from a small cart by the sink and quickly snapped it behind his neck. I felt much better once his body lay hidden under shapeless black vinyl. "How short are you going to go?"

He shrugged under the smock. "I'm not here to have my hair cut. I came here because I wanted to talk to you. Your friend from the hospital told me to wait back here. A shampoo is really not necessary."

"Yeah, well, my boss is going to get upset if people keep dropping by to see me. If you want to talk," I pushed his head back against the sink's porcelain neck rest, "you're getting your hair washed. And you better leave a tip. Thirty percent should keep the Nair out of your shampoo."

His mouth twitched. "Fair enough."

"Good." I caught a movement over my shoulder, and a quick glance to my right showed Quentin peering through the curtain. I opened my mouth to give him a piece of my mind, but he ran away before I could get the words out. He was *so* dead.

I turned back to Kim and started the water. "So, how did you know I worked here?" I did my best to sound casual.

He smiled. "I can't reveal my sources."

I snorted. "What a surprise. Kim Gimhae has more secrets."

Kim's brown eyes sparkled with amusement. "Yes. It took some work, but I managed to hack into your personal records."

My eyes widened. "What kind of records? From school? Medical?"

He laughed. "No, more top secret than that. I found your profile on Facebook."

"That's really funny," I told him, forcing myself to bypass the bleach and instead grab the shampoo. If only I could dye Kim's hair pink without getting fired. "Maybe if this whole samurai thing doesn't work out for you, you could start a career in comedy."

"Maybe." He smiled, folding his hands over the smock.

I dug my fingers into his scalp, not caring if I was

a little rough. "Did you come here because you want something? Or are you just going to make harassing me a daily occurrence?"

He flinched, and I couldn't tell if it was from my fingers or my words. "You're absolutely right," he said. He waited for me to finish rinsing the shampoo from his hair before he sat up. "Last night didn't exactly go as planned. I wanted nothing more than to guide you through the awakening process with as little stress as possible. It seems I handled it all wrong, and for that I apologize."

I felt my calm defense crack at the mention of the awakening. "No problem," I told him, failing to steady my shaking hands as I dried his hair with a towel. The smell of sandalwood gradually left no trace of the grapefruit-scented shampoo I'd used. Even the towel picked up his warm, earthy smell. Fearing that the scent would soak into my skin, I dropped it on the floor. I walked around the chair so that I stood in front of Kim and put one hand on my hip. "Listen, I'm over it already."

Kim raised an eyebrow.

Feeling courageous, I placed my other hand on my hip. "That's right. I'm tired of being attacked. I'm tired of mysterious notes. It's making me crazy. Last night I was so freaked out that I thought I saw someone sneaking around my house."

Kim's eyes widened and he opened his mouth to speak, but I cut him off. "This isn't good for me. The best thing I can do is go back to living my life exactly the way it was before I ever met you."

"You can't."

I tapped my foot impatiently against the granite floor. "Yes, I can."

"No. You can't."

"And why not?"

"That could have been a Noppera-bō sneaking around your house."

"A what?"

Kim didn't answer, warning me that this was not going to be a revelation I would enjoy. Instead, he stared at his hands, lacing and unlacing his fingers until he let his breath out in a loud whoosh and met my gaze. "Rileigh, you were once a powerful samurai. If you transcend, you will be again. The Noppera-bō—which is Japanese for 'faceless ghost'—would prey upon you for your power."

"What is this, Scooby Doo? Are you telling me that *ghosts* are after me?"

Kim gave me an impatient look. "Of course not. The Noppera-bō are as real as you and me. It is only the name they call themselves because of their ability to avoid capture."

"Oh." I thought about this and smiled. "I don't see the problem. If the Noppera-bō want my power, they can have it."

Kim shook his head. "You don't understand. Your power is tied to your spirit, and your spirit is housed in that body." He pointed at me. "If they were to take your power, then they would have to remove your spirit. There is only one way to free a spirit from a body."

Even as the hair on the back of my neck stood on end, I made a disgusted sound and pulled a bottle of hair gel from the cart. I wouldn't fall for another of Kim's lies, especially not one as outrageous as the Noppera-bō. "That's the most ridiculous thing I've ever heard."

"Rileigh, you are in danger."

My mind replayed the image from last night of the shadow outside my window, and I failed to suppress a shudder. "How do I know it wasn't you sneaking around my house?"

He frowned. "Why would I do that?"

I squirted gel into my open palm and rubbed my hands together. "That *is* the question, isn't it? Maybe you could be honest for once and tell me what exactly it is that you want from me."

"What I want?" With my hands in his hair, he twisted around so that he could face me. "I've only ever wanted one thing!" The desperation in his eyes pulled at me. The longer he held my gaze, the more the pressure built until I was forced to look away just so I could breathe.

The curtain swayed as someone walked by, so he cleared his throat and continued in a much softer tone. "Your safety."

Startled by the fierceness in his eyes, I jerked back, bumping into the cart and knocking several bottles of shampoo onto the floor. I wanted to argue with him, but I could feel the truth of his words like a jagged rock in my throat. I wanted to ask why a guy who had just met me would care so much about my safety. But I didn't say anything. Instead, I crouched down, softly trembling, as I picked up the plastic bottles.

"I'm so sorry," he said, pulling the smock from his neck. "It appears that when we're together, I can do nothing but upset you. I'll go now, and we can talk later."

"Wait," I told him before he had a chance to stand up. "What if you have the wrong girl? What if I'm not this samurai?"

Kim leaned back against the chair. "There is no—" He stopped, smiled to himself, and tried again. "We won't know for sure unless you transcend."

Curiosity got the better of me, and I sat down in the chair next to him. "What does that mean?"

"If awakening is the act of your past life making connections with your present life, then transcending is the two lives fusing together in complete assimilation." He held up his hands and linked his fingers together as an illustration.

Was he crazy? Becoming one with the spirit inside of me? That was the last thing I wanted. I only hoped that by learning more about the process, I could uncover the secret to undoing it. "And how does that happen? How does a person transcend?"

He took a deep breath before he answered. "It only occurs one way: you have to become reacquainted with an object that belonged to your past self."

I sighed. "What does that mean?"

He leaned forward, and I met him halfway so he could whisper in my ear. His breath on my neck raised goose bumps down my back. "Simply put, you must touch it. The physical object acts as a bridge that connects your present self to your past self. By touching it, you can join the two together."

I whispered back. "So you're saying that if I really am who you think I am, I have to find something that belonged to me in my past life, in ancient Japan, in order to transcend?"

"Technically, yes," he answered, leaning back again and smiling.

"What do you mean, 'technically'?"

"Well," he leaned forward again, "'technically' that's exactly what a person would have to do to transcend. But if you are who we think you are, you don't have to do all that."

"Why?"

"Because I already have the katana that belonged to Senshi."

I felt lightheaded. "But how? That would make it—"

"More than five hundred years old," he finished for me. "Braden, Drew, Michelle, and I belong to a group made up of others like us, known only as 'the Network.' It has an entire division for monitoring antiques should the need to find a specific one come up. Like Senshi's katana."

"Senshi, huh?" I rolled the name across my tongue. "It just seems a bit unlikely. If we were together long ago in Japan, what are the odds that we would find ourselves within miles of each other in America?"

"In every life, you create soul ties with the people who

surround you. The stronger the tie you have with a person, the more likely it is that you will follow them into the next life." Kim dropped his eyes to his lap. "It's no coincidence that we live so close to each other. Where Senshi goes, I will follow." He met my eyes and I had the irresistible urge to reach for him. Instead, I balled my hands into fists and shoved them inside my apron. "We are forever linked."

I swallowed the sour taste on the back of my tongue. "But you don't know for sure that I'm Senshi."

"Not until you transcend," he answered.

I shook my head. "That's not going to happen." The fear of losing any part of me, no matter how small, was too big a risk to take.

He shrugged. "I won't force you to do anything you don't want to do. Unfortunately though, I am afraid no matter what you choose, your life will never be the way it was."

I frowned. That wasn't the answer I was hoping for.

He continued. "The awakening process has already begun. Those feelings, thoughts, and talents are here to stay, and I can't say they won't increase. Not to mention, your life is in jeopardy. We have much to do to ensure your safety."

My hopes of salvaging what was left of my normal life were shaking with my knees. "Like what?" I asked.

"Until we find the people who left that note for you, I must insist you start training with us at the dojo. Though you do not have all the skills of your former samurai self, you must hone the ones you have awakened. It is imperative you know how to defend yourself."

"And if I say no?"

He stood up and shrugged. "I guess I'll have to camp out on your front lawn so I can watch over you."

I sighed because I believed him. When Whitley picked me up for our date, how could I explain to him what the brooding Asian guy was doing roasting marshmallows in my yard? I also had to consider which was worse—training a couple hours a week or having Kim continue to spy on me. "What time did you say this was?"

Kim's smile was too smug for my liking. "We train every night at eight."

"Fine," I told him. "I'll start tomorrow."

"We train *every night* at eight."

"I heard you the first time, but I can't make it tonight. I have a date."

His smug expression melted away, leaving his face blank and unreadable. Even though I enjoyed taking him down a notch, his reaction made me wonder if there was more at stake than he was letting on. "Kim, what if I am Senshi? Then what?"

He shifted in the chair. "I don't understand what you are asking."

I licked my lips, considering the best way to handle such an awkward subject. "Were you two … close?"

He swallowed hard. "I do not expect the same from you."

I took his failure to answer my question as proof that

they had been more than friends. I nodded. "Good. That's good. It's just that I'm not crazy about the whole past life thing. Even if I was this Senshi girl, I don't think I could possibly be the same person you knew. I'm me now. Rileigh—not Senshi—and I make my own choices. I won't let the past make them for me."

"I understand," he said. He closed his eyes but continued to talk. "I would be a liar if I told you that I'd never hoped to find Senshi and be with her again." His dark lashes lifted, revealing eyes that held no emotion, no longer showing the pain that was there only seconds ago. "But I do understand that different lives have different outcomes. If you want a life separate from mine, I won't stop you. Senshi would know that, above all else, nothing matters more to me than her happiness, even if that happiness is shared with another."

Without saying anything, I stood up and moved the shampoo bottles into straight lines in an attempt to give my shaking hands something to do. Maybe he wasn't the arrogant jerk I initially presumed him to be. He was broken, and there was nothing I could do to help him.

The back of my arm tingled and I glanced over my shoulder to see Kim pulling back from a touch he never made.

"Rileigh, I will leave you now. Until tomorrow." He stood up and put a twenty-dollar bill on the chair.

Why did this have to be so complicated? Now that I saw him for the guy he really was, the guy he could be if he wasn't so damaged—there might have been something there that would have worked for us. Maybe in another life. I giggled at the irony of my own thought, which I quickly masked with a cough when Kim cocked an eyebrow. "Sorry, tickle in my throat."

He nodded, unable to hide the skepticism in his eyes. "Right. See you tomorrow."

He turned to leave, but I couldn't let him go before I asked him a question that had plagued me since the day we met. "Kim?"

He looked over his shoulder.

"Why are you afraid to touch me?" I asked.

He rotated back toward the curtain. For a moment, I thought he would leave without answering my question. Instead, he pushed his shoulders back and reeled around to face me, closing the distance between us in two strides, leaving only enough room to breathe. "I'm afraid," he whispered.

"Of what?" I whispered back. I was afraid myself, but I couldn't think of why I should be.

"I'm afraid that if I touch you, even for a moment, I might not be able to let go." Before I could react, he turned and strode out of the room.

21

Kim was still on my mind later that night when a knock sounded at the front door. "Coming!" I shouted, hurrying to slip on my dangling earrings. After Kim left, work got crazy, and I was happy for the distraction from my thoughts and Quentin's curious glances. Luckily when my shift ended, Quentin had been too busy with a client to notice my escape. I knew I was going to have a lot of explaining to do later.

But I didn't want to think about all that. Despite my earlier lack of enthusiasm, I was now excited about going out. It would be a relief to do something so normal when my last couple of nights had been filled with sword fights, biker bars, and samurai. This was just what the doctor ordered. I did a quick appearance check in the mirror above my dresser. My makeup was still smoky and flawless from Quentin's earlier application. I hurriedly ran a brush through my hair and tugged my black lace shirt down to ensure my midriff wasn't exposed between the bottom hem and my denim skirt. "Good enough," I whispered to my reflection. I concentrated on every step I took out of my room. It was my first time wearing the black five-inch knee-high boots I snatched from Debbie's closet, and the last thing I wanted was to twist an ankle.

"I got the door," I heard my mother call. "It's probably Jason."

I stepped up my pace, skirting in front of her and grabbing the doorknob from under her freshly painted hot-pink nails. "It's for me." I smiled.

Debbie raised a perfectly arched eyebrow. "A skirt? I never thought I'd live to see the day. Where are you and Q off to?"

I took a deep breath. This wasn't a conversation I wanted to have at the moment. "Ha ha. I'm not going out with Q tonight."

"Oh?"

I stared at the ground as I tugged at the skirt, remembering why I never wore the things—so drafty. "I have a date."

Debbie cocked her head. "Rileigh, don't mumble. It's very unladylike. Now, what did you say?"

There was another knock at the door, followed by a confused and muffled inquiry.

"Just a minute," I called through the door before turning back to Debbie. "I *said*, I have a date."

Debbie made a small choking noise and took a step

back. "You what?" She then thrust an arm in front of me, pushing me aside as she wrenched the door open. I watched, dismayed, as the surprise on her face melted behind her professional mask. "Why hello there. I'm sorry you had to wait so long, but you know how we women love to take our time."

Whitley smiled at her. "Well, any time spent for Rileigh is worth the wait."

I felt the fire of a blush ignite my cheeks. Debbie measured Whitley up and down with her eyes. "Aren't you sweeter than a sugar cube on a snow cone," she said. "Come inside, please."

"He can't!" I answered, darting around Debbie and grabbing Whitley by the arm. Debbie hadn't been around enough to see me off on many dates, but what she lacked in physical presence she made up for with grueling interrogations. Getting pregnant at seventeen had jaded her against men—or so I'd thought until Dr. Wendell walked into the picture. I knew she thought it was her motherly duty, but I also knew I needed to get Whitley away from her before she did something to *really* embarrass me. "We're going to be late."

"Next time, then." Debbie watched from the door as I pulled Whitley down the walkway. We almost made it to the driveway when she called out to me.

I groaned inwardly. "Can you give me a sec?" I asked Whitley.

"No problem." He inclined his head to the black BMW sidling the curb next to our house. "I'll just wait in the car."

I gave him an appreciative smile before walking back to the porch where my mother waited. "Did you need something?"

Debbie frowned. "Rileigh, he's gorgeous."

I clenched my teeth. "And that's a bad thing?"

"He looks smooth. Did you see his car?"

"Yes, Mom."

She met my eyes. "You're a good girl, Rileigh. I know you'll be careful." She paused a moment before digging into her pocket and pulling out a business card. "On a side note, he has fantastic bone structure. If he's interested in doing some modeling, tell him to give me a call."

"Sure thing." I took the card, careful to not let her see me crumple it in my fist as I turned and made my way back to Whitley's car.

"Have fun," Debbie called after me. "I have a date myself, so I'll probably be home late."

Without answering, I threw my hand up in a backward wave as I made my way to the passenger side of the car.

Whitley smiled as I slid into the seat. He wore jeans, a blue-striped collared shirt, and a brown corduroy jacket. "You look..." He stopped and tried again. "You look... God, I can't come up with anything to describe how amazing you look." He wore his hair down, styled back from his face, the ends brushing his collar.

I felt the heat of color burn my cheeks to almost painful degrees and quickly turned my head, pretending to study the armrest. Those damn dimples were back and once again wreaking havoc. Quickly, I ran a list through my mind of things that would help me calm down: spiders (ew), picking gravel out of road rash (so nasty), and that colon-cleanse infomercial. (I realized too late that the last one was overkill and I shuddered.)

Finally, with my composure restored, I settled back into the cushy leather and buckled the seat belt. "Nice car."

He shrugged. "I inherited it."

I flinched. Real smooth, Rileigh. "I'm sorry."

He shrugged again. "That's okay, you didn't know." He waved his hand dismissively. "So what do you want to do? I was originally thinking coffee … but with the way you look, now I'm thinking we should go someplace nicer."

"Coffee's perfect." And it was. It avoided the awkwardness of an expensive restaurant or the uncomfortable silence of a movie. It was the perfect place to sit and talk.

So we left my house in South St. Louis and ventured deeper into the heart of the city. We arrived at a colorful coffee bar only blocks away from the Anheuser-Busch Brewery. The aroma of roasted coffee beans nullified the smells of hops and barley that filled the darkening night.

Inside, we ordered our lattes and perched next to each other on an overstuffed, stained loveseat. From there, we could hear each other above the music from an acoustic guitar player with enough piercings to skip the rod and line and catch fish with his face.

I learned Whitley had come to St. Louis from Los Angeles to stay with a relative after his dad died. His mother died when he was a baby. Despite these tragedies, he had a great sense of humor. After one particular joke, I laughed so hard that I had to place my hand on his shoulder to steady myself. My heart skipped as the heat from his body and my fingers mixed. Slowly, I forgot how screwed up my life was and actually felt like a normal girl on a date with a cute guy.

We continued to talk and laugh until the coffee bar had cleared out and the employees, wiping the already clean tabletops, shot nasty looks in our direction. I gasped, looking at a clock behind the counter. "It's a quarter after eleven!"

"Yikes!" Whitley jumped to his feet. "I've got an early morning." He held out his hand. "I hate saying this, but, ready to go?"

"Guess we better." I smiled, slipping my hand inside of his. He curled his fingers around mine, pulling me gently to my feet and leading me through the door.

Once outside, Whitley released my hand and searched through the front and back pockets of his pants.

I stopped beside him. "Is something wrong?" I asked.

He looked up with a sheepish grin. "Can't find my wallet. I probably left it at the counter."

"No biggie." I shrugged. "If you want to go inside and grab it, I can wait out here." The breezy summer night felt delicious against my skin.

"I'll hurry. Promise you won't go running off with a better-looking guy while I'm gone?" His smile was dazzling. A giggle erupted from my mouth before I could smother it with my hands.

Whitley gave my hands a quick squeeze before

explaining his situation to the girl outside cleaning windows. After he smiled at her, she appeared more than eager to escort him back inside, abandoning her squeegee and glass cleaner on the stairs like an afterthought.

Alone except for the occasional passing car, I settled down onto the concrete steps and enjoyed the warm gust that blew in from the river. It carried a sweet smell, like clay and damp wood, and I breathed deeply. The night was quiet, but that was typical for a Tuesday evening. I had visited this Soulard coffeehouse before, but I hadn't been able to hear the soft whoosh of cars traveling along the nearby interstate like I could now. Come the weekend, I knew no one would hear anything over the laughter and shouts from people leaving the bars and restaurants that stayed open until the early hours of the morning.

I no sooner leaned against the cool concrete with a contented sigh when a shrill voice called out to me. "Oh. My. God. I don't believe it."

I tensed. There was only one person who had a voice similar to the squeal of car tires braking at eighty miles per hour. Quentin's sister Carly.

The five-foot-ten-inch captain of the cheerleading squad marched up to me with two Bratz doll clones in tow. She lifted her hand and made an exaggerated effort to push her curtain of hair behind her back, making sure to call attention to the nightclub band tied to her wrist. The same neon-green band was tied to the wrists of her minions.

"How are you?" She pulled me up into the kind of hug you'd give someone with leprosy. I made a show of returning the gesture. This was how it had worked with us since junior high. It was no secret that she hated me and that I returned the sentiment, but we had an unspoken agreement to never let our feelings show directly. Since Carly was Quentin's twin and I was his best friend, an out-and-out war would get us both in big trouble with Quentin's mom. So we relied on cold war tactics like spreading rumors through anonymous Internet profiles.

But now, as I pulled away from the smell of beer and cigarettes, the whole thing seemed ridiculous.

"I'm good." I forced a toothy smile that I hoped didn't look too much like a snarl.

"Oh, thank God." Carly splayed cotton candy pink nails against her chest. "After Quentin told me about your attack, I was sooo worried. We all were." When the dolls on either side of Carly didn't move, she shot them a narrowed glance. A moment of silent confusion passed before the dolls recovered and voiced their agreement.

"See?" Carly smiled proudly. "We would just hate it if something happed to you, Rileigh. You're such a good friend." She gave me another half-hearted hug.

"Thanks, Carly." My smile wavered, strained from being stretched over my teeth for so long. "You're too sweet."

She opened her Coach clutch and pulled out a compact. "What are friends for?" After studying her reflection for a moment, she snapped the compact shut and gazed at something over my shoulder. "Ugh. Great." She curled her lip in disgust.

I looked behind me to find a broad-shouldered man in a long jacket lumbering toward us. The first stirrings of a cool breeze blew a flutter through the ends of my hair. I knew what that meant—someone was waking up.

My smile vanished. "Please no. Not in front of Carly," I whispered under my breath. I could feel each pop and snap of electricity as the message to prepare for a fight circuited through my nerves. My muscles twitched and tightened in response.

The stranger picked up his pace and called out to us, his voice sharp enough to cut glass. "Hey! You there!"

Before I could answer, Carly huffed and shoved her compact back into her clutch. "Keep on moving, loser. We don't have any change!"

He stopped in the middle of the road and pointed at me. I could feel the malice in the gesture as if he had jabbed the finger into my chest. "You there." The overhead streetlight illuminated two red devil horns that had been tattooed on both sides of the man's shaved head.

The dolls tensed behind Carly, but she only scoffed. "Whatever, dude. Look, we're not joining your church of crazy or buying anything you have to sell, so you better beat it before I call the cops."

She pulled a cell phone from her pocket and held it up, but it vanished from her grip and wound up wedged in the wooden door behind me, secured by a silver-pointed star.

22

Carly's scream sounded distant as the spirit took over and pushed me deep into my mind. Once again, the ribbons of silk unfolded into my limbs, but this time something felt different. As the spirit flexed each of my muscles and sunk my weight back on my heels, I curled my hand and produced a fist. Though it wasn't complete, I had maintained some control.

The man threw his jacket into a heap at his feet. "Nobody's going anywhere, except *you.*" He locked his yellow-brown eyes on me. "You're coming with me."

I descended the stairs and widened my stance on the sidewalk, my fear replaced by eagerness. I wanted to punch this guy's face in.

But wait. That wasn't right. I didn't want to fight... did I?

I couldn't remember.

It was like I was taking a test labeled *Who is Rileigh Martin?* And instead of answers there were pictures floating inside my head. Pictures of my skateboard, a katana, Quentin, the hair salon, Kim, Whitley, school, the skate park, the dojo—and the problem was, no one told me if the test was single answer, multiple choice, or essay.

"You can have her!" Carly squealed, pulling me from my thoughts. Two sets of slender fingers grasped my shoulders and shoved me forward. "Just don't hurt us!"

So much for being friends. I stopped her advance by wedging a heel into a crack in the sidewalk. As she continued to push at me, I snagged one of her wrists and twisted it at the same time I lifted her arm. Carly stumbled to her knees, yelping, helpless to move without snapping her wrist.

The tattooed thug stopped his advance and smirked as he appeared to drink us in with his eyes. "Ladies, by all means, if you're going to fight, go ahead. I can wait."

I made a disgusted sound. "Don't worry, I'll get to you next." I turned my attention from him and lowered my lips to Carly's ear. "Listen carefully. We're done pretending to be friends. From here on out, you will not look at me, you will not talk to me, and most of all you will not *touch* me. Got that?"

She nodded, hiccupping through the sobs that shook her body.

"Good." I released her arm. She scrambled backward and nearly knocked over the frozen dolls. They regained their balance, but still none of them moved.

“What are you still doing here?” I pointed a finger down the street. “Run!”

They didn’t need to be told twice. They bolted, but not before Carly shouted over her shoulder, “Rileigh Martin, you are such a freak!”

“You’re welcome,” I mumbled. Then I turned to face Devil-boy, who stood staring at me with a bemused grin. “Now, where were we?”

The smile vanished as he reached behind his back. When his hand reappeared, he held a strange weapon that looked like two wooden rods connected by a chain.

The voice swirled in my head like a winter fog: *nunchaku.*

Devil-boy held the weapon over his head and charged. I had only a second to duck to avoid missing the heavy wood as it whizzed over my head. Sneering, he swung the nunchaku again, low enough this time that I could feel the weapon pulling at a few unruly hairs curling around my part. A centimeter lower and I would be spoon-fed lime gelatin in a hospital somewhere as I drooled into a pillow. Not cool.

Devil-boy grinned. “Slippery little thing, aren’t ya?” He licked his lips. “Let’s see you dodge this!” Instead of swinging the nunchaku as before, he bore them down on top of me.

I watched the arc of his arm as it came down and waited until the last possible moment. I could feel the rumble of my heart as it sped up, like a distant train, but it was too far away to distract me. I could see in his eyes that Devil-boy thought he had me, so he added a bit of last-minute power to his blow. And that was exactly what I wanted.

I dodged to his side, but because of Devil-boy's last-minute power surge, he stumbled forward when his nunchaku swept only air. I had enough time to see his eyes widen in shock before his broad shoulders were in front of me. I pushed as hard as I could.

The combination of his momentum and my added shove sent Devil-boy staggering into the brick wall of the coffeehouse. His neck snapped back violently as his forehead collided into the building. I thought for sure he'd go down, but after taking a moment to regroup, he shook himself like a dog getting out of a bath.

When he finally turned around, I thought I might be sick. A thick line of blood trailed from a gash in his forehead and down the bridge of his nose, where it wound down the side of his nostril and onto his lips. He smiled, his teeth red and glistening. He spit a crimson glob on the sidewalk next to his boot. "It's not going to be that easy," he growled.

I sighed and spread my stance into a ready position. "It never is."

He spun the nunchaku in his hand and thundered toward me again. But this time he moved like a drunken bull, his feet scraping the ground in a clumsy shuffle. The head injury had done more damage than he was willing to let on. He swung the nunchaku wide, and I ducked under them, but this time, when I rose to my feet, I planted my left fist into the back of his head.

We both cried out in pain at the same time. Who knew that punching someone hurt so much? Devil-boy staggered, which was good because I was too busy waving my sore hand in the air to dodge an immediate attack.

He spit several more wads of bloody goo onto the sidewalk before swinging at me again. This time, however, I could tell that he was struggling to keep upright and the strike was easy to avoid. When I righted myself, I answered his attack by planting my knee into his stomach. He doubled over and I used that moment to punch his left temple with my right hand.

He cursed and I bit my lip to keep from doing the same as tears of pain dotted my eyes. I looked down at my hands and noticed that not only were my knuckles red and swollen, but one of my freshly painted nails had a chip in it.

"Dang it!" Anger burst through the numbing calm burning through my blood with enough heat that I wondered if I might spontaneously combust. It was stupid to be upset over a chipped nail—I knew that. But my life was unraveling at the seams and for that, someone was going to pay.

I launched myself at Devil-boy as he staggered to his feet.

Before he knew what'd hit him, I lashed out with a backhand to the base of his skull and followed it with a spinning kick to his spine. Devil-boy took one wobbly step, then another, before sinking to his knees.

He shook his head. "This isn't over." Slowly, he rose to his feet.

I knew he would keep coming at me as long as he held the nunchaku. Scanning the street, I looked for something to disarm him with. When I saw the cleaning supplies the coffeeshop employee had abandoned on the steps, I had an idea.

As Devil-boy worked his way to his feet, I dashed up the stairs and grabbed the squeegee. When I descended, he was glaring at me, his face a road map of blood. He held the nunchaku up and began to spin them wildly over his head as he made his charge.

I dug my heels in the ground and waited, fear a thick knot in my throat.

Devil-boy let out an anguished cry as he bore the weapon down on my head, but this time, instead of dodging, I lifted my arms and met the blow with the squeegee. One of the wooden rods wrapped around the long handle. When I pulled back, the flat rubber squeegee locked Devil-boy's weapon in place. Another tug and I ripped the nunchaku from his grasp.

Devil-boy stared at his empty hands as if he couldn't figure out what had happened.

With an expert throw, unlike my usual girlish tosses, I launched the squeegee-nunchaku knot into the neighboring alleyway. Afterward, I dusted my hands. "Are we done here?"

He spit more blood onto the walk. "Not even close." He reached back into his waist pocket and pulled out a gun.

Oh. Snap.

The ribbons of silk unraveled from underneath my skin, leaving me cold and drowning in fear. Why now? Why would the spirit abandon me when I was staring down the barrel of a gun? I took a step backward and tripped on the stairs, landing sharply on my butt.

Devil-boy cocked the trigger. "You're going to pay for what you did to me. Maybe I'll shoot you in the leg. Boss says you're supposed to be left unharmed, but I can say it was an accident." He licked at the blood still flowing down his face and spit again, his eyes wild.

I pressed myself against the concrete while my pulse beat divots into my veins. How do you fight a bullet? I opened my mouth to scream, but the sound only knotted inside my throat.

Devil-boy leaned in. "I'm going to enjoy this."

It was at that moment I learned a fun fact: When a gun is pointed at you, it is physically impossible not to stare at it. Seriously. The closer the barrel moved to my head, the more desperate I became to close my eyes. But they refused to budge. It was like someone had stapled my eyelids to the top of my skull.

The gun moved nearer, the barrel growing larger until its black depths filled my vision.

"Nighty-night," Devil-boy whispered.

I held my breath and waited to die.

But Devil-boy never pulled the trigger.

Instead, he shrieked and dropped the gun to the sidewalk.

As if by magic I could move again, breathe again. But I couldn't understand why, and what I saw didn't make sense.

Where Devil-boy had once been standing, he was now hunched over, pawing at his face as he moaned.

"What the—" But before I could finish my sentence, a woman wearing a dirt-smeared shirt and tattered sweat-pants stepped in front of me, her canister of pepper spray held high.

"Beat it!" the woman advised in a gravely, cigarette-damaged voice. "Or I'll give ya another dose! Ya hear?"

Devil-boy pressed a hand into his watering eyes but didn't move. Down the street two guys exited a bar, the music from the band spilling out onto the street behind them. They were too far away to know what was going on, but lucky for me their presence was enough to send Devil-boy scrambling away. He cast me one last heated look before he knocked into a parked car and then into a light pole before finally disappearing into an alley.

I stood. The movement must have startled the home-less woman because she raised her canister in my direction. "Don't spray me!" I ducked my head and raised my hands. "I just wanted to thank you. He—he was going to shoot me."

"Humph," she muttered, pocketing her pepper spray. She grabbed the discarded gun from the sidewalk and tossed it into a nearby trash can before turning to leave.

"Wait!" I called after her.

She ignored me and kept walking.

"I just—how can I repay you?"

She snorted and bent over to retrieve Devil-boy's abandoned jacket from the road. "Don't need to be paid for being a decent human." She tucked the jacket under her arm and wandered down the road without looking back.

Un-freaking-believable.

My knees wobbled and I sank against the steps before the reality of what just happened could set in.

"Right where I left you! Sorry I took so long."

A yelp escaped my mouth and I whirled in the direction of the voice. Whitley paused just outside the door as the barista locked it behind him. Whitley took one look at my pale, shaking figure and the smile fell from his face. "Hey." He rushed to me and enveloped me in his arms. "What happened?"

I shook my head and leaned my weight against him, knowing that there was nothing I could say, no explanation I could give, that wouldn't make me sound crazy. Though the St. Louis streets weren't exactly the safest, I couldn't think of anyone other than me who'd been attacked with nunchaku. I just hoped Whitley wouldn't glance over his shoulder at Carly's cell phone still wedged into the door.

"Shh." He stroked the back of my hair with one hand and pressed me closer to him with the other. In the past, I'd put myself in a swooned-out state just by imagining the feel of Whitley's arms. But now that they were actually around me, I couldn't feel anything past the numbing cold of shock that filled my body. I was only vaguely aware of the spicy cinnamon cologne that tickled my nose.

Whitley continued. "This is my fault. If I hadn't taken so long… I couldn't find my wallet. I searched the whole place from the counter to the bathroom only to find it wedged between the couch cushions. I should have known better than to leave you out here so long. Of course you were scared—alone on a dark street—especially after what happened to you last weekend."

I pulled away so I could look up at him, careful not to blink and risk spilling the tears building in the corner of my eyes. "It wasn't you. I had a really great time… but I think I've had too much excitement for one night." I offered him a weak smile. "I hope I didn't ruin our date."

He smiled. "Impossible."

A blush warmed my cheeks. "Thanks."

Whitley wrapped an arm around my shoulder and gently guided me down the sidewalk toward his car. "Come on. Let's get you home."

The drive back to my house was uncomfortably silent.

Whitley pulled into my driveway and drummed his thumbs nervously on the steering wheel. "So… "

What a night. I was so relieved to be home, but at the same time, there was a part of me that hated ending the date I'd been waiting three months for. Hoping to gain an extra minute or two, I took longer slipping out of my seatbelt than was necessary.

"Can I call you?" he asked.

I stopped fidgeting and turned to face him. "I'd like that."

A smile lit his face. "Great." He reached around to the backseat and pulled up a backpack, shuffling through it before finally pulling out a legal pad with a pen clipped to it. "Your phone number?"

I gave it to him, and while he finished scribbling it down, I opened the door and stepped out. Sure, I was a little disappointed at our casual goodbye, but I didn't want to seem too eager. Then I heard his car door slam behind me.

"Wait!" he called. "I'll walk you to your door."

I couldn't help but smile into the dark. My door was only fifteen feet away. I stayed where I was until I felt his hand take mine and lead me the short distance to the concrete porch.

"Well, I guess this is good night," Whitley said.

I swallowed, my throat suddenly dry and my tongue thick. The tension scratched along my skin like an itchy sweater. It wasn't that I didn't want to kiss him—my body warmed to the thought—it was just the awkwardness that led up to it. Could he feel how much my hand was sweating in his? Maybe he was disgusted but too polite to let go. Should I slip my hand from his so I could wipe it on my skirt? Or would that hurt his feelings?

Whitley leaned forward. I closed my eyes and stopped thinking. A few agonizing seconds passed before I felt my hand lifted. Confused, I opened my eyes to find Whitley's sparkling blue irises locked onto my own as he laid a gentle kiss across my knuckles.

"I had a great time," he whispered. He dropped my hand, which I quickly clasped behind my back before he noticed the damage that remained from punching Devil-boy.

"Me too."

He smiled, flashing those incredible dimples. "I'll call you tomorrow."

Heat burned in my cheeks and I forgot how to talk. I could only raise my hand in farewell as he made his way back to his car and pulled out of my drive.

"Bah!" I cried when I was sure he could no longer see me in his rearview mirror. "I'm such an idiot." Leaning my forehead against the door, I continued to mutter as I fumbled with my keys. At the very least I could have said "bye" or some other attempt at verbal communication. Anything but standing paralyzed like the dummy I was.

Sighing, I turned the key in my deadbolt when a heavy feeling wrapped around me like a lead jacket. I leaned back and locked my knees to keep from falling down.

I was being watched.

I spun on the steps, leaning my back against the door so I could scan the neighborhood. The only noises came from buzzing cicadas and a distant barking dog. Most of the neighborhood had retired for the night, leaving the dim streetlights as the sole source of light.

That's when I saw the silver Trans Am parked in front

of Mr. and Mrs. McKinnley's house across the street. The McKinnleys, a retired couple, owned an older Lincoln Town Car. How long had the Trans Am been parked there? I couldn't remember seeing it before I left on my date, but then again, I hadn't been looking.

I pushed off the door and marched across the small yard toward the mysterious car. Maybe I should have called Kim, or at least the police, but I was too angry and tired to care anymore. If the tattooed stranger followed me here to start another fight, I'd save him the trouble of having to come after me.

I was halfway into the street when the car engine roared to life. The sound, like the growl of a giant beast, startled me but didn't stop me. I wanted this to end. The tires crunched into the gravel as they turned out toward the road.

"Oh no you don't!" I shouted at the black-tinted window. "Don't you go anywhere!" I jumped forward, but only managed to beat my fist against the window once before the sports car peeled out, narrowly missing my toes in its retreat. "Coward!" I shouted as it screeched around a corner and out of sight. I screamed in frustration, picked up a fistful of gravel, and threw it into the empty street.

Dogs barked and several of the neighboring houses flicked on their bedroom lights. Cursing softly, I turned and ran as fast as my heels would allow me, praying that they wouldn't see me before I was either inside or crumbled on the ground with a twisted ankle.

So much for a nice normal night out.

Once inside, I sucked on my bottom lip to keep it from trembling. No amount of wishful thinking was going to change anything. Ignoring it would not help. As much as I hated to admit it, Kim was right.

My life was never going to be the same again.

23

My ringing phone ripped me from the depths of dreamless sleep. The clock read seven in the morning. Groaning, I pulled my pillow over my face to muffle the noise. It was the first day since the start of summer vacation that I wasn't scheduled to work. I'd planned on staying in bed until noon. It wasn't enough that Kim wanted his dead girlfriend back, a reincarnated samurai spirit wanted my body, and a tattooed freak wanted God-knows-what. Now someone wanted to take away the only thing I had left: sleep. "What?!" I shouted into the receiver.

"Ri-Ri!" Quentin exhaled loudly. "Oh, thank God. You had me so worried. What was going on with you yesterday?" He was speaking so fast his sentences fell on top of each other. "You got the whole salon in a tizzy over your little exchange. I thought this Kim guy had a thing for you. But it's more than that, isn't it? Carly said you and some tattooed freak threatened her last night. It's not that I blame you, I just thought you were on a date with Whitley. What are you keeping from me? How could you—"

"Q!" I interrupted. "Breathe!" I reluctantly pulled myself up against my headboard, propping two pillows behind my back. He was really worked up, so I knew I might as well get comfortable.

I heard him suck in air. "You're right." He took another deep breath. "Okay. That's much better."

"Good. Now start over."

There was a pause. "What the hell is going on?"

I flinched back from the anger coming through the phone. I'd never heard Quentin so mad before. "Q, I'm so sorry. I—"

He cut me off. "I've been worried sick, you know."

My apology didn't work, so I was going to give reason a try. "I tried to tell you the other day in the sink room, but Jeannine interrupted us, and the same thing happened yesterday with Kim. Not to mention," I sighed, "a part of me is worried that if I do tell you… you might not understand."

The anger left his voice. "It's me, Ri-Ri. What on earth could you possibly tell me that I wouldn't understand?"

I opened my mouth to answer but couldn't form the words. This was all wrong. I couldn't divulge my deepest secrets while a cluster of stuffed animals stared at me from across the room. I wanted to look him in the eyes and read the thoughts that played behind them. I needed him with me, holding my hand—where he should have been all along. "I can't do this over the phone."

There was a sudden intake of breath. "How big is this, Ri-Ri?"

"Big," I answered. "And even though I wanted to, I just don't know how to handle it alone."

"I'll be over first thing after work."

It was tempting. I needed a friend so badly right now, but I remembered my promise to Kim to train at the dojo. "Q, I can't tonight. And I'm thinking about calling in sick to work tomorrow." Getting my life back on track wasn't going as well as I wanted, and I could use an extra day off to regroup. "Ask Jeannine if you can take an early lunch tomorrow and meet me at the sub shop. I'll tell you everything then."

His silence was heavy.

"Please, Q?"

He sighed. "Eleven okay?"

I smiled. "That's perfect. And I promise, I'll tell you everything." When I hung up, I felt a weight lift from my shoulders. No more secrets. I needed Quentin. I had learned the hard way that trying to get through this on my own was too much to handle.

But then I had another thought. What if I told him all about awakening and transcending and he didn't understand? Would he think I was crazy? Was our friendship worth risking by telling him my secret? And if I didn't tell him, would my lies become a wedge between us?

I chewed on my thumbnail as I padded out of my bedroom and into the kitchen to eat a bowl of cereal. A massive bouquet of yellow roses sat in a vase on the counter next to my much smaller bouquet from Whitley. Curious, I lifted the card open.

Debbie,
You light up my life.
—Love,
Jason

I closed the card and pushed her monster bouquet aside, not caring that it put them in direct sunlight so they were sure to wilt, and opened the cabinet they had blocked. It wasn't that I minded Debbie having a relationship with a guy. She deserved someone to care about her after all these years. But why Dr. Wendell? Why was she suddenly so interested in the one guy that gave my gut the same reaction as dissection day in biology?

I pushed all thoughts of Dr. Wendell aside. I had bigger things to worry about at the moment. After snagging a bowl and filling it with cereal and milk, I walked into the living room to enjoy my toasted flakes and watch TV. I was in mid-squat over the sofa when I caught a silver gleam outside the front window.

The Trans Am was back, parked precisely in the same place it had been last night.

Unbelievable! I ignored my pulse thundering in my ears as I set my breakfast down and made my way outside, just like I ignored the morning dew as it soaked through my socks. I couldn't believe the nerve of the guy—coming back so soon after I called him out the night before.

I stood right in front of the driver's black window, fist poised, before the first inkling of doubt seeped into my mind. I brushed it aside. Would this guy really try something in broad daylight with so many of my neighbors shuffling through their morning rituals? Then again, how long did it take to shoot someone? He could be halfway down the road before someone noticed me bleeding to death on the asphalt.

"Genius plan, Rileigh," I mumbled as I wiped my now-slick palms on my sweats. There was no point in running back inside my house. If he was in the car he'd have already seen me. I rapped my knuckles against the tinted glass. Nothing happened. I knocked again. I didn't hear or see anything from inside the car. Maybe no one was in it. I cupped my hands around my eyes and leaned against the glass, only to jump back, heart pounding, as the electric window rolled down.

"You!" I pressed my hands against my chest in an effort to keep my heart from jumping through. "You're not the tattooed man!"

"Who?" Kim frowned as he squinted in the morning sun that spilled into his car. He looked terrible. Heavy bags pulled at the bottom of his eyes, and his hair was flat in spots where he had laid it against the car's headrest.

"Are you spying on me?" I demanded.

He sighed before opening the car door and stepping out onto the road.

Goodie. He was back to not answering my questions. I squeezed my hands into tight fists at my side, afraid to open my mouth and release the angry scream that hung in my throat.

Without making eye contact, he laced his fingers together and rested them against the back of his head. His shoulders lifted in a shrug. "I don't know why you are so mad. I told you I was going to watch over you."

"But I agreed to train with you," I growled. "I thought that was the deal."

He dropped his hands and looked at me. "You didn't train last night."

I cried out in frustration. "Are you kidding me? This is how it's going to be?"

He nodded to my driveway, where my busted-up Fiesta waited for its appointment at the auto body shop. "What happened to your car?"

"I hit a deer."

Kim snorted and turned back to me. "You're oblivious to the danger you're in, aren't you?"

Maybe I had been, but after spending a night dodging nunchaku and having a gun pointed at me I was starting to get the picture. "I understand that there are people after me, Kim, but that doesn't mean I'm ready to give up my privacy. Besides, this road gets a lot of traffic and my neighbors are nosey. Somebody would have to be pretty stupid to start something with me at my house."

"Is that so?" he asked. He reached into his back pocket and pulled out a piece of paper that looked like the one I'd found on my doorstep. "I didn't want to show you this. You are under so much stress already, but you need to understand. I found this on your porch." He handed it to me. Only one word was written on it, but I could tell the handwriting was the same: *Soon.*

"Soon? What's soon?"

Kim held his arms wide. "I don't know. But I suspect nothing good."

This was crazy. I dropped the note and refused to watch it fall to the ground. I didn't want to see it ever again. "When did you find it?"

"Early this morning. After you chased me away, I came back an hour later and found it."

I hugged myself, suddenly cold despite the warm summer morning. What did it mean? Was this a note from the tattooed guy warning me that he was coming back? Or was it something else entirely? "So tell me, then, why did you leave in the first place? Why didn't you just let me know what was going on?"

He shrugged and stared up into the sky. "You looked mad."

"Let me get this straight. You peeled out of here like a bat out of hell because I looked *mad?*" I laughed. "Aren't you supposed to be some samurai badass or something?"

His eyes lowered in shame. "Not just mad. *Really* mad," he emphasized.

I shrugged my shoulders. "So?"

"Look, I know you don't trust me. And that's partly because of the way I've handled our last couple of encounters."

"You can scratch the *partly,*" I grumbled.

He ignored me. "So here you come, storming at me, and I just… panicked. I didn't want you to think I was spying on your date. That wasn't my intent at all. I just wanted to keep an eye on your house. To make sure no one was waiting for you when you got back."

"Really?" High-pitched laughter bubbled from my throat. "That's so funny." I laughed some more, causing Kim's eyes to flash with unease. "You were *here* protecting my house. Meanwhile, I'm at the coffee shop getting attacked by a guy with nunchaku. Honest-to-God nunchaku!" I kept laughing until I was out of breath and tears sprung from my eyes. "I mean, *who does that?*"

"Nunchaku?" Kim looked horrified and I couldn't tell if it was from my behavior or the fact that I was attacked. Finally he said, "It looks like someone else was conducting a test of their own."

For no reason that I could think of, I found this funny and laughed all over again. "Rileigh." Kim ducked his head low in an attempt to meet my eyes. "You are coming undone."

"Tell me something I don't know," I answered, dabbing at my eyes with the back of my hands.

"Are you still planning to train tonight?"

"Would you stake out my place if I didn't?"

He nodded.

"Well, gosh." I clasped my hands together in mock enthusiasm. "Wild horses couldn't keep me away."

He frowned, arching an eyebrow.

I sighed. "I'll be there, okay? Eight o'clock. Got it."

"Good. Then I'll leave. See you at eight." He opened his car door.

I nodded again, happy to be *alone,* before realizing what that would mean ... I'd be alone. Now that there were people actively hunting me down, spending time by myself didn't hold the appeal it once did.

"Wait—do you think that's such a good idea?"

He reached to the side of his seat and hit the trunk-release button. "I do not believe that whoever it is would be foolish enough to come for you during the day." He walked around to his trunk and lifted out a black bag slightly longer than the length of my arm and double the width. "But just in case, I want you to have this." He held the padded nylon bag out to me.

I stepped forward curiously. "What is it?"

"Senshi's katana."

I jerked back, stumbled, landed on my butt, then scrambled to my feet again while dusting off the gravel that clung to my cotton pants. "Wait. No. Won't that—isn't that—I thought I couldn't touch it," I finally spit out.

Kim smiled. "Nothing will happen to you if you take it. It's in a bag."

I frowned. I'd been tricked by him before.

He sighed and held the nylon strap out to me. "I promise nothing will happen to you."

I crossed my arms and narrowed my eyes. "You said I didn't have to touch it if I didn't want to."

He nodded once. "You don't."

"Then why give it to me?"

"Because it's yours."

I narrowed my eyes at him. "We don't know that for sure."

"Of course," he answered. He set the bag down in the road and climbed into his car, pulling the door shut behind him. He leaned out the window. "Take the sword. Touch it. Don't touch it. It's your call. I'll just feel better knowing you have it if you need it."

"Kim, don't you leave this thing here," I warned.

He smiled again. His smug expression disappeared behind the black window as it rolled up.

"Don't you do it!"

The car roared to life.

"I'm warning you!"

He pulled forward onto the road. I watched him, frozen, until he turned at the corner and disappeared from view.

Great. Just great. I stared at the black bag. Was the key to my past really three feet in front of me? And if that past were unlocked, would it be the end of the person I knew to be me? Or was Kim wrong? It could just be an ordinary sword. An ordinary five hundred-year-old sword, sure to be worth a small fortune. I should just leave it where it was and let whatever happens to it happen. Maybe a car would run over it. That would show Kim.

I turned to leave, but found myself rooted to the road. I couldn't do it. I couldn't leave something so valuable lying out, a fact Kim was probably counting on. Damn him.

That left me with the dilemma of how to get it inside

my house. I closed my eyes and stuck out my foot. I flinched when my toe brushed against the nylon—nothing. So I pressed my luck further, nudging it against the pavement—still nothing. I relaxed. This was good, but I still wasn't completely convinced.

I circled the thing once before an idea came to me. Last week, I'd brought home a box of latex gloves so I could dye Quentin's hair. Aha! I ran into my house, emerging minutes later with the dusted-latex safely covering my hands. I scooped the sword case up confidently and brought it into my house, where I laid it on the breakfast table. Now what?

I pulled the gloves off with a snap. I suppose I could put it in my closet, but what if I needed to get to it fast? The kitchen was in the center of the house, so that made it the ideal spot. But then I had to wonder if Debbie would mess with it. Somehow I didn't think so. I couldn't remember the last time we had eaten a meal together, let alone at the kitchen table. Suddenly tired, I sank into a wooden chair. What had happened to my life that I needed to figure out the best place to store a weapon? My hands wanted to fiddle with something while I thought and I almost reached for the bag's zipper. I caught myself and jumped out of my chair, knocking it over in the process. This was a dangerous place to be.

I scurried into my bedroom and climbed back into bed. I curled into a tight ball and pulled the covers up to my chin. It wasn't just the kitchen; my whole life was dangerous, and I sure couldn't run from myself. I wrapped the blanket tighter around me. If I was attacked at home, could I do it? Could I grab the sword and merge with the past? What would I lose? Nothing? Everything? I was so preoccupied with losing myself to the past that I didn't put my own death into the equation. Wouldn't that be worse? If you had to weigh it—dead vs. not dead—I thought not dead came out ahead every time.

I shuddered and yanked the blanket over my head, using the faded quilt as my shield from the world. I would do it if I had to. If my life was at stake, I would touch the sword, and if my past self took over I'd still be alive. At least, I hoped the person I knew to be me wouldn't fade into the blackness of my subconscious. I wanted to ask Kim and the others how it worked, but I wasn't sure they would tell the truth. If their past selves had taken them over, why would they warn me that mine would do the same? As I trembled, I said a silent prayer that I would never have to find out.

24

I pulled into the dojo parking lot a little before eight, surprised at how hard it was to find a parking space. Before I could exit my car, my phone buzzed from its perch in the cup holder. I picked it up and opened the text message from Whitley.

Great time last night. Call me.

With a groan I put the phone back in its place. It wasn't fair that I'd finally won Whitley's attention only to have to put my love life on pause. It wasn't like I could call Whitley and tell him, "Hey, sorry I can't go out tonight. I'm trying to figure out how to exorcise a fifteenth-century samurai spirit from my body. Oh, and did I mention that by hanging around me there's a good chance you'll get something sharp and pointy thrown at your head?" Yeah, that'd go over well.

I grabbed my gym bag and pushed through a swarm of

children and parents exiting the building. Michelle was in the lobby and gave me an encouraging wave forward when she saw my struggle.

"What's going on?" I asked, carefully maneuvering around a child sitting on the floor pulling on dirty tennis shoes.

"Pretty wild, huh?" Michelle said. "Kim is the best instructor around. Most of his children's classes are full." She gave me a sly wink.

"That's nice," I said, feigning interest.

"Don't worry, they'll be gone soon, and we can get started." She jutted her chin toward me. "Cute outfit, by the way."

"Thanks," I answered automatically. I didn't really see what was so "cute" about it. I was wearing black cropped yoga pants with a plain purple tank top. I didn't look all that much different from Michelle, who wore a yellow tank with tight spandex workout pants.

"Come on," she said. "The guys are in the dojo."

I followed her in to find Kim instructing several middle school kids on the proper stance for delivering a spinning back kick. Beads of sweat glittered like tiny diamonds across his chest and neck. I wondered if his muscles would feel as tight under my fingertips as they looked.

A grunt from behind me snapped me from my thoughts. I turned to find Sumi, the receptionist from the other night, glaring at me with her hands on her hips. She wore the same traditional white martial arts outfit as the other kids in the dojo, but her belt was brown unlike the kids' blues and reds. Her eyes blazed.

"What's *she* doing here?" I whispered to Michelle.

"Sumi? Oh, she helps teach the kids' classes," she answered. "I think she's got a little hero-worship thing going with Kim." She giggled.

"You don't say," I mumbled to myself, rolling my eyes.

"What's *she* doing here?" Sumi echoed my question to Kim when the last of the children had left.

"Hmm?" Kim turned toward the direction of her stare, his mouth curving in a slight smile when he spotted me.

My stomach fluttered. Stupid Rileigh, get a grip! I had to shake my head several times to snap out of the trance.

"How nice of you to join us, Rileigh." Amusement flashed through his eyes.

"Wait a minute." Sumi shook her head. "She just started here. How comes she gets to train in the advanced class? I've been here for three years and you won't let me train with you."

Kim turned back to her. "Rileigh has a lot more experience than you, Sumi. You will train with us when you are ready."

"But when—"

"When you are ready." His tone left no room for argument.

Sumi huffed loudly and spun toward the door, fanning her hair like a long black cape as she walked away. In the doorway, she gave me one last withering glance over her shoulder before she left.

"You know," I said, "I think she's starting to like me."

Kim grinned.

"Hey, Rileigh!" Drew tossed his long braid over his shoulder as he walked through the same door he'd used when they'd originally attacked me. He wore red leg and arm pads over his T-shirt and shorts. Braden followed behind him, securing a Velcro strap on an arm pad as he walked.

"Here you go." Michelle came up beside me with a set of blue pads in her arms.

"Uh, thanks," I said, reluctantly taking them. I wasn't psyched to do *more* fighting, but now that my life was at stake, I was learning to get over it. It took me a minute to decide which pad went where, but they were patient, making small talk with each other while I figured it out.

"All right." Kim clapped his hands together when I finished tightening the last strap. "Let's get started. I'll lead us in stretching today."

I soon learned that my skateboarding, while it was a good workout and taught me balance, did little to prepare me for the physical demands of martial arts. As Kim bent and twisted, I mimicked his movements as best I could, ignoring the twinges of my protesting muscles. If I was a samurai in the past, my current body was nowhere near that level of athleticism, despite what I was able to do. Pain, like an electric current, shot through both my legs as I tried to touch my elbows to the floor with my knees locked. Sighing, I collapsed to the floor. "I can't do this."

Before I could look up I was encompassed by the scent of musk and sandalwood.

"You're right." Kim crouched on the floor beside me. "You can't do this."

My mouth went slack.

Kim continued. "You can't defend yourself from muggers. You can't fight off three samurai. So you sure as hell can't *stretch*."

Cute. He was using my sarcasm against me. I grunted and rolled my eyes.

He didn't even flinch, but his tone was softer. "I know this is hard on you and your body. Your mind is telling you that you can do one thing, and your body is trying to convince you that you cannot. It will take time and training for the two to come together. But it will only happen if you try." He smiled and left to resume his position in front.

I thought about casting him another nasty look, but what was the point? He didn't flinch anymore, and that took all the fun out of it. But that didn't stop me from swearing under my breath.

When we finished and my muscles were on fire, Kim paired us off in two groups for sparring: Drew and Braden versus Michelle and me.

Kim brought me the katana I had used my first night at the dojo. "We know that you work well fighting on your own; let's see how you do with a partner. The rules are simple: no striking the front of the face or hitting the groin, understand?"

I nodded.

"Yeah, Michelle," Braden said. "No hitting the groin!"

She laughed. "Last time was an accident."

"Accidentally on purpose," Drew added.

"All right then," Kim interrupted. "Let's arm up."

Braden and Michelle approached the weapon wall, each taking down a pair of wicked-looking forked weapons with two small prongs on either side of a third, longer, center prong.

Michelle turned to me. "When I fought you, Kim wanted us all to use a katana, something he thought you'd remember." She twirled the weapon in front of her, one-handed. "But the sais are my weapon of choice."

"Good to know," I answered, watching her twirl the two sais around her body with ease. I made a mental note—don't make Michelle angry while she's holding the giant forks.

"Sais are not typical weapons for samurai," Braden said, coming to stand beside me.

"Unless you're a cartoon turtle," Michelle added.

Braden laughed. "In our last lives, Michelle and I were raised on a farm in Japan where we used them to shovel hay." He twirled a sai in his hand. "When war split the country, the working class learned to use their everyday tools as weapons, and we were no exception. We were so comfortable using them during our chores that later on, when we joined the samurai, we'd carry a pair into battle along with our swords."

"We raised quite a few eyebrows on the battlefield," Michelle added. "But the sais were only half of the reason."

"What was the other half?" I asked.

Braden answered. "Sons of farmers were not allowed to be samurai."

I was going to ask why again, but Drew walked by with a weapon that distracted me. On top of a four-foot polished staff gleamed a two-foot-long curved blade. My palms grew slick with sweat. What kind of practice was this? Where were the foam nunchaku and wooden swords the children exiting Kim's class had carried? "What the heck is that?" I nodded my head toward the weapon.

Drew smiled. "It's a naginata."

"A *girl's* weapon," Braden teased.

"Watch it," Michelle warned, poking the tip of her sai into his rear.

Braden yelped and jumped forward. "Hey!"

Michelle blew on the tip as if it were a smoking gun, spun it, and stuck it into an imaginary pocket. I was starting to like her.

Drew rolled his eyes at Braden, who rubbed his bottom. "Anyway," Drew continued, "it *was* mostly used by women. The length makes it possible to fend off an opponent while keeping them at a safe distance."

"Makes sense," I muttered, my eyes transfixed on the gleaming edge.

Drew shrugged. "Even so, I've always been partial to it. It just suits me. Here," he said, offering me the staff. "What do you think?"

I placed the katana on the floor and accepted the

weapon that stood taller than I did. The weight of the blade surprised me, and I fumbled with it to keep it upright.

"Anything?" Drew asked.

I wasn't sure what he meant by that, but there was none of the familiarity with the naginata that I felt with the katana. I shook my head.

He laughed. "Senshi never liked to use the naginata. Maybe it was the stigma that it was a woman's weapon, or maybe nothing suited her quite like the katana."

I scowled and thrust the weapon back at him. Another test and another reference to Senshi. "You know," I told him loud enough that everyone could hear me, "what everyone seems to be forgetting here is that there still is a chance I'm not this Senshi person. I'm sure there were millions of people throughout history who could fight and used a katana. I could be any one of them." I looked around the room, making sure to make eye contact with everyone, daring someone to challenge me.

"Tell me, Rileigh, do you really believe that?" Kim answered. "Or are you so scared of the truth that you're going to keep lying to yourself?" He walked over to me, forcing Drew to take a step back until there were only inches separating my raised chin from his chest.

Of course I was scared. I'd be stupid not to be. "I like who I am. I don't want to be taken over, or whatever it is that happens, and lose myself."

He sighed. "It doesn't work like that. Who you were *makes* you who you are. It doesn't change anything."

"Well, coming from Mr. Truthy-trutherton himself, it must be true."

Kim opened his mouth to answer, but a snicker from Braden cut him off. Kim shot him a look of warning and Braden quickly masked the rest of his laughter behind a series of coughs. Kim shook his head before looking at me. "Rileigh, I—"

"Save it. If this is the lecture where you explain that you lied for my own good—blah, blah, blah—I've already heard it." I bent down and picked up the katana. "I thought we were going to train, or was that just another trick to get me to come here?"

A muscle flexed in Kim's jaw. He nodded. "You're right. Let's get started. You and Michelle start over there." He pointed to the side of the room closest to the mirrors.

Michelle gave me a nervous glance as we walked to our side of the room. I did my best to ignore her. I came to train and nothing else. But when I reached the designated area, a new thought hit me—I didn't have the slightest clue what I was doing. I was seconds away from sparring and the voice inside of my head remained quiet. In front of me, Drew leaned back, preparing to strike, while Braden drew his sais together in front of him with a menacing hiss. But me? I stood with my hands at my sides, awkwardly clutching a sword with hands that were more accustomed to working iPods and cell phones than pointy weapons.

"Psst," Michelle whispered to me. "What are you doing? Get into position."

I stared blankly at the sword in my hands as if by

looking at it hard enough I could somehow remember how to use it. But no such luck. The only cool breeze sliding along my skin came from the A/C duct overhead. "Um, I have a slight problem," I whispered back.

"Can it wait?" she asked without looking at me.

"Uh, no."

She sighed. "What's the problem?"

"I … don't know how to fight."

Michelle looked at me, her eyes wide. "Wait, what?"

But I didn't have time to explain. From across the room, Kim shouted for us to begin.

The fight was on.

25

I took a step backward. "Michelle, what do I do?"

She jerked her head past her shoulder. "Get behind me!"

Before I could take a step back, a pressure began to build inside my chest. I immediately recognized the sensation. "Oh no," I whispered. "No no no no."

"What are you doing?" Michelle hissed. "Get out of the way!"

I tried, but my legs refused to cooperate. The pressure rolled against my ribs like a tidal wave and I cried out in pain.

"Rileigh?" Michelle said.

I hugged myself with one arm. "It hurts," I panted. Like it had the night with the bikers, a heaviness stretched and pulled from my chest to my stomach.

"I think we need to stop," Michelle called to Kim.

He shook his head. "Keep going."

I shot him a seething look. Before I could give him the words to match, the pressure left my body in the form of a powerful wind, fluttering my hair and stinging the lines of sweat running down my temples. My muscles reflexively tightened, and my body coiled like a wire ready to spring.

Michelle, still holding her sais, ran her fists along her bare arms as if fighting off a chill. "What the heck was that?"

My eyes, I knew, were as wide as hers. "I don't know," I whispered. "But be happy you're still standing."

"I don't believe it," Michelle said, her face a paler shade than usual. "Did you just move your ki?" Before I could ask her what she was talking about, she snapped her head over her shoulder, and turned to meet Braden's sais with her own. The two twisted against each other, breaking apart only to clash together again.

I ducked just in time to miss the naginata's blade as it bore down on me. Luckily the shift from clueless shampoo girl to skilled fighter happened in a matter of seconds. I knew what to do and, better still, the inner voice was quiet. Interesting. Unfortunately, I didn't have the time to figure out the change.

I spun to the right, bringing my blade up in front of my face as the naginata appeared close enough for a shave. Apparently Drew, like Michelle and Braden, fought better with his weapon of choice, and this was not going to be as easy as the other night when we all held katanas.

He stooped low, sweeping the naginata with him, trying to catch my feet. I jumped over the rod and answered him by bringing my sword, broad side down, on his shoulder. We weren't, after all, trying to kill each other.

He cried in surprise, and then the gloves came off. He lashed out like a whirlwind, answering each of my blocks with another attack, his speed not allowing me the chance to make an advance of my own. Not that I would have been able to make much of one anyway. Just as he said, the naginata kept me well out of striking distance. If this continued, he would wear me down before I landed another blow. Then I had an idea.

He struck out again, but this time, instead of blocking the blow, I dropped to my knees and tumbled forward. I rose to my feet behind him. Before he could turn to face me, I brought my free arm up under his arm, over his shoulder, and behind his neck, bending him over in a painful angle that put me safely out of range of his flailing arms. He was bigger and weighed much more than me, but the angle of the lock I held him in left him helpless to counter.

After a minute of struggling, he gave a frustrated cry and dropped the naginata onto the floor.

"Drew, out!" Kim ordered.

Drew bowed to me before retrieving his fallen weapon. He left the ring and joined Kim.

Michelle's in trouble. I groaned as the voice blew inside my head. I knew the silence had been too good to be true. I pivoted and instinctively jumped over the fallen girl, sensing her placement on the floor without looking. I crouched down and fed my blade to the sai arcing toward her.

Braden hesitated. "How did you move so fast?"

"Beats me," I grunted through clenched teeth. With a yell, I pushed Braden back a couple of steps, which gave Michelle time to scramble to her feet.

Braden regained his footing and came back at me. He swung a sai up, caught my sword, and attempted to wrench it from my hand. It almost worked, but I tightened my grip and pulled my katana back toward my chest. The sai spun from his hand onto the floor.

Michelle came up beside me, smirking at Braden. His eyes darted nervously between the two of us while he twirled his remaining sai. I wanted to wait for his next move, but Michelle didn't have my patience. During her charge, Braden caught her two sais with his single one, twisting his arm to lock them in place. While she struggled to free her weapons, he brought his leg back and planted a side kick into her stomach.

She grunted, dropping her weapons as she flew backward. Crap. I jumped forward, catching her around the waist, spinning us both around, before releasing her safely to her feet. I turned to Braden.

"Nice," he told me, smiling.

"Thanks." I smiled back.

I watched Michelle sneak up behind Braden during our exchange, but by the time he noticed, it was too late. The roundhouse kick to his back knocked him forward. As he stumbled for balance, I gave him an additional spinning back kick to the side. He crumpled with a thud, his remaining sai landing a good ten yards from his hand.

"Match over!" Kim smiled.

Michelle turned to me. "Nice match, girl!" She held up her hand.

I hesitated, not sure how to respond. I finally shook my head and returned the high-five. I didn't need to overthink everything.

She beamed.

"Nice job, Rileigh," Drew said, patting me on the back.

I suppressed the flinch. I could do this. I could act friendly around these people even if trust was still an issue.

"Yeah," Braden chimed in. "Nice job saving Michelle's ass!"

"Hey!" Michelle poked the handle of her sai into Braden's stomach.

"Well done," Kim said. He turned for the break room, stopped, gave me a wink, then continued on his way.

To my annoyance, a heated flame licked the inside of my stomach. I was getting a little tired of the way my body warmed and my heart fluttered when he was around. I stuck my tongue out at the back of his head as he walked away.

Michelle, who watched the exchange, giggled. "Come on. We have a locker for you." She motioned for me to follow her and the others as they headed toward the door in the back.

Drew and Braden were already stripping off their sparring pads when I entered the plain, windowless room and looked around. A short counter complete with a sink lined the side wall. In the middle of the room, a card table was set up with several folding chairs scattered about. Along the far wall stood a row of full-sized lockers, twice as big as the half lockers we have in school.

"That locker is yours," Michelle said, pointing to the farthest one against the wall.

I counted the lockers. "Why are there only five?"

She just shrugged and smiled. "That's all we need."

I fought the urge to huff at her answer that wasn't an answer. Instead, I stripped off my pads and loaded them into the locker. When I finished, I turned to find Drew creeping up behind Kim, who was pulling on a black T-shirt. I started to ask what he was doing, but Drew placed a finger to his lips. A sinister grin spread across his face.

Michelle appeared at my side and elbowed my arm. "Brothers," she said, rolling her eyes.

Was she crazy? There was no way Drew, with his lily-white skin and blond hair, could be blood-related to Kim. "Was Kim adopted?" I asked.

She smiled. "No. In the old life, Drew's name was Seiko."

I didn't bother to hide the skepticism in my voice. "Are you kidding me? Psycho? Like the personality disorder?"

She laughed. "It's spelled differently, but it's fitting, right? He was Kim's older brother. I guess some things never change."

Together, we watched Drew as he slowly crept forward. When he positioned himself behind Kim, he crouched low to the ground and gave us a thumbs-up.

Michelle snorted.

"What is he doing?" I whispered.

"Getting his ass kicked," she whispered back.

Just then Drew let out a cry and kicked his leg out. He would have swept Kim's legs out from under him—only Kim was already in the air lashing out with a roundhouse kick.

Drew fell back and had to flatten his spine to the ground to avoid Kim's foot from smashing into his face. After Kim landed, Drew pushed off the ground and landed on his feet in one fluid movement. He held his palms flat and across his body in a defensive stance and laughed. "Thought I had you that time."

Kim grinned and moved his arms apart like he was pulling an arrow back on an invisible bow. "Not in your wildest dreams. How do you expect to sneak up on someone when you have the stealth of an ox?"

Braden stepped up next to Drew and opened his arms wide. "Don't worry, Drew, I got your back."

Kim laughed. "I think you were better off by yourself."

Michelle jerked me back by the arm just as Braden leapt at Kim.

"What the—" I tried to flatten myself against the lockers in an effort not to be hit by flying limbs. "We need to get out of here!"

"Nah." She tugged my shirt to get me to follow her. "They do this all the time. Drew and Braden have been trying to best Kim for … " She smiled sadly. "As long as I can remember. Come on. Do you want something to drink?"

I followed her to the small kitchenette, flinching every time a foot or a fist entered my personal space.

I watched as Kim caught Braden's sidekick and used his foot to thrust him backward. Braden fell to the ground and tumbled backward into Michelle who stood at the sink filling two glasses with water.

She gasped and dropped the plastic cups into the sink. "Braden!" She spun around, pulled a sai from her waistband, and twirled it in her hand. "Unless you would like to meet the pointy side of my sai, I suggest you play somewhere else."

Braden grinned and lifted his eyebrows. "I would love to get to know the pointy side of your sai."

Michelle huffed and tucked her sai back into her pants. "You're stupid. That doesn't make sense." But as Braden shrugged and jumped back into the fight, I watched Michelle's eyes soften into … adoration? Or was it something more? Love? She turned to me and shook her head. "Stupid boys. Wanna try this again?"

While Michelle refilled the cups with water, I carefully maneuvered the card table around the fighting boys and set it up against the wall along with two folding chairs. Once I sat down, I watched a laughing Kim duck under Drew's spinning kick.

Michelle set a cup in front of me and sat down.

"Why don't they do this out in the dojo where there's more room?" I asked.

She snorted. "Because that would make too much sense."

Braden yelped as Kim twisted his arm behind his back.

Michelle took a drink. "At least it looks like they're winding down."

I nodded, even though, to me, they appeared to be fighting with just as much vigor as they started with.

"Did you have fun tonight?" she asked.

I shrugged. "I guess so."

She sighed and ran her finger absently around the rim of her cup. "I know it sucks."

I looked at her.

"I'm just saying that I know how you feel. Like at school, you hang out with the skaters. I never see you without that blond guy by your side. What's his name?"

"Quentin."

"That's right." She nodded. "Anyway, it's not like that for me at school. I don't really fit in and I was wondering if you might feel the same way. Sometimes—" Her voice trailed and her eyes lowered to the table.

"What?" I waved my hand in front on her face.

"Sorry." She blushed and met my eyes. "I just thought it would be cool if we became friends."

I blinked at her. Friends with motor-mouthed Michelle? I wondered if it would be easier to buy a talking parrot.

She looked away. "Never mind. It's stupid, I know."

A knot of guilt tightened inside my stomach. Way to be a jerkface, Rileigh. "No, Michelle," I said, tapping her clasped hands with my fingers. "It's not stupid. Of course I want to be friends." And the weird thing was, I really did.

"Really?" She glanced at me, the corner of her lip curling into a half smile. "You mean it?"

I smiled back. "Totally."

"Yay!" Michelle clapped her hands together. "I just know that we'll be great friends! We're going to have so much fun. We can have sleepovers and talk about boys! Oh!" Her face lit up. "Speaking about boys, you see Braden there?" I followed her gaze to the mop-haired boy that Kim held in a headlock. "We're a couple." She leaned her chin against her hand as a coy smile played on her lips. "Are you seeing anyone?"

"I went on my first date with Whitley Noble," I said, shrugging. "But I think it's too early to call us a couple."

"Whitley?" She wrinkled her nose. "Ugh. He asked me out a bunch of times last semester, but he's not my type."

I hoped my face didn't show my shock. Whitley had asked out Michelle I-need-a-hot-oil-treatment Walters? Crazier yet, she turned him down? "You have something against tall and gorgeous?"

"Looks aren't everything." Her eyelids lowered dreamily and her chin sunk deeper into her hand as she continued to stare at Braden.

When she didn't move for several seconds, I cleared my throat loudly.

"Huh?" Her eyes fluttered wide. "Oh, sorry." She rubbed her hand along her burning cheek. "Have you ever been in love, Rileigh?"

I tried to respond, but the answer lay thick and sour on my tongue. It wasn't that I didn't want to be in love, but I seemed unable to choose a guy who saw me for who I was. Maybe this time, with Whitley, it would be different.

She opened her mouth to say something, but seemed to think better of it. "Never mind. What were we talking about? Oh yeah—boys. By the way, I was a boy once."

I choked on my water.

Ignoring me, Michelle continued. "In my other life, my name was Yorimichi. My twin brother Kiyomori and I were the youngest samurai in our army."

My throat burned, but I managed to form words between gasps for air. "That can happen?"

"Yup," Drew answered, pulling up a chair and flopping down next to us. "Some people believe in karma and its effect on who you will become in your next life. As far as I can tell there's no pattern between who someone was in the past and who they are at present. Rebirthing is a mystery."

I turned back to Michelle. "How do you do it? You were a boy, and now—isn't it confusing?"

She smiled. "You know, it's not as weird as you think. It really doesn't matter who or what I was in the past." When I made a face, she laughed. "Look, I remember who I was in the past, but that person's dead. A shadow. By transcending, I'm able to remember the past, but that doesn't bring it back. Who I am now is who I'm supposed to be for this life. Nothing can change that."

Both Braden and Kim pulled up chairs next to the

table. Braden collapsed into his, panting, but the only sign that Kim had been fighting was the sweat glistening on his skin.

"Nobody can be the same person they were," Drew said. "Each new life brings new experiences, which, in turn, shape the person you were into someone who can deal with the current world. A person is like the earth itself, covered in different layers and always changing. At the core we're the same molten fire rock that blazed to life millions of years ago, but we transform through each phase."

"Our souls make us who we are," Kim added. He pressed a hand against his chest. "This is only a shell. Inside, our souls have no shape. No gender. The only thing we carry from life to life is our essence." When I made no sign of understanding, he continued. "Think of it in terms of color. Our shells may change from life to life, but what's inside stays the same. Our souls may fade or darken depending on our experiences, but the color, the essence, never changes."

I frowned. "This sounds a little too new age for me."

"There's nothing *new* about this way of thinking," Michelle said with a giggle. "But that's beside the point. From the moment I saw you fight, I had no doubt in my mind that you were Senshi."

I opened my mouth to argue, but she stopped me with a raised hand. Surprised, I leaned back in my chair.

"There's also the way you act and the faces you make," she said. "They're the same. And the attitude—it's been a lifetime, but Senshi's attitude isn't something easily forgotten."

Braden snickered, but stopped after I shot him a dirty look.

Michelle continued. "There's also your fighting style." She tilted her head. "But there is a difference. I just can't put my finger on it." She squinted her eyes, and I had the uncomfortable feeling that she was trying to see through me.

"It's her eyes," Drew spoke up. "They're not haunted."

"Haunted?" I repeated. This was getting weirder by the minute, and I couldn't help but think how unfair it all was. It wasn't even a week ago when I'd been perfectly happy living my nice, normal life—before everything fell apart. What I wouldn't give for some glossy-toothed TV host to burst through the door and tell me I was on a hidden-camera show.

"Yes! That's it!" Michelle said. She focused her attention on my eyes, which I disliked even more.

"She hasn't killed in this life," Kim said.

"Of course not." I looked at him. "Look, I like to skate and I like to hang out with friends. A good time for me does *not* involve murder. That's insane."

Braden laughed. "Wanna guess what the number-one duty is under a samurai's job description?"

I shrugged. "Do I really care?"

Kim ignored me. "Senshi was a gifted fighter. Even though she killed protecting her family and loved ones, I saw how haunted the stain of death left her." He leaned back in his chair. "She didn't have much of a childhood. When she was fifteen, her mother decided she was old enough to begin work as a prostitute. But that didn't really work for her," he said, chuckling, "because Senshi assaulted her first patron."

My heart quivered under the pain of a memory that refused to surface. Surprised, I hugged myself, hoping that the others wouldn't notice the slight tremors that shot through me. "Stop that," I whispered.

Kim sat forward again. "These stories are hard to hear, I know. You need to know that when you transcend, you'll relive them again. You've heard the expression 'My life flashed before my eyes'?"

I nodded.

"That's exactly what happens. At rapid speed, you will experience your past life firsthand. Your childhood, the killings, all your memories—both good and bad—will resurface together, all at once. It can be a bit ... overwhelming."

And he was just now telling me this? I felt my cheeks flush. "I can't believe you didn't bother to tell me any of this when you left the sword with me yesterday!"

Michelle gasped. "You gave her the katana?"

Kim casually shrugged his shoulders. "It belongs to her."

"Yes, but—" Braden bit off the rest of the sentence after Kim sent him a warning glance.

"But you didn't ... I mean, obviously ... you haven't touched it yet, right?" Michelle asked.

I dropped my chin and rolled my eyes up at her.

"Right." She paused. "Er, why not?"

I sighed. "I'm not convinced that transcending would be in my best interest."

Her face scrunched in confusion.

"I get it," Drew said. "You're worried that you won't be the same person after transcending that you are now."

"But that doesn't happen," Michelle said. "The memories and abilities you gain through transcending are already in your head. They've already shaped who you are. Transcending just, like, unlocks the door that keeps them stored in your subconscious. That's not to say it's not hard and painful. But you don't have to go through it alone. You have all of us to help you."

I looked around the table at each of them. Their smiles were genuine. I wanted so badly to believe them. To accept their offered help and friendship. But I couldn't let my guard down. My life was being threatened and I couldn't afford to make myself vulnerable.

You can trust them.

I jerked upright. That was the other thing to take into consideration. I wasn't about to trust anyone until I knew for sure I could trust myself.

Michelle frowned. "Is something wrong?"

I shook my head a little too quickly. "No—no. I'm fine." I plastered a smile on my face and thought of a way to change the subject. "So, you were a twin, huh? That's pretty cool. Do you know whatever happened to your brother?"

"Kiyomori?" Michelle smiled. She leaned over and gave Braden a nudge. "You're looking at him."

For the second time of the night, I almost choked, but managed to mask it as a cough. "You're dating your brother?" I struggled to keep my voice neutral. This development was a bit much for me to process. Not to mention just plain gross.

Michelle bit her lip and dropped her eyes to the table. "It's not what you think," she said softly.

Ew. I knew if I lost one ounce of control I would shudder, and I could tell Michelle felt bad enough. I took a deep breath. And then another.

She twisted her hands together. "It's true, Braden and I were brothers. We were so close—even had our own language." She looked at Braden and their eyes locked. "From the moment we were born, we did everything together. We even died together."

Braden flinched and closed his eyes.

Michelle turned back to me. "For whatever reason, in this life, Braden and I were not born into the same family. But that doesn't matter. A soul mate's connection can transcend a lifetime." She gave me a knowing glance. "I imagine you understand a little about what I am talking about?"

I wasn't about to admit my involuntary attraction to Kim, but I had a feeling my burning cheeks gave me away.

She gave a satisfied smile and continued. "I met Braden before I transcended. I knew I loved him from the first moment I saw him. We didn't *fall* in love. It was there already, I just didn't know it yet."

Braden spoke up. "You ever hear people talking about 'love at first sight'?"

I nodded.

"That's usually what occurs when connected souls from the past reunite in the present."

"Connected souls?" I repeated.

"Or soul mates," Michelle added. "Your relatives and your gender are strictly physical. And since souls move beyond the physical plane, so do your connections. When you're reborn into a new life, the connection with your soul mate is still there, but it might show up differently than it did in your past life."

I considered that. Even if Kim and I were indeed soul mates, in my book that wasn't an automatic engagement. Maybe in this lifetime we were meant to be friends. Just friends. I could live with that. But one thing still didn't quite make sense to me. "Why now? Of all the possibilities, why were we brought back now?"

"Are you familiar with the Chinese yin yang?" Drew asked.

"The black-and-white tadpoles that form a circle?"

Drew laughed. "Actually, it's a symbol for balance. The Earth can only exist with balance. Equal light for equal dark. We believe a great evil has returned and we're meant to fight it. And that's why you're here, too."

A great evil? It was hard to comprehend, considering that up until the attack, the only things that scared me were cooking that didn't include a microwave, Quentin's hair-styling experiments, and zits on picture day.

"Rileigh?"

I looked up from the spot on the table I had been staring at and turned my attention to Kim.

"Is something the matter?"

I gave him my best "Are you insane?" look. "How can you even ask me that? With everything I've been through—everything I've learned? No, Kim, nothing's the matter. I'm just peachy." He opened his mouth to reply, but I cut him off with a sigh. "I'm sorry, okay? I'm exhausted. I promise I'll be better after a full night's sleep."

"Me, too," Drew said. He tossed his braid behind him as he stood.

"Where do you have to be?" I asked.

"Nowhere. Drew's just lazy," Michelle answered. "He owns this comic and gaming store, so he sets his own hours. He's twenty, but he likes to sleep even more than I do."

Drew smiled and shrugged.

I stood up with them. Even though I wasn't going in to work in the morning, I knew driving would become dangerous if I stayed much longer. "I guess I'll see you guys later."

Kim stood and folded his arms. "You mean you'll see us tomorrow—at training." The tone of his voice didn't make it a question.

I rolled my eyes and turned for the door.

"Eight o'clock," Kim shouted.

I held my hand up in acknowledgement as I exited the dojo.

Once inside my car, I jammed the key into the ignition and spit gravel from my tires. As I crossed the JB Bridge into Missouri, I replayed the night's revelations in my head, startling myself each time my tires ground against the divots on the side of the road designed to wake sleeping drivers. This was not how I wanted to spend the summer before my senior year. I was supposed to be shopping and hanging out with Quentin, not training with samurai. I breathed a sigh of relief when I pulled into my driveway. I was lucky I didn't get pulled over.

Then I noticed the strange Mercedes in the driveway. I guessed my luck had run out.

26

I braced myself for a sword-wielding ninja, but when I opened the door I saw something worse: Dr. Wendell.

"Rileigh!" My mother sat up from where she lay against Dr. Wendell on the couch and straightened her hair. "You surprised me."

"Hey there." Dr. Wendell lifted his hand from her thigh to wave at me before dropping it back in place.

I felt like crying. After the night I had, I now had to come home to this? It hardly seemed fair.

"I noticed the condition of your car this morning," Debbie stated. "Is there something you'd like to tell me?"

"Deer," I answered automatically.

Her brow folded. "But the side mirror and the passenger window are shattered. How—"

"Pieces went flying. It was a mess. I've already called the insurance company and made an appointment with a body shop, so you don't have to worry. It's all been taken care of."

Dr. Wendell glanced at me, a frown on his face, before darting his eyes back to the TV.

Debbie crossed her arms. "A deer did all that?"

"A *big* deer," I corrected.

"Uh-huh." But she didn't look convinced. "So where have you been? On another date?" She gestured toward the loveseat. "Sit."

My shoulders slumped. "Mom, I'm really tired. If you don't mind—"

Debbie cut me off. "I know I've been busy lately and we keep missing each other. You can't talk to your mother for five seconds?"

I sighed. There was no trumping the guilt card. "I didn't have a date."

"Oh." Debbie's face relaxed for a moment before tightening back up. "Wait—why didn't you have a date? Did that boy try something last night? I knew he looked like trouble."

"Mom," I groaned, "last night went ..." I thought about the attack and the fact that I was still alive. "Pretty good, actually." Well, it could have gone worse.

"Oh." She thought for a moment. "Then where were you? Surely you weren't at the skate park this late? It's dark out."

"Where was I? Well ... I ... uh ..." I scanned my brain for a feasible explanation while she waited, frowning. "You see, Dr. Wendell was right. I had some things to work out, so I decided to take up martial arts." It was close enough to the truth.

"Really?" Debbie cocked her head to the side. "I have to say, I'm a little surprised. This is a very mature decision you've made. You're not playing the victim. You're taking control of the situation."

"Rileigh, this is great news!" Dr. Wendell turned off the TV and focused his attention on me. I should have known he'd have to get his opinion in. "This is just the thing to help you get over the attack. You know, I take martial arts myself." He turned to Debbie and winked. "I'm a black belt."

"Oooh," Debbie marveled. "That sounds so dangerous."

"It is." He sat back, nodding.

I wondered how many naginatas he'd had lobbed at his head tonight. Maybe I could volunteer …

"Just think." Debbie clasped her hands together. "Now you and Rileigh have something in common."

"Yeah." Dr. Wendell smiled. He turned to face me. "If you like, I would be more than happy to give you a few pointers. You know, show you the ropes." He jabbed the air with his hand.

"Er, great." I stood up and pretended to stretch, to keep them from seeing my disgusted expression. "Boy, I'm tired. I think I'll head off to bed now."

"Okay, honey," Debbie said. "But one more thing before you go."

I froze halfway between the living room and the kitchen. So close.

"You really need to be more careful when you leave the house. Jason got here first and said the door was wide open. Someone could have robbed us."

Dr. Wendell smiled at me. "But you don't have to worry. I checked the house and gave it the all clear."

An icy jolt ran down the length of my spine. "The door was open?"

"You probably forgot to shut it when you left, and the wind blew it open." His smile didn't waver. "But just in case, I'm going to stay the night again—only as a precaution."

The sword! Without a word I turned and sprinted into the kitchen. I could see the vacant spot on the table even before I turned on the lights. This couldn't be happening! My breathing came out in quick gasps as I paced the room and chewed on my thumbnail. I jumped when I felt a sharp sting followed by the coppery-sweet taste of blood.

"Mom!" I called out, trying my best to hide the frantic edge to my voice. "I had something on the table earlier. Did you move it?"

"I didn't touch anything," Debbie called back.

I felt the blood drain from my face. What was I going to tell Kim? That sword must be worth—well, I didn't even want to think about it—more than I had, to be sure. Not to mention it was the key to my transcending. True, I wasn't sure that transcending was in my best interest, but I hadn't completely decided against it, either. Now it appeared the choice had been made for me.

A beep from the corner of the room made me cry out.

"Are you all right in there?" Debbie asked.

"I'm fine!" I answered, in a pitch higher than I'd intended. Damn cell phone! I retrieved it from the kitchen counter with an impatient huff. The screen said one missed call. I dialed my voicemail and listened to the message.

"Hey, Rileigh. It's Whitley. I texted you earlier, but maybe you didn't get it. Just wanted to tell you what a great time I had last night. And I hope we can do it again soon. Give me a call when you can. Bye."

I deleted the message and struggled not to cry. Why did my life have to be so complicated? Why couldn't I just be a normal girl and have a normal summer vacation, without getting attacked, stalked, and having my house broken into? Then there was Whitley—a very normal and very cute guy—whom I couldn't have a relationship with because "dating" was being pushed to the bottom of my priority list in order to give "staying alive" the top spot. "Not having my stuff stolen" was a close second.

Dr. Wendell appeared in the doorway and jumped when he caught sight of me. "I'm sorry, Rileigh, I didn't know you were still in here. Boy trouble?"

I wiped my eyes with the back of my hands and shot him a look I hoped would boil water. "Nothing I'd talk about with *you*."

He didn't flinch. "Fair enough." He looked down at a cell phone vibrating in his hand. "Look, uh, I hate to ask, but I've got to take this call, and I could really use some privacy."

It took me a second to realize he was asking me to leave my own kitchen. I thought about telling him that if he was at his own house he could have all the privacy he wanted, but I didn't feel like risking Debbie's wrath. Instead, I settled for "Whatever" before spinning on my heels and marching down the hall to my room.

"Thanks!" he called after me.

I ignored him and reached for my doorknob, only to freeze before my fingers grasped the metal. My heart beat impossibly loud, drowning out the sounds of the TV down the hall. I didn't know how I knew it, maybe another premonition of sorts, but something was definitely not right. I wiggled my fingers, itching to twist the knob and get it over with, but at the same time felt terrified at what I might find.

I bit my lip. So what was my other option? Spending the night in the living room with Dr. Wendell? As if. I'd take my chances with the unknown.

My fingers grasped the cool metal knob, the same one that I'd grasped thousands of times before, but still, it felt foreign in my grasp. After a quick turn, I pushed the door open and surveyed what lay before me.

All the oxygen left my lungs at once. My room had been torn apart, literally. The contents of my dresser were strewn about the room and the drawers themselves lay discarded on the floor. I even spotted a pair of my underwear looped across the ceiling fan and spinning lazily over my head. My mattress had been shoved against the wall and my box spring harbored the clothes and shoes ripped from my closet.

Struggling to breathe, I tiptoed across the shredded remains of several stuffed animals and climbed onto my box spring. From there, I removed the underwear from the fan and climbed down. My lip trembled and I quickly bit down on it. I would *not* shed another tear. The time of crying and hiding under my covers was over—the time for action was now.

I launched the lacy fabric against the wall and clenched my shaking hands into fists. "Easy, Rileigh," I whispered to myself. "Gotta calm down." But every time I looked at the wreckage of my room, a new wave of anger crashed down on me.

I decided the best place to start putting things back together was closing my wide-open window. However, as I drew near the fluttering curtains, I heard someone talking outside. With breakneck speed, I darted to the window and flattened myself against the wall. From my new vantage point, I could hear the speaker better, but not enough to understand his words. His voice was disturbingly familiar, and I knew that if I could just get a look I'd know who ransacked my room.

Sucking in a breath, I decided to risk it. Using the move I'd seen in countless crime dramas, I curled myself against the windowsill and chanced a look outside.

What I saw was a bald head with two tattooed horns illuminated by the moonlight. Devil-boy! He continued to talk into his cell phone as he crept along the side of my house with a sword case strapped to his back. My katana! My vision hazed in a cloud of red and I gripped the windowsill to keep from launching myself at him. Even in the dark, I could see the silver gleam of the handgun in his back pocket and I doubted there were any Good Samaritans with pepper spray nearby. Stretching my neck out the window as far as I could without being seen, I managed to grasp a few pieces of his conversation.

"No. I didn't forget what you paid me for," Devil-boy grumbled. "But she wasn't here like you said she'd be." There was a pause, then, "How am I supposed to know? I can't snatch someone who isn't here. I did find the sword, though." Another pause. "Fine. Get the girl yourself." Devil-boy slammed his phone shut and rammed it inside of his jeans pocket. He stopped at the edge of my house, looked left and right, then disappeared in front of it.

My pulse pounded a rhythm like the bass beat of a dance mix inside my head. I had to get my sword back ... but how? I growled, pounding my fist against the window trim, cursing myself when pain exploded like a thousand needles in my hand. I couldn't sit and do nothing. Devil-boy was my direct link to the person responsible for trying to ruin my life. If I couldn't confront him head-on, I could at least follow him to wherever he was taking my katana and call Kim with the location.

I had one leg swung over the sill when a knock at my bedroom door sent me tumbling into a pile on my bedroom floor. "Oof," I complained, rubbing my sore elbow.

"Rileigh?" It was Dr. Wendell. "Is everything all right in there?"

Great. Just what I needed. I brushed myself off and climbed to my feet. "Just, uh, doing some decorating."

He was silent for a moment. "Well, I just got off the phone and I was thinking, you looked so upset earlier... would you like to go out for ice cream with me and your mom?"

An alarm signaled inside of my head, but Devilboy was getting away, leaving me no time to analyze it. "Thanks, but no thanks." I slipped my foot back over the sill. "I'm pretty tired and have to work tomorrow morning, so if you don't mind, I'm just going to go to sleep."

"All right, then. Good night."

"Night." I slid both feet out and landed softly in the grass. I was about to take off when Dr. Wendell spoke again. "Rileigh, if there's anything going on with you, that's—I don't know—too much to handle, you know you can always come to me, right?"

With a sigh I leaned back inside my window. Seriously, what was up with this guy? "Good to know. *Night.*"

It wasn't until I heard the soft shuffling footsteps of Dr. Wendell retreating from my door that I began to creep along the side of my house. When I reached the corner, I poked my head around and surveyed the street. At first, nothing moved, but then I heard the soft jingling of dog tags as old Mr. Lewis and his dachshund, Pretzel, came ambling down the sidewalk. He eyed me curiously when Pretzel stopped to sniff a light pole.

So much for my super spy skills. With my head ducked low to avoid eye contact, I peeled myself from my hiding spot as nonchalantly as I could and made my way to my car. There was no point in hiding any longer. Aside from Mr. Lewis casting me suspicious glances, the street remained quiet—thanks to Dr. Wendell, Devil-boy was long gone.

Now what?

My body hummed. I couldn't sit in my room all night—not to mention that in its current state, there was nowhere to sit. So what's a girl to do when she's all juiced up with no one to kick in the face? My answer was to go for a drive to cool down. Who knew? I might even spot Devil-boy while I was out.

27

Once I had rolled out of the drive in neutral and coasted to the end of the street, I slammed my foot against the gas. I pressed down the button for the two remaining windows and the warm summer air quickly enveloped me, but for once, it did little to ease my tension. In fact, after an hour of driving aimlessly, I was still shaking, and also coming to the realization that locating Devil-boy was no more likely than finding anything cute on a seventy-percent-off department store rack. Discouraged, I pulled into a deserted parking lot to turn my car around when I found myself staring into the glass doors of Kim's dojo. I hadn't even realized I'd crossed the bridge.

I picked up my cell phone to call Kim. Now was definitely the time for reinforcements. I dialed his number, but it went straight to voicemail. "Perfect," I muttered, ending the call.

I wished I could call Quentin, and I felt a pang of regret that I hadn't had a chance to tell him what was going on. If ever I needed my best friend, now was the time.

I turned off the Fiesta and climbed out. I wasn't sure what I was going to do, but it felt right to be here. I walked up to the door and peered into the dark lobby. Empty. I pulled at the door. It didn't budge. Had I really thought it would? I shook the door several more times before leaning my head against the cool glass in defeat. Brilliant plan, Rileigh.

We can open the door.

I pushed myself off the glass. "Oh yeah?" I asked. "Then do it. Open the stupid door."

Concentrate, the voice ordered.

I balled my hands into fists. "Not the deal. You've done enough to ruin my life. I'm not helping you do anything."

CONCENTRATE.

I cringed against the thundering in my head. "All right! You win!" The last thing I needed was a migraine.

Close your eyes.

I felt ridiculous, but I did what I was told.

Still, nothing happened. Maybe the voice got its kicks by having me make a fool out of myself?

Visualize it.

Visualize what? No sooner did the question pop into my head than the image of the inner workings of the lock appeared inside my mind. The gears tightened, pulling each other along with metal teeth, until they had sucked the deadbolt from its resting place. I knew what to do.

"Open," I whispered.

From the pit of my stomach, I felt the first stirrings of the same icy wind that had breezed through me during the sparring match and with the biker chicks. I held my breath and stiffened against the tickling sensation. Gradually the butterfly wings stopped tickling my stomach.

I sighed. I could see where this was going. I closed my eyes again and focused on relaxing. The wind rose again, but this time flipping and twirling hummingbirds replaced the butterflies. I gritted my teeth, afraid of doing something to make it go away but not enjoying the uncomfortable feeling of having a tornado inside my chest. Just as I opened my mouth to scream, I felt a ripping sensation followed by the rush of wind pushing itself from my body.

I stared at my own wide eyes reflecting back at me in the glass. As the wind poured from my skin, it tore the scream from my throat and twisted my hair into knots, forcing me to double over.

When I thought I could bear it no more, the lock made a soft click and the wind vanished as quickly as it had come.

I stood up and smoothed my tangled hair out of my face. What just happened? I was scared to touch the door, afraid that I was going crazy and had imagined the whole thing. Tentatively, I reached out for the handle and pushed. The door swung inward.

I hung my head. Part of me had hoped that I *did* imagine the whole wind thing. It was nice that I unlocked the door, but that did not make me thrilled to add another item to my list of *Things that Make Rileigh Not Normal.*

I walked into the dark lobby, fumbling my hand along the wall until I found the light. I flicked the switches, and the front lobby lit up in welcome. I had to admit, it felt right to be here. It was as if the building had called to me, and subconsciously, I answered.

I wondered briefly what Kim would do if he found me here. True, I was trespassing, but I hoped he wouldn't see it that way. I had nowhere else to go. He'd understand, right?

I left the main dojo lights off as I walked across the mats to the far wall with the punching bags. This was why I was here. I marched along the line of bags, taking my time to look each over until I settled on one. Most of the bags were filled with water and grounded to floor stands. The one I selected was bigger than the rest and suspended from the ceiling with several metal chains. I tested it with a shove. It moved sluggishly away from me, but then returned with more force. Perfect.

I gathered all the anger inside of me and ripped it out, piece by piece, as I launched my assault. I pummeled the bag with an uninterrupted stream of punches and kicks. The release was exquisite. Punch. Jab. Side kick. Hook. Spinning back kick.

From a far-off place, I realized my hands were throbbing, but I didn't just ignore the pain; I embraced it. Every time my hands connected with the bag, the biting sting that followed felt like a victory against the rage.

Finally, after I'd purged myself of the fury boiling my

blood, a heaviness crept through my body and I became aware of my aching muscles. I readied myself to lash out one last roundhouse kick to the bag when I caught the outline of a man in my peripheral vision.

I froze, silently choking on the breath that my throat refused to swallow. Devil-boy hadn't driven away after all! He'd only waited for me to get in my car, then he'd followed me!

With my leg still in the air, poised to strike, I watched the dark figure edge closer to my back through the mirrors along the wall, all the while cursing myself for not turning the lights on. I waited, counting the seconds until he stood directly behind me. Then, using my senses as my guide, I pivoted on my foot and released my paused kick.

He effortlessly sidestepped the blow and reached for my outstretched leg. Snagging my foot, he twisted it, knocking me to the floor on my elbows. "Stop," he ordered.

I grunted into the mat. "As if *that's* going to happen." I didn't remember Devil-boy moving so fast in our last encounter, or maybe I was tired from my workout and moving slower. Either way, I had to get my act together and quick. I pushed off the ground and swung my free leg for his head. The man released my foot as he jumped back to avoid my strike. As soon as I was free, I scrambled to my feet and launched myself at him with a barrage of punches and kicks.

Unfortunately, Devil-boy must have consumed his V8, taken vitamins, and eaten all his vegetables, because he fought with an expert's skill that he clearly lacked the night before. He sidestepped every hit and kick with ease. In fact, he was doing more damage to me than I was to him. Each time he blocked my strikes, I ended up with another bruise on my arms or legs.

My muscles screamed, but I refused to listen. Hit after hit and kick after kick. I felt like a machine, fueled on rage alone. For several more minutes, I continued to throw myself at him, a flurry of thrusting arms and legs until, finally exhausted, my right leg shuddered and my ankle gave away. I careened sideways into the mat.

He used my loss of balance as an opportunity to grab my right wrist.

With an angry cry, I swung my free hand for his face. He seemed to humor me then, letting the blow come inches from his face, teasing me into thinking I might have a chance before spinning me sharply by the wrist and snatching my striking hand out of the air.

I found myself locked against his chest with my own arms. I struggled for a moment, pulling and twisting, locking myself tighter until, finally, I slumped against him, defeated. "Just get it over with already."

He said nothing, but the scent of sandalwood enveloped me.

An electric current ran through my body. It couldn't be…

"Are you finished?" Kim asked.

I was. My legs gave out from under me and Kim stepped into my fall, tightening his grip to keep me from collapsing.

"Why did you sneak up on me?" I asked between gasps. My lungs seemed unable to get enough oxygen.

"Last I checked, this was my dojo. Besides, you attacked *me*." He held me until I regained my balance, and even then didn't let go. "What is going on?"

Tears streamed down my cheeks, but I was too tired to care. So much for my vow not to cry. "Someone tried to kidnap me, tore apart my room, and stole the katana!" I sobbed.

Kim went rigid against me. He was silent for several moments before finally whispering, "It appears our time has run out."

28

Rileigh." Kim twisted me in his arms so I faced him. "Are you all right?"

I rubbed my burning eyes with the palms of my hands. His hair was in disarray, but his eyes were clear and alert. "Of course I'm not all right. Didn't you hear what I said?"

"Are you hurt?"

I almost told him no, but noticed my burning hands. My knuckles looked like they had been run through a cheese grater.

Kim followed my eyes. He gently lifted each of my hands, ignoring my blood as it dripped onto his skin. "You know, you're really supposed to wear gloves, or at least wrap your hands when you train with the bags."

I tried to think of a snarky response but came up blank. Instead, I wondered how someone who worked out so much could have such velvety soft skin. And yet, his actual hands were solid, like granite wrapped in satin. He moved his thumbs in circles from my knuckles to my wrists and I shivered in response.

"Kim!" I jerked my hands from his grip. "You're not listening to me. You're getting distracted." And he wasn't the only one.

He didn't move. The heat between our bodies was inviting, like sitting next to a campfire on a cold night. But if I moved any closer, I knew I'd get burned.

"Someone is trying to kidnap me." My voice was barely a whisper. "And the katana is gone."

"One thing at a time." He looked around the room and raised a curious eyebrow. "How did you get in here, anyway?"

"Do you have ADD?" I asked, stamping my foot. "With everything that's happened, you're worried about how I got in here?"

He folded his arms across his chest and waited.

I let out a cry of frustration. "Fine. If you must know, you forgot to lock the door."

He narrowed his eyes. "Try again."

Crap. Why did I have to be such a terrible liar? I sighed. "I don't really know. Besides, it's not important."

"Actually, it's *very* important. *You* opened the door."

I laughed nervously. "Kim, how could I have done that? I don't have a key."

He stared without blinking. "You didn't need a key, did you?"

I fought the urge to flinch under the weight of his gaze.

Instead, I threw my shoulders back and lifted my chin. Locking my eyes with his, I said, "Nobody can open a door without a key."

Kim smiled and straightened his stance, apparently not one to lose a staring contest. "*You* can."

"No, I can't." I never considered brown eyes to be anything special, but then, I'd never before seen eyes the color of melted milk chocolate.

"Yes, you can. Senshi could manipulate ki." Kim nodded his head once, as if that settled it.

I grunted and folded my arms. "Why can't you ever explain things in a way that makes sense?"

The corner of his mouth twitched, but he managed to suppress the smile. "Ki manipulation is the ability to control the energy around you. You were quite good at it in the past, and now it appears you are awakening to it again. How long have you known you could do it?"

I opened my mouth, then closed it. What was the point of arguing further? "A couple of days." I eyed the ground as I spoke. "Totally by accident."

He laughed. "I bet that was a surprise."

I thought it over. "It was ... painful."

I looked up to see him staring at me with soft eyes. He nodded. "I remember, from the old life, when Senshi began training in ki manipulation. It was painful at first, when she was learning control."

"How did she make the pain go away?"

"Our daimyo, Lord Toyotomi, was a great master in the art of manipulating ki. He taught you how to push and move it, without it pushing and moving you." He didn't seem to notice when he stopped using the name 'Senshi,' and I shifted uncomfortably.

"Right," Kim said, waving his hand. as if pushing the past memory to the side. "If you would allow it, I'd like to get your hands taken care of."

I shrugged. It wasn't like I had anywhere better to be, or even a place to stay.

"Not to mention you're bleeding all over my mats."

I pulled my hands against my chest before the realization dawned on me. "Wait. Did you just make a joke?"

He shook his head, his face as straight as the lines on notebook paper. "No, these are really expensive mats." Slowly, a wicked grin tugged his lips into an upside-down smile.

"No-nonsense Kim cracks jokes?" I threw my hands in the air. "It's the end of the world!" There might just be hope for him after all, I thought.

He appeared pleased. "We can leave after I lock up."

I froze. "Wait a minute—we're going somewhere?"

"My apartment. It's just around the corner. You can see the dojo from the kitchen window."

I frowned and folded my arms. Alone in his apartment? I knew that wasn't a good idea, but as I stood close to him, his warm scent and golden skin clouded my judgment and I struggled to think of the reasons why. I felt a danger around Kim that I didn't feel around any other guy I'd ever dated, including Whitley. With my past relationships, I learned that most guys weren't interested in anything deeper than finding out the color of my underwear. So I'd built a wall around myself and projected only the snarky, tough skater chick that everyone expected me to be. Unfortunately, when I was around Kim, I got the feeling he saw right through my crispy, flaky crust. I wondered if my dislike of Kim wasn't because he was so arrogant and pushy, but because I knew he could hurt me.

Yes, alone with Kim was a dangerous place to be. Maybe I could find Devil-boy and challenge him to another street fight instead.

He sighed. "Rileigh, you have my word—I mean you no harm. I have bandages here, but your wounds require antiseptic. Allow me to treat them, and then I will find you safe lodging for the night."

I stopped short. I knew I couldn't possibly stay in my room until I'd put it back in order, but another thought occurred to me. "My mom's at my house. What if the person coming after me tries again? I don't want to put her in danger."

Kim frowned. "Then you see why you can't go home. She's safer with you gone."

Crap. He had a point. "I guess . . . "

"Good." He cut me off. "Then let's get going."

I followed him, but stopped short before walking into the lobby. "Wait!"

His shoulders slumped, as if bracing for another argument.

I crossed my arms. "How did you know I was here?"

"Truthfully . . . " He appeared to search for the words as

he ran a hand through his disheveled hair. "I'm not sure. I was sound asleep when a feeling of alarm woke me up. I don't know how—but I knew something was happening at the dojo. When I looked out my window I saw a car in the parking lot. I walked over to find out what was going on, and I got attacked by some crazy person."

I cocked my head. "So now you think I'm crazy?"

He laughed, and my body warmed like bathing in sunlight. "No more than I am, Rileigh. But how about a deal? Next time you want in, come get me. I've got a key."

I turned away from him so he wouldn't be able to see my cheeks burn.

He laughed again. "Let's go."

I followed him outside and around the building into the big grassy lot between his dojo and a small apartment complex. As we crossed the field, I admired the night. It amazed me how Kim and I were only separated by twenty miles, and yet his night sky was completely different than mine. My sky always looked like an out-of-focus photograph; the stars dull, like diamonds caked in grease. This sky was open, endless, the stars pulsing with life like lightning bugs lit on fire.

It wasn't until Kim put his key into the door lock that I noticed we'd arrived at his apartment. That's when my stomach sank to my knees. Just the other night I'd stood on my porch waiting for Whitley to kiss me. And now I was on a different doorstep, with a different guy and entirely different feelings.

Kim caught my hesitation. "What's the matter?"

How could I begin to explain? Things were changing between us faster than I could figure them out. I felt overwhelmed, almost to the point of suffocation. I knew if I just moved closer to Kim, if I touched him, I would be able to breathe and the heaviness would subside. But that was wrong. That wasn't me. I was independent. I didn't need anyone, let alone ache to stand in their presence.

There had to be an explanation. Maybe the voice in my head was gaining more control over me, and like the overwhelming desire I had to fight Devil-boy, it was influencing my feelings toward Kim. But what if the longing to press myself against Kim's chest and let his arms envelop me was my own? I couldn't decide which scared me more.

Kim's forehead knit into worried lines.

My pulse quickened. "You know, it's late." I held up my shredded hands. "This is no big deal, really. I'm sorry I woke you up and then attacked you. Really sorry. You don't need to worry, though; I bet I can bunk with Q." I turned from him before he had a chance to argue, but wound up almost bumping my forehead against his chest from the other side. Startled, I took several steps backward, which put me inside his living room. "How do you *do* that?" I demanded.

He frowned, ignoring my question. "Rileigh, you can go if you like, but I would feel much better if you'd let me dress your hands first. I have no other motive." He held three fingers up and marked an invisible cross over his chest with the other. "Samurai honor."

I tried to suppress a laugh, but failed. "Fine, but I'm just staying long enough for you to fix up my hands."

"Deal."

He moved past me and I followed him the rest of the way into his apartment, which, though small, made me feel like I was walking through an art gallery. The first thing I noticed was a colorful kimono, folded in half with the arms wide, laid out under glass and mounted against the wall over a plain brown sofa. Without invitation, I walked over to the kimono and placed my hand against the glass. I closed my eyes and could almost feel the lines of embroidery slide against my skin. I shivered.

Turning from the display, I examined the various Japanese prints that surrounded it. Large black brushstrokes portrayed majestic mountains overlooking a crystal lake. I could feel the crunch of rocks under my feet and hear the chiming melody of exotic birds. The next picture showed a peaceful creek twisting through a valley; the crash of rushing water sounded close enough to dive into.

The different noises collided inside my head, leaving me dizzy. The room swam in a mix of mountain breeze, rushing water, and chirping birds. My world tilted to one side and then the other. I reached out blindly for something to grasp, and Kim was suddenly there, cradling me in his arms.

"Rileigh?" His worried face loomed over me.

"Did you plan this?" I accused, at the same time willing myself not to throw up.

"I swear to you I did not." His expression left no doubt.

I nodded and pushed myself out of his arms. "It's a little intense here. Can we go somewhere ... calmer?"

He led me by the hand toward the back of the small kitchen. As we drew closer to a rice paper screen, I could hear the screaming horses and samurai battle cries emanating from the war scene painted on it. The thundering of hooves grew so loud, I thought my head might burst. I squeezed my eyes shut and didn't open them again until I felt the linoleum under my feet give way to carpet. The sounds of battle disappeared. I opened my eyes and a king-size bed lay before me. I turned to Kim, who had the decency to look embarrassed.

He gave my hand a tug. "It's a small apartment," he explained. "There's only one bathroom and it's in the bedroom."

I started to follow him the rest of the way to the bathroom, but I caught sight of something that made me stop dead in my tracks. "What are those?" I gently pulled my hand out of his and walked to the foot of the bed. Mounted on the wall over the headboard, and crossed so they formed an "X," were two of the most magnificent weapons I had ever seen. The first blade was a katana, but unlike any I had seen before. I clenched my hands into tight fists at my side, fighting the urge to touch it. The handle had been wrapped in gold thread, embedding a nickel-sized blue sapphire at the base. The second blade was identical, only larger. It appeared to be as long as I was tall, and then some.

Kim appeared at my side. "The larger blade is a nodachi." He smiled, admiring the weapon along with me.

"Nodachi," I whispered. The light filtering in through the thin screen reflected off of the blade, making it look like it was made from blue flames instead of steel. "It's beautiful."

"Yes." He smiled. "It is." He moved to the side of the bed and stared down the length of the sword. "It's my favorite weapon. It was designed to kill the horses the enemies rode, but I found it more useful for beheading the riders when I fought from the ground." His eyes were lost and I realized he was speaking to me from another place, if not another time.

I shivered, hoping that this artifact wouldn't talk to me as the others had.

After a moment, Kim chuckled and shook his head. "Sorry. It looks like you're not the only one getting swept away by the past." He rubbed his hands together. "Let's get you taken care of."

I followed him into the small bathroom, which was as neat and tidy as the rest of the house. He closed the toilet lid and motioned for me to sit down.

While Kim rummaged through the small linen closet, I waited, sitting on the cool porcelain, staring at the crusty flakes of blood that had dried around my knuckles. Finally he emerged with peroxide, gauze, and medical tape in hand.

"I meant to ask you," he said, kneeling in front of me and moistening a cotton ball with peroxide. "Before you tried to pummel me, why were you beating the snot out of my training bag?"

I smiled at his phrasing. "I'm not exactly sure. I was so worked up over everything that happened tonight. I thought I'd try to follow the guy who stole the katana, but he slipped away before I could get outside. I didn't know what to do, so I started driving. I didn't set out to go to the dojo." I shrugged. "I just ended up there."

Kim nodded without looking up from the cotton ball. He dabbed the antiseptic against my tattered skin, and the pain that followed blurred my vision. I sucked in a quick breath to keep from yelping.

"Sorry," he said, tapping the cotton ball lightly against my skin. "I'll try to be fast." He threw the bloody cotton into the trash and went about wetting another one. Before he went back to work on my hands, he asked, "What would you have done if you walked in on the intruder while he was in your room?"

I squeezed my eyes shut in an effort to keep them from tearing up. "I don't know," I hissed through clenched teeth. "Ever since this whole possession thing started, I never know what I'm going to do next." When Kim frowned, I made a correction. "Sorry. I forget you call it an *awakening*. You say po-tae-to and I say po-tah-to."

He continued to dab at the blood on my hands as the tendons on his jaw flexed slowly, like a horse chewing on a lemon. "So you would not have touched the sword? Even if your life depended on it?"

I shifted uncomfortably on the toilet lid.

Kim threw more bloody cotton away. "I will tell you a secret, Rileigh. I used to envy those who went through this life completely unaware, happy in their dormant mind state."

That was a shocker. If anyone in the world could be a spokesman for transcending, I thought that person would be Kim.

He laughed at me. "You look surprised."

"I am," I answered. "Did the awakening disrupt your life, too?"

"Yes." He smiled, but there was a heaviness to his eyes. He looked past me as he reached for a box of gauze. "But I guess I had time to get used to it."

"When did you awaken?"

"I was three, almost four years old ... " He brought both of my hands up to his mouth and my heart froze inside my chest, waiting for the brush of his lips.

Instead, he blew lightly across my knuckles, forcing the breath from my throat. Only when he released my hands to get the gauze was I able to inhale again.

"What?" My voice cracked.

He nodded, his eyes focused on the gauze he wrapped around my hands. "It's rare for it to happen to someone so young." He shrugged before reaching for the medical tape. "I guess I was just unlucky that way."

"I don't get it. I would think it would be a relief to know right away, and so much less confusing."

"That's where you're wrong," he replied. "Some of the first memories of this life that I can recall are of remembering the old one. I was only a young boy, and to have all of those images ... the battles alone." He shook his head and cut the tape. "It was very difficult. I didn't have a chance to establish myself."

"What do you mean?"

Kim gathered the medical supplies and stood up. "Because I awakened at such a young age, this isn't really a new life for me—it's a continuation of the old one. I didn't get to grow up like a normal teenager. I tried to date, but it was pointless. No one could measure up to the girl I lost in Japan—the girl that haunts my dreams, my heart, and now my toilet."

I blushed and pretended to study the tops of my tennis shoes.

Kim continued. "I gave up on school too, because in my mind, school is for people who have choices. I have none—I am a samurai." He sighed and turned away, but it was too late. I'd seen the pain in his eyes.

"What about your parents? Didn't they want you to have a life and go to college?"

His lips pressed into a weary smile. "They died two years ago in a car accident. They never knew. I did everything I could to hide it from them." He crossed the room to the closet. After placing the supplies back inside, he turned to me with a smile. "Don't look so sad," he told me. He walked over to me and crouched down in front of me, meeting my eyes. "I've made my peace and moved on."

Liar. The sorrow that etched his smile and tightened

his back was undeniable. "How do you make your peace with something like that?"

"My parents were wonderful people, and I am grateful for the time I had with them in this life."

"But you didn't *have* much of a life!"

He smiled again, but his eyes strained from the forced effort. "When I was a child, the memories of the past were difficult because they reminded me of everything I had lost. It wasn't until after my parents' death that I realized it didn't have to be that way. I didn't have to be alone. By meeting others like me—like us," he corrected himself, "I learned that my friends, my family, all the people that I loved were still out there." He sat back against the wall opposite me. "I just had to find them."

I folded my hands together to keep from reaching out to him. "So you've spent your whole life looking for people from the past?"

"Well, mostly just for you," he answered.

My throat tightened. I distracted myself by picking at the new bandages on my hands.

Kim continued. "I didn't care if you experienced the awakening or not. It didn't matter to me if you would ever remember me. I just wanted to find you and make sure you were happy." He looked down at the ground. "There are many things I can handle, Rileigh, but not having you in my life isn't one of them. Look, I know you barely know me, and you are dating ... *some guy*." His mouth twitched slightly. "I'm not asking anything from you, except that I could be your friend." He tilted my chin and forced my reluctant eyes to meet his own. "That would be enough for me."

The tension in the room had built to an overwhelming level, and I had to fight to keep from squirming. "Are you sure you don't want anything more?"

The corner of his lip folded into an upside-down smirk. "The truth? I've wanted nothing more than to hold you from the second I saw you." He shrugged. "I'm not saying that this won't be hard on me, but I want to try if you'll let me."

Before I could answer, the cool wind stirred inside of my mind. *Remember.*

I shivered. It was as if a veil was lifted from my mind, just enough that I could see Kim for who he really was. I remembered. I saw his brilliant smile from across a garden of falling cherry blossoms. I felt his muscled arms pluck me off a blood-stained battlefield and secure me onto his horse's saddle. I smelled the musk of his sandalwood cologne as we awoke every morning, intertwined like the branches of a tree.

I remembered how much I loved him. No, that wasn't right. I curled my fingers around the toilet lid in an attempt to remain upright under the flood of memories. I gasped. That was it. While the experiences were memories, the feelings weren't. My need for Kim, my longing, surpassed anything I'd ever experienced before. I wondered if my heart would break under the strain.

"No," I heard myself whisper.

Kim flinched, and then lowered his eyes to the floor. "I understand."

"No." I stared at him, my eyes heavy with unshed tears. "You don't understand at all." I slid off my perch and kneeled on the floor. "I don't want you to try to be my friend, and I don't want to be yours."

Kim reached out and traced my jawline with his thumb. The sensation made my breath catch in my throat. "Then tell me, Rileigh, what *do* you want?" His face inched closer to mine until I could feel the warmth of his breath against my neck.

I shivered, lifting my chin in invitation. He obliged, weaving fingers in my hair as his teeth grazed the tender spot below my ear. "I want," I whispered, not quite knowing how to finish the sentence. It was suddenly so hot in the tiny bathroom, I couldn't think.

I tried again. "I want—" But I never finished.

Kim's arms were around me. One hand knotted in my hair, and the other pulled me onto his lap. I braced a hand against his unyielding chest, enjoying the sensation of hard muscles flexing beneath my fingertips. He kissed the skin beneath my ear, then worked his way along my jaw, into the corners of my mouth, and finally ended on my lips.

I felt my body ignite. The world seemed to move. I wrapped my arms tightly around his neck to keep us from falling apart.

Kim tightened his grip and I could no longer determine where he ended and I began. It was like we were melting together.

I pulled away with a gasp.

Kim grinned, and it was nothing short of heart-stopping. "I'm sorry, but I've waited a lifetime for that." He reached behind me for what I thought was going to be another kiss, but instead lifted my hair up with his hands and let it spill through his fingers around my shoulders like a curtain. "This can't be real. I've dreamt of this for so long. And now you're here, my Senshi. I'm so afraid I'm still dreaming."

"Yoshido," I replied, then jerked upright and out of his arms. "Holy crap!" I dropped my forehead into my palm.

Kim snapped forward. "What is it? What is wrong?"

I shook my head. "Oh no. No. No. No."

He frowned and reached for me.

I scurried to my feet. "Don't you get it?" I asked.

His eyes widened, but he said nothing.

"That wasn't me! That was the other girl. Senshi! She's trying to take over, just like I thought!"

29

Kim slowly rose to his feet. "Rileigh, calm down. Tell me—"

"I'll tell you!" I shouted, then took a breath to steady myself. "I would never call you Yoshido. I don't know a Yoshido. I only know Kim."

"Yes, you do. You know my name was once Yoshido."

"No, I didn't! Drew, Braden, and Michelle told me their names from the past, but I never knew yours. I had no way of knowing." I struggled for a moment to make sense of the thoughts tumbling inside of my mind. "*Senshi* knew," I whispered.

"You're not making sense."

My pulse skipped in my veins as I pulled the pieces together. "It makes total sense. Senshi knows your name was Yoshido so obviously *she* was the one who spoke it out loud. It couldn't have been me, even subconsciously. I'd never even heard the name Yoshido until it came out of my mouth. It's proof that I'm losing control!"

Two lines pinched the bridge of Kim's nose as he frowned. "Rileigh, it doesn't work like that."

I jabbed a finger into his chest. "That's what you *want* me to believe."

He took a step back, not bothering to mask the hurt on his face. "Rileigh, I would not lie to you about such things."

I crossed my arms. "Oh yeah, then why am I so out of control when this girl takes over? Why does she do things that I wouldn't normally do? Is that what's going to happen when I transcend? Is Senshi going to be completely in control, and Rileigh just … disappears?"

"You won't disappear." Kim took another step forward, but stopped when I almost tripped over the tub in an effort to back away from him.

I had to keep distance between us. It was the only way I could think. When I was near him there was only the scent of sandalwood, the heat of his touch, the velvet of his lips … How did I not see it before? Kim was infecting my head just as much as the spirit!

"There is no other girl in your head," he said. "I know it may feel like that, but there is only one you, just different layers. The voice you hear, the actions you do, that is all you."

I shook my head.

"Rileigh, you are worried about being taken over?"

I nodded.

"Well, in a way you are being taken over—but by the

real you. Your mind is locked right now. The person you are, the real you, is shut away. The person you think you are now is only a fraction of who you are, and she's holding you hostage. Rileigh, you will lose nothing by transcending, but gain everything."

I ran a finger along my temple, unable to think through the forming headache. "I'm so confused," I whispered.

"I know," Kim answered back. His hands hung loose at his side.

"Look, about all this—"

Kim lifted a hand to stop me. "I understand. This is not our time. No need to discuss it further." He motioned toward the door. "Please stay here tonight." I started to argue, but he cut me off again. "As my guest. You can stay in the bedroom, and I'll take the sofa. Later, we will find you somewhere to stay where you will be more comfortable. At least until I discover who is after you."

I tugged at the bottom hem of my shirt, partly to mask my trembling and partly to keep my betraying fingers from reaching out to him. "But what about Senshi's katana?" I asked. "What if we can't get it back?"

Kim shifted awkwardly. Meeting his eyes, I caught that unmistakable look of guilt that I was growing all too familiar with.

I narrowed my eyes. "What is it?"

"It's nothing." He gripped his elbow and studied a spot on the ceiling.

"Kim Gimhae," I growled. No longer afraid to close

the distance between us, I took a step forward and poked my finger against his chest. He looked down, surprised. "I know you aren't telling me something, and I'm in no mood for any more of your secrets." I jabbed my finger against him one more time for emphasis.

He ran his hand through his hair. "Senshi's katana was not stolen."

I crossed my arms. "What are you talking about? I saw it slung across Devil-boy's back!"

"Devil-boy?"

"That's what I call the scary guy with horns tattooed on his head." I shook my head. "But don't change the subject!"

"Right." He swallowed hard. "The katana I gave you was stolen."

I tapped my foot against the floor. "You better start making sense and *fast!*"

He sighed. "Senshi's katana is in my bedroom, mounted on the wall with my nodachi."

I glanced over my shoulder at the golden-hilted katana braced against the larger sword. "What? If *that's* Senshi's katana," I turned back to him, "what did you give me?"

He dropped his gaze to the floor. "A decoy."

"Excuse me?" I took a step back. "You lied to me!" Anger coursed through my body, burning through my veins like acid.

"No!" He reached for me, but I stepped beyond his grasp. He let his hand fall to his side. "I mean, yes, but it wasn't intentional."

I glared at him. "You knew it wasn't Senshi's katana, but you told me that it was. Are you sure you know the meaning of the word 'intentional'?"

Kim closed his eyes and leaned his head against the door frame. After a deep breath, he said, "I did lie to you, but I did not do it to hurt you. I did it to protect you. You *must* understand that."

"Go on."

He continued. "There is a Noppera-bō after you, Rileigh, and we do not know who this person is. It could be a friend, a teacher, or the mailman. I thought that if whoever was targeting you thought that you had your katana back and had completed your transcending, they would move on. I never meant to hurt you."

"How many times are you going to say that to me, Kim? How can I trust you when you don't trust me?" I hugged my arms against my body, remembering the feel of his hands pressing me against him. I shivered. How could I have been such an idiot?

He moved closer and raised his arm to cup my chin with his hand. I didn't move, but clenched my teeth under his fingers.

"In order to have the Noppera-bō believe it," Kim said, "I needed you to believe it—and with the theft of the decoy, it looks like it worked." He frowned and dropped his hand to his side. "It is only a matter of time before the Noppera-bō realize they have a fake and come looking for the *real* katana."

My head ached from the emotions twisting within.

Half of me wanted to pull him against me and curl against the warmth of his chest—the other half wanted to drop-kick his face. "How do you know the Noppera-bō won't believe the decoy is real?" I asked.

"Rileigh, did you not even unzip the bag?"

"No. I was afraid to touch it."

Kim sighed and tilted my chin up with his thumb so that our eyes met. "If you had opened the bag, you would have seen the answer to your question spelled out plainly on the handle."

"What's that?"

"Made in China," he said. Then he turned off the bathroom light.

30

Japan, 1493

Now that the smoke was gone, Senshi could clearly make out the approaching figure. What she saw made no sense to her.

"Zeami?" Senshi used her katana as a crutch to push herself back on her feet. It was unusual to see him alone. Zeami had fought side-by-side with Yoshido for as long as they'd been samurai. They were practically brothers. But now, Yoshido was nowhere in sight and Zeami was not dressed in armor. In fact, the red silk robes he wore were spotless and far beyond the reach of a samurai's pay. The pieces fell into place.

"You!" Senshi failed to keep the rage from grinding her voice into a growl.

Zeami laughed. "Your magic tricks are always amusing. Toyotomi was a fool to have you trained as a samurai. What a waste of talent. You would have made quite the entertainer. I doubt, however, you would have been as gifted as your mother." He licked his lips.

"I have no mother!" she spat.

"Oh, that is right." He nodded, his small black eyes glittering. "She would not claim you."

Rage boiled through Senshi's blood, and before she realized what she was doing, she'd raised her katana to attack. She took a step forward, but a hand from behind grabbed her shoulder and stopped her advance.

She twisted to face her oppressor, who in turn spun her back to face Zeami with an arm protectively blocking her chest. Senshi blinked, the furious fire extinguished by Yoshido's cool gaze. She shivered as his fingers brushed down her arm when he dropped his hold on her. She could think again.

"Ah, Yoshido, why do you bother with her?" Zeami sneered. "She is the daughter of a courtesan. Surely you could have done better."

Yoshido turned slowly, giving Zeami the weight of his full stare. "Hold your tongue, Zeami. If not, I will gladly remove it for you."

"Yoshido, that is why I have always liked you." Zeami put his hands on his hips. "So direct. You are absolutely right, of course. The time for talking has passed. These walls are surrounded by ninja and you will soon be defeated."

Senshi felt the tingle of tension creep along her shoulders. Dozens of samurai lay slain around her. The garden stank of sweet copper from the blood glittering on the grass like midnight dew. Only a handful of ninja joined the dead. Where was the rest of the army? Captured? Dead? Were she and Yoshido the only ones left? She pushed a trickle of her ki energy outward, searching. She only found ninja—too many to count—waiting in the darkness.

Yoshido shook his head. "I do not understand. Why, Zeami? We fought side by side for years. We were family."

Zeami snorted. "Family? You are disillusioned, my friend, if you think that we were ever Toyotomi's family. A samurai is nothing more than a glorified slave."

Yoshido's eyes widened. "That is absurd!"

"Is it? Slaves have no choice but to serve, and neither do samurai. What happens if a samurai chooses not to fight? Are they not executed?"

Yoshido narrowed his eyes. "Why would you not want to serve? There is no greater honor."

"Bah!" Zeami threw his arms in the air. "Honor means nothing if you are dead, and death is of no interest to me, Yoshido. In case you have not noticed, the invasions have increased. We have been successful in stopping them, but each battle has been worse than the one preceding it. It was only a matter of time before we were defeated. I was not going to stay and wait for death."

"You disgrace yourself!" Yoshido screamed, his nodachi trembling in his hand. "You disgrace your ancestors! You swore an oath of loyalty!"

"I am loyal, Yoshido ... to myself. I have enough money now to own land. I am my own master and will never have to fight someone else's battle again. Toyotomi could not give me that."

"Maybe not," Yoshido said, "but he treated us like family. Few daimyo treat their samurai so well."

"Wrong again," Zeami said. "My current employer paid me not only in money, but power. I have been bestowed the gift of dark magic. Toyotomi was always so proud of Senshi and her gift. Well, her power cannot stand against my new strength. My only regret is that Toyotomi did not live long enough to see me, Zeami, defeat his two favorite warriors." A giggle escaped his throat before he could clamp his hand over his mouth to stifle it.

"Toyotomi is dead?" Yoshido's face folded into lines of disbelief. "You lie."

Senshi held back a sob and placed her hand on Yoshido's arm.

Startled by her touch, Yoshido's eyes widened as he searched her face for the truth. Her silence told him everything. "No," he whispered, turning back to face Zeami.

"Do not be so sad, Yoshido," Zeami sneered. "You will join him soon." He held his arm out and a ninja appeared to his right. "But first, a surprise."

"Cheap ninja magic," Senshi muttered under her breath.

"Ah-ah," Zeami scolded. "Do not spoil the surprise."

The ninja strode toward Senshi and Yoshido, a bundle of something, masked by darkness, hanging from his hand. He stopped a few yards away.

Yoshido drew his sword, and Senshi readied her own.

"Go ahead." Zeami nodded at the ninja. "Please give my gifts to my old friends."

The ninja nodded and threw the objects into the air. They fell with a wet thud at the feet of Yoshido and Senshi.

At first, Senshi's mind refused to make sense of the horror of the severed heads at her feet. As she stared at the milky eyes before her, the puzzle clicked into place, one anguishing piece at a time. The twins, Kiyomori and Yorimichi. The two young boys had not quite finished their training under Yoshido. They spent most of their days following Senshi around like starved puppies, convinced they could learn the art of ki manipulation if they watched her every move.

The third head Senshi had trouble making out, as it was bruised to a plum purple. Then she saw the identifying birthmark half-hidden under a swollen gash—Yoshido's brother Seiko. Her body trembled from the strain of holding back tears. She would not give Zeami the pleasure of seeing them fall.

Yoshido was unmoving, his chest not even rising in breath. "No measure of pain can describe what I am going to do to you," he growled through bared teeth. His eyes burned with feral rage, and Senshi, terrified, no longer recognized him.

"You do not like your present?" Zeami asked in mock disappointment.

Yoshido roared. "Enough of this! Enough of your games! We finish this here, and we finish this now."

"As you wish, Yoshido," Zeami said, no longer smiling. He bowed his head to the ground. When he lifted it up a moment later, his pupils had dilated to encompass his entire eye, making his sockets appear empty.

The air in the garden prickled with hot energy that pulled at the hair along Senshi's arm and neck, giving her the sensation of a thousand daggers digging into her skin. She grimaced in pain. "What is this?" she asked.

"I have told you, my lovely Senshi," Zeami replied. "I have been given great power, power even you cannot comprehend."

Wide-eyed, Yoshido turned to her. "What is going on?"

Senshi shook her head, a feeling of helplessness weighing her down. "This is no magic that I know."

Zeami smiled. "What did I tell you? So much for the great powers of Senshi." He turned his attention to Yoshido. "Come, old friend, let this be done." Streaks of blue electricity snapped around Zeami's body in hissing and popping rings. He held his arms out, laughing as he embraced the power.

Zeami was right. Never before had Senshi seen or felt anything like it. Her own magic was a cool wind that blew out from her center. Zeami's energy was sharp and hot, seeming to come from everywhere at once. Zeami turned back to Senshi. He raised his arms and reached for her, lightning raining from his fingertips. Her shoulder was struck, and she marveled that Zeami's energy felt like a physical blow before she realized Yoshido had shoved her to the ground.

She screamed his name, watching her lover's eyes widen in surprise as he took the hit meant for her. His neck snapped up, pulled back by the lightning coursing through his body with sickening cracks. He jerked upright, twitching like a puppet shaken on its strings, before he crumpled into a heap on the ground, his eyes never once leaving her face.

The smell of burned flesh mixed with the scent of blood already hanging in the night air.

31

I woke with a start and had to shield my eyes from the sun glinting off the two swords mounted above the headboard. With my eyes closed, I was even more aware of the scent of sandalwood coming off the comforter I had wrapped around myself. I jerked the covers off, but I could still smell Kim's scent on the clean T-shirt and boxer shorts he'd given me to wear.

I flopped onto my back and tried to fall back to sleep, but the nightmare was too fresh inside my head. I tried to push the images from my mind, but that only allowed my earlier conversation with Kim to slip in. He said I had nothing to lose by transcending, and everything to gain. Was he right? Was the real me being suppressed and held captive?

Even more distracting were the memories of how his arms felt. They made my heart trip and my blood uncomfortably hot. If I thought about it, I could almost feel his lips beneath my ear, rising higher and higher … I sat up with a gasp.

Dropping my legs over the side of the bed, I grumbled the entire way into the bathroom. I knew Kim wouldn't mind if I took a shower; I just hoped he wouldn't realize how cold I intended it to be.

After my shower, I picked up my soiled workout clothes and held them up for inspection. They were spotted with the blood from my torn knuckles and smelled like sweat—but I didn't care. Anything was better than having Kim's scent sinking into my skin. I slipped my clothes on and left the bedroom in search of caffeine. Kim sat at the kitchen bar, studying his laptop. He looked up at me when I entered.

"You didn't sleep long. Were you not comfortable?"

"I'm not very tired," I lied. "Care if I use your phone? I need to call work and tell them I'm not coming in today."

"What about your mom?" he asked. "Do you think she's worried?"

I made a face. "I doubt she's noticed."

Kim frowned, but kept quiet. He inclined his head toward a phone on the counter. "It's all yours."

After I called, I returned to the counter opposite him. He looked like hell. I smiled. It was nice to see I wasn't the only one who didn't sleep.

He narrowed his eyes. "What?"

"Nothing." I gave him my best innocent look. "You got any coffee?"

He returned his focus to the computer. "The coffeepot is behind you, and coffee is in the cabinet directly above it."

"Thanks," I said. I hesitantly grabbed the pot and filled it with tap water. I'd never made my own coffee before, but I'd watched Debbie do it enough that I thought I could wing it. The tricky part was deciding how many scoops of ground beans to use. Eight seemed like a good number. After snapping the filter compartment shut, I glanced at Kim. "What are you doing?"

"Hmmm?" Kim finished typing and closed the laptop. "Just finishing up some things with the Network. I'm trying to track down our thief. Nobody has heard anything yet, but it's not uncommon for these things to take time."

"The Network ... " I set the pot into place under the dispenser. The name alone was enough to make me distrust it. "Exactly what is it, again?"

Kim shrugged. "It's an agency like any other—we just keep a lower profile."

"Okay. But what does the Network *do?* Who's in *charge?"*

He cleared his throat. "The identities of the higher-ups are kept classified for security reasons."

"Uh-huh."

"But I can tell you that the sole objective of the Network is to keep watch over people who have transcended or show signs of transcending."

I clapped my hands in mock delight. "You mean to tell me that a secret agency is watching my every move?

I feel better already! Not to mention I'll never shower naked again."

Kim made a face. "Rileigh, it's not like that."

"Then what *is* it like, Kim?"

He took a deep breath before answering. "Most people, when experiencing some form of awakening, are confused and scared, wouldn't you agree?"

I shrugged.

He continued. "There are people in the Network who have access to the patient records of doctors, psychologists, sleep clinics, and so on. They will flag anyone in the system who's showing … symptoms."

"Symptoms?"

"Sure. The symptoms can range from a person having constant dreams of places they've never been to a sense of familiarity with a culture they've never known. Or, like in your case, unexpected … talents."

"And how do you find all of this stuff out?"

Kim fidgeted in his chair. "It's not like we have cameras in people's homes or anything like that. We have highly classified computer software—developed by the military."

I could only blink. This was a lot heavier than I thought. Kim opened his mouth, but I cut him off with a wave of my hand. "I don't think I can handle anymore about the Network right now. Just tell me what we do in the meantime."

"Well." He folded his arms. "It's your choice, but I would really like it if you stayed with Michelle."

"I don't know." I liked her, but didn't know her well enough to be comfortable. "Why can't I stay with Q?"

"Your friend from the hospital?" When I nodded, he said, "We don't know who's after you, Rileigh. I think until we know more, it would be best if you stay with experienced fighters. If you don't want to stay with Michelle—" he shrugged—"you can always stay here."

"Uh, that's okay." I had to get away from Kim and fast. Last night proved that the closer we were, the better the chance of a Senshi takeover. It was a risk I couldn't afford to take. "I'll stay with Michelle."

Kim looked relieved. "Good. When you're ready, I can drive you home to pack a bag."

I rolled my eyes. "I can drive myself."

Kim made a face.

"I promised to meet Q for lunch."

"Fine," Kim said. "I'll follow you to your house. I'll go once I'm certain you're safe. After your lunch, drive straight to the dojo." His tone left no room for argument.

I poured coffee into a mug and held it up to my nose and cringed. It smelled like nail polish remover. "Is all this really necessary?"

"Unfortunately, yes. I won't gamble with your life."

I took a sip and struggled not to choke. They didn't make battery acid that strong. It took me several tries before I was able to swallow, but once I did, I asked, "So we don't do anything? I go stay with Michelle and … that's it? That's the whole plan?"

"For now," Kim answered. He reached behind him

and pulled a coffee mug off a hook beneath the overhead cabinet. He turned and pointed the mug at me. "But I promise you this. I will find the person who has been targeting you."

"What if you can't?"

Kim snorted as he walked past me toward the coffeepot.

"Okay. So you find the person, then what?"

"I'll deal with them as necessary."

I drummed my fingers along the mug. "What's that mean?"

Kim ignored the question by taking a sip of coffee. He dropped his gaze into the mug as he inclined it toward me. "Did anyone ever tell you, you make a great cup of coffee?"

I grunted and poured the rest of mine down the sink.

Later that morning I was home again, stuffing my gym bag with the toiletries I would need for a week-long stay at Michelle's. I didn't want to think about packing for longer than that. I called Debbie at work to tell her that I would be staying with a friend over the weekend. To my surprise, she sounded disappointed.

"Oh no, Rileigh! Jason is going to be so upset. He owns a timeshare at the Lake of the Ozarks and seemed really adamant about the both of us going down there for the weekend. He made such a big deal about wanting to get to know you. I think it's so sweet that he's involved, don't you?"

I rolled my eyes. "I guess."

"Are you sure you won't reconsider? We can go jet skiing and lay out by the pool. Lord knows you could use a little color on your skin."

"Can't, Mom. Some, uh, other stuff came up." I glanced at my pasty arm. But now that she mentioned it, if I made it out of this alive, a little more vitamin D was definitely in order.

"Well, that's too bad." But then she giggled, a sound in all my seventeen years I'd never heard before or cared to hear again. "I guess Jason will have to deal with having me all to himself."

Ew. I wanted to hang up the phone right then, but an uneasy feeling came over me, like a fly that insists on buzzing in your face even after you've swatted at it. "Are you sure this is such a good idea, Mom?"

Her voice dropped. "What do you mean?"

"It's just that you've known him less than a week. He could be a psycho killer."

She laughed. "Please, Rileigh, you'd be amazed how well I know Jason."

Double ew. The uneasiness I'd felt moments ago was buried by a tidal wave of nausea. As if my stomach hadn't been victimized enough by the strong coffee at Kim's. "It's just that Dr. Wendell is a far cry from the underwear models you usually date."

Debbie sighed. "And that was the problem. You have

no idea how refreshing it is to go out with someone whose IQ isn't less than or equal to a box of Pop-Tarts."

I didn't know what to say to that.

Debbie continued. "I love you, Rileigh, but sometimes you can be a drama queen. Someday you'll understand what true love is, and you'll know that how a person looks and how much time you've spent with them has nothing to do with it."

I bit my tongue so hard that my eyes watered.

"Anyway," she continued, "have a good time with your friend, and I'll see you Sunday night. Okay?"

I sighed. At least with her out of town she would be safe from whomever was lurking around here. "Okay."

"Good girl. Hugs and kisses."

"Bye, Mom."

I hit the end button and began searching the kitchen for junk food to bring along. After all, what good is a hideout without chocolate? Unfortunately, my search of the cabinets turned up nothing snack-worthy. And the fridge only held a carton of eggs, a tub of margarine, and a months-old carton of Chinese food. Forget it. I slammed the fridge and sat down in a nearby kitchen chair.

My house didn't seem like the cozy fortress it once had. It had been violated. *I* had been violated. I hugged myself to suppress a shiver.

I looked around at the various oddities I'd left lying around the kitchen. A *People* magazine, an ink pen, a dying cactus. Did Devil-boy touch them? Did he go through the cabinets? What if he came back during the night? What if he was hiding in my room right now? I jumped from my chair, knocking it over, and ran to my bedroom and flung the door open. I squeezed myself tighter. It looked like the same mess that I'd left last night, but I couldn't be sure.

I snagged an outfit out of my closet and changed out of last night's workout clothes. Then I began cleaning. It took several hours to straighten up my room after its ransacked makeover, and the entire time I bagged, folded, and sorted, I couldn't shake the feeling of being watched. When I finished, I sat in the middle of my bed, hoping to relive the feelings of security I'd felt inside my bedroom walls growing up. Despite all the tokens and reminders that I'd once had a normal life, comfort didn't come. I reached to my nightstand and picked up a picture of Quentin and me laughing at last year's Mardi Gras in Soulard, running my finger along the frame. We wore matching pink feathered boas along with hundreds of beads. Quentin had done a lot of flashing that year.

A tear splattered onto the glass, startling me as it blurred out Quentin's face. I hadn't even realized I was crying. I flipped the picture over and laid it down. Time to move on.

After wiping the remaining tears away, I finished packing my bag and prepared to leave. Outside, I paused midway to the Fiesta and gave the house one last look. There it stood, small and blue. It used to feel so safe and cozy, but

there was a darkness to it now. I sighed. Why did everything have to change?

I climbed into my car and drove away. It was hard not to look back when the danger lay in the past.

32

Before I could go to the dojo, I had to talk to Quentin. The hard part was getting ahold of him. I couldn't call the salon because I'd told them I was sick. I hoped he'd answer his cell.

He picked up on the second ring. "Ri . . . ." His voice wavered. "An!" he finally finished.

"Ryan?" I asked.

"Ryan, how good to hear from you. Have you heard our dear friend Rileigh is sick? Tsk tsk."

I could take a hint. "Jeannine's standing behind you, isn't she?"

"Why yes! Yes, she is," Q answered, sugaring his words. Jeannine would be ticked if she knew Q was talking to me on the phone when I was playing hooky. "So what's up, man? I've been meaning to call you." I heard him cover the phone with his hand and say, "It's my cousin." Jeannine must have given him a questioning look.

"Q, are we still on for lunch today?"

"Well, you know what, Ryan? Today is your lucky day because I just had a cancellation. Can you be here in like fifteen minutes?"

"I assume that when you say 'here' you mean Bread Company?" I asked.

"That's right, Ryan."

I shook my head. "Q, I think you should stop saying 'Ryan.'"

"Whatever you say, Ryan."

I groaned. "You're going to get both of us fired. See you in fifteen."

It was a little before eleven when I walked into the crowded café. Bread Company was a relatively safe place to meet, since we'd never seen Jeannine binge on anything other than greasy fast-food burgers and fries.

"Ri-Ri!" I heard him call my name but couldn't see him over the crowd of customers. I did, however, see a long arm raise a Styrofoam coffee cup into the air. "Got ya your fix!"

I laughed and worked my way through the suits standing in line. When I reached Quentin, I gave him a giant bear hug.

He pushed me back and gave me a horrified face. "Ri-Ri!"

I didn't bother to hide my hurt feelings. "What?"

"You smell like," he put his face close to my ear and whispered, "you've been macking with somebody."

I gasped and stumbled back. How did he know?

"Oh my God!" He clapped his hands in delight. "I was just joking."

Crap! I'd played right into his hands. "It's not that big a deal." I lifted my chin indignantly.

"Oh my God. Oh my God. Oh my God," Q repeated as he tugged me over to a corner table. He shoved me into the booth before settling in across from me, his eyes dancing the entire time. "Tell. Me. Everything."

I groaned.

Q clapped his hands. "It was that Asian guy, wasn't it? I could feel the heat coming out of the sink room all the way to the dryers. That's why all the drama, right?" He made a show of fanning himself.

"Enough, Quentin!" I reached across the booth and grabbed his shirt collar, pulling him forward and forcing him to sit up straight.

He was undeterred. "I want to know what happened, where, and when."

"I'm not going to tell you that!" My cheeks burned.

"Hmpff." He sat back against the booth with his arms crossed. "You're no fun."

"It's just that I don't really feel good about the whole thing."

“Oh, don’t tell me.” He stuck out his bottom lip in a pout. “Bad kisser?”

“Not at all. In fact—” I stopped myself when I realized he’d tricked me again. “Quentin!” I grabbed a couple of sugar packets off the table and threw them at him. “Be serious!”

“I’m sorry, I’m sorry.” He laughed as he plucked my discarded ammunition from his chest. After placing them back on the table and dusting himself off, he cleared his throat. “I am now serious.”

“Yeah, right,” I told him, grinning. “And I am now Miley Cyrus.”

He stuck his tongue out.

“Whatever.” I waved my hand in the air. “I just think the whole thing was a giant mistake.”

He blinked, waiting for me to continue.

“It was too soon,” I went on. “I have a lot going on right now. I’m still dealing with all these … changes. Plus there’s Whitley … as if trying to date one guy isn’t hard enough! And then last night, I don’t know what happened, I was upset with Kim one minute, and the next we were all over each other.” I shook my head. “But then I found out that he lied to me—*again*.”

“Oh, Ri-Ri!” He threw his arms on the table and collapsed on them dramatically. “Do you have to overanalyze everything?”

“I’m just telling you how it is!” I cried. “I can’t have a relationship with two guys—especially if one is a liar.”

Quentin smiled. “Well, actually … ”

I narrowed my eyes.

He threw his hands in the air. "All right! Calm down. This is all really simple."

I waited.

"Who do you like better?"

I gave an exaggerated sigh. "It's not that easy. Whitley is so nice and drama-free. But Kim, the way I feel around him ... it scares me. It's like gravity ceases to exist and he's the only thing I can hold on to."

Quentin put his hand under his chin. "That is *hot*."

"Yeah, well." I rolled my eyes. "It may be hot, but it doesn't change the fact that I can't trust Kim. Yeah, part of me is drawn to him, but that doesn't mean I like it."

"Because you're scared. You've never been in love before."

I almost choked on my coffee. "And I'm not in love now."

He smiled and shrugged. "All right, you can keep lying to yourself."

I folded my arms. "You don't get it. Even if I could trust Kim, I don't think he likes me for who I am. I'm pretty sure he thinks I'm somebody else."

Quentin's smile faded, and he collapsed his head back onto his folded arms. "Are you kidding me?" he asked.

"What?"

He sat up. "This is your problem? Kim doesn't like you for who you are? Who does he think you are?"

"Some kick-ass fighter chick," I told him.

"Okay, and why did Whitley ask you out?"

I thought about how excited Whitney was when he mentioned the story of my fight in the parking lot. "Um, because he thinks I'm some kick-ass fighter chick."

Quentin cocked an eyebrow.

"Bah!" I waved my hand. "Then I guess neither one of them *really* knows me."

"That's one answer. Here's another: I think the only person who doesn't know you is *you*."

I glared across the table at him. The last thing I needed was another person telling me who I was.

"Listen, Ri-Ri. When I found out you were part Bruce Lee, I wasn't really that surprised. You're an incredibly strong, confident girl. Your mom really did a number on your head if you can't see that."

His insight brought goose bumps to my skin. Wasn't that exactly what Kim had said? This life had locked away my inner warrior, and the awkward, uncertain girl was left holding the key. "Q," I whispered. "There's more."

He settled himself against the back wall, smiling. "Ooh details, bring 'em on!"

"Not about that!" I swatted his arm. "This is serious."

He ran a hand over his face, pretending to smooth his smile into a frown.

My throat went dry. This was it. But what if it was too much for him to handle? Would I lose the best friend I ever had?

He cocked his head at my hesitation and then placed a reassuring hand on my arm. "Ri-Ri." His tone was quiet. "Whatever it is, you can tell me."

"You're going to think I'm crazy."

"Not an issue. I already do."

I smiled, despite myself. "This has to do with Kim."

He clapped his hands together.

I ignored him. "Anyway, it turns out that I knew him in a past life." I stopped and waited for a reaction. I didn't get one, so I continued. "And it's not so much that we knew each other, but apparently, we were pretty heavy." Still no reaction. I talked faster. "Not only that, but we were also samurai!" I sat back, bracing myself for the worst.

He folded his arms and leaned back against the wall. "I don't believe it."

I dropped my eyes to the table. I figured this was how it would go.

"This has to do with the attack, doesn't it?"

I wasn't sure how to answer that question. I opened my mouth to ask, but he cut me off.

"You awakened that night, didn't you?"

I blinked several times before I answered, sure I hadn't heard him correctly. "How—how do you know about that?"

He inched closer to me so that he could whisper. "Remember Dillon? That guy I met when my parents took us all to Jamaica? He told me all about it. He said he was an Arabian concubine in a previous life." He wagged his eyebrows. "Very exotic."

"You believe me?" I couldn't have been more surprised if the President of the United States walked into the café and did his own personal rendition of *Lord of the Dance.*

"Honey," he scolded, "you should know me better than to think I'd ever judge anyone. If you say you're a samurai," he shrugged his shoulders, "then you're a samurai."

"Okay, so you're not judging me. But I need to know, do you *believe* me?"

"Truthfully," he began, "at first, when Dillon tried to explain things to me, I thought maybe he'd spent too much time smoking up. But after getting to know him, the things that he knew and the dreams he had, it was impossible to argue. And you—" He laughed. "Who can argue after seeing what happened to those muggers? It makes perfect sense. What I can't believe is that you didn't come to me sooner."

"I was afraid you'd think I was crazy."

He waved the notion away with his hand. "Is this all you wanted to tell me?" he asked.

"I wish. But there's more… I was attacked *again* while on my date with Whitley. Then the next day the attacker came back, broke into my house, and trashed my room."

The blood drained from Quentin's face, leaving his face the color of the Styrofoam cup he held. "You mean my sister wasn't exaggerating? And you're just telling me about this now?"

"Like I said, it's complicated. Do you know what transcending is?"

"Trans-what-it-who?"

I thought back to the explanation from the dojo. "It bridges the gap between your past and present lives with an object from the past. When you touch this object, supposedly you can unlock the part of your brain that keeps the past hidden. You'll be able to remember everything."

"Wow," he said.

"Yeah, wow," I agreed.

"What does this have to do with your house getting broken into?"

I filled him in on everything that preceded my first visit to the dojo up until I met him at the café.

"Wow," he said again when I finished. "After I sweep the salon, I'll go home and pack a bag."

"What? Why?"

He shrugged. "You're supposed to be there at four, right?"

I nodded.

"Well, I'm going with you. I'm not going to let you hide from some bad guys all by your lonesome. It'll be fun. Like a sleepover!"

I shook my head. I'm sure with Quentin there, it *would* be more like a sleepover than a hideout. I bit my lip to keep it from quivering.

"Oh no. No-no. Don't you start that up!" Q got out of the booth and slid in next to me, laying his head on my shoulder. He sniffed. "Now look what you did." He dabbed his eyes. "You got me going, too."

I hugged him. "I love you."

He put an arm around my shoulder. "I love you, too."

I smiled.

"Ri-Ri?"

"Hmm?"

"Do you think I have a past life, too?" he asked.

"I don't know." I shrugged. "What do you think?"

"I think," he said, bumping me with his hip, "that I'm the reincarnated Marilyn Monroe!"

I laughed.

"One more question," he said. "What are you going to do about Kim and Whitley?"

I sighed. "Nothing. I can't afford to think about a relationship if someone's after me."

"Whatever." Q rolled his eyes. "You are so hot for Kim."

I felt my cheeks burn. "I am not."

"Liar, liar," he sang. "I could cut the heat in the salon with a knife. I know that guy greases your gears. Hell, he greases mine, and all I get to do is look at him."

I grinned. "Both guys *are* fun to look at."

"This is true." Q grinned back. "All I'm saying is that, for once, you need to listen to your heart. Because your head is all screwed up."

I frowned. "Thanks a lot."

"Your heart knows what it wants. Just listen, okay?"

I suddenly felt nervous. Was the voice in my head not a different person at all, but the voice of my heart? Doubtful. I mean, if it was really my heart talking, wouldn't it tell more about who to love and less about whose ass to kick? "I wish I was as confident about it as you are."

He cast a tortured look up toward the ceiling. "Oh God in heaven, what did I do to deserve such an exasperating best friend?"

"Stop it!" I swatted at him.

"Then listen to me," Quentin said. "True love, the stuff in the fairy tales, it's really out there! I'm not saying that Kim is the one for you. I don't know him well enough for that, but you would be stupid not to try and find out. Please, Ri-Ri." He grabbed my hands. "I couldn't bear it if you let another opportunity pass you by."

I gave him another squeeze. "Sorry I'm such a pain in the ass."

He shrugged. "You'll always be my best friend. This samurai business—it doesn't change a thing."

I gave him one last hug before sliding out of the booth. I hoped he was right.

33

I arrived at the dojo a little before four, and again cars filled the parking lot. Like the previous night, I walked into a lobby full of parents watching their children in the dojo through the separating glass. The only difference from last night was that the children training in the dojo with Kim were much younger, maybe around five or six.

Five girls about my age, with designer purses and heavily applied makeup, eyed me as I moved closer to the glass. When I looked in their direction, they huddled together, whispering.

"Which one are you here to pick up?"

I turned to the plump brunette girl who had walked up next to me. Her thick glasses magnified her eyes to the point of making me dizzy.

"Which one?" she repeated, jutting a hand at the class going on in the dojo. Her other hand clutched a key chain that contained more plastic bobbles and dangles than actual keys.

"Excuse me?" I asked.

"Which kid? Isn't one of them your brother or sister?"

"Oh!" I laughed and shook my head. "None of them. I don't have any siblings."

A couple of the girls in the designer-purse crowd leaned in to listen.

"I'm here because my little brother takes lessons," the girl continued. "My mom makes me pick him up. I don't mind because his instructor is really hot." She smiled.

I looked out into the dojo and locked eyes with Kim. He grinned, and my body temperature rose immediately. From my peripheral vision, I could tell that I was on the receiving end of several dirty looks.

"I know I don't have a shot with him."

I reluctantly brought my attention back to the girl beside me.

"You see how pretty all those girls are?" She inclined her head toward the glaring clique. "Every one made a play for him, and he rejected them all." She grinned again. "It was pretty funny."

"I'll bet." I grinned back.

Kim chose that moment to surprise the both of us by appearing at my side. "Patricia," he said, smiling, "I see you've met our school's new instructor."

"New instructor? Oh, I—uh, I—" she stammered, her face turning scarlet.

The cluster of girls gave a collective sigh of relief.

I raised my eyebrows and waited. What was he up to now?

"Why aren't you dressed?" he asked, eyeing my jeans and tank top.

I folded my arms.

"That's right." He snapped his fingers together. "I forgot to give it to you. It's in the break room. Go suit up. You can help me finish this class." He winked and walked back into the dojo.

I was going to kill him.

Before I could head off, Patricia tugged on the back of my tank top. "About what we talked about—can you just forget I even said anything?"

"Don't worry about it," I said. At that moment, I would have told her anything for a chance to get away.

Inside the dojo, Kim motioned me toward the break room with a tilt of his head. "It's in your locker," he said.

Goody. Another surprise. I walked past Kim and into the break room, where I skidded to a halt. I knew Kim told me that I'd find it in my locker, but did he really mean for me to find Sumi tugging on the handle? "What are you doing?"

Sumi gasped and let her fingers fall from my locker. She tightened her hands into fists and turned to face me, her face pinched with loathing. "None of your business," she spat.

I walked toward her. "Actually, you're screwing around with *my* locker—so that makes it my business."

"It was supposed to be *my* locker." Sumi stalked

toward me, letting her hair fan behind her like an angry shadow.

We met in the middle of the room, leaving only inches between us. I could feel the anger radiate from her skin in hot prickly waves.

She curled her lip into a snarl. "I don't know why Kim thinks you're so special."

I crossed my arms and lifted a single eyebrow. "And *you* are?"

She leaned in closer. "Some people are meant to be together—like me and Kim. There's nothing you can do to stop it. You can't fight destiny."

Before I could respond, she pushed past me and stormed from the room.

Gritting my teeth, I fought the urge to go after her and rip out that silky hair. Instead, I went to my locker to find out why she had been trying to get inside. "What a total bi—" But the word died on my tongue as a sweet, familiar scent wafted through the vented door. What now? I tried the handle, but it stuck. Aggravated, I jiggled it until it finally gave way. Inside, I found a single cherry blossom perched on top of an envelope.

Curiosity replaced my anger as I plucked the pink flower and brought it to my nose. The soft scent swirled inside of me, dancing its way into my head and tugging on memories just beyond my reach. I tucked the blossom behind my ear and sat down on the floor with the envelope, folding my legs underneath me. I pulled out a handwritten note.

Rileigh,
As a warrior, all I know is to fight for what I want.
Last night you showed me there was a chance.
I won't give up now.
—Kim

The scent of sandalwood mixed with the blossom, and I knew without looking that Kim had sat beside me. I folded the note and tucked it into my pocket. "About last night ... I hope you don't think things have changed between us."

"Rileigh, I am sorry for deceiving you again." He clenched his hands into fists. "You have every right to be upset with me."

"Damn right I do. You keep asking me to trust you, but how can I? Every other word out of your mouth is a lie."

"No. The way I feel about you is not a lie."

I shook my head. "How do I know that? Maybe you're just a player looking for a score."

His mouth fell. "How could you say that?"

I waved my hand dismissively, wanting to change the subject. "What happened to your class?"

He sighed. "It's over. I hope you don't mind me telling everyone you are the new instructor. You looked like you could use a little saving out there."

I laughed softly. "Is that what you're here to do, Kim? Save me?"

"No." He shook his head. "I think I am the one who needs to be saved."

I looked into his eyes, and the longing I found there made me shiver.

As if sensing what I saw, Kim averted his eyes. "I trust everything is well at your home?"

I tore my eyes from his face, making it easier for me to concentrate. "Yeah. My mom is going out of town."

Kim looked thoughtful. "This is good. She will be safe."

I nodded but wasn't so sure. Something about Dr. Wendell struck me as not right, but the reason why lay beyond my grasp. It was like trying to look outside through the gauze of lacy curtains.

"The others will be here soon. We can have a short training session before you get settled at Michelle's."

I cleared my throat. "Q is going to meet me here. He's coming with us." I wanted to make sure he knew by my tone that I wasn't asking permission.

Kim raised his eyebrows. "He understands the danger?"

"Probably not, but there's no talking him out of it."

"He's a good friend."

I smiled. "My best."

Kim opened his mouth to say something, but appeared to think better of it and snapped it shut. After a moment, he reached out a finger and traced it along my jaw.

My breath caught in my throat, which annoyed me. Why couldn't I control myself around him? He was a jerk, right? But with his finger igniting sparks along my skin, I couldn't be sure of anything.

Kim laughed. "Still frowning after all these years ... I

promise you, I will take care of this." He leaned forward and my heart jumped in my chest as if reaching for him. "Rileigh," he whispered, breath warm against my neck, "I wanted to tell you—"

"Hey guys!" Braden called, entering the room with Drew in tow.

Kim abruptly straightened.

Braden stopped walking, his brow furrowed. "What are you guys do—" But before he could finish, Drew shoved his elbow into his ribs. "Ow!" He hugged his stomach. "What was that for?"

Drew groaned and turned back for the door. "We'll see you in the dojo," he said over his shoulder.

"What's going on?" Braden asked.

Drew hit him on the back of his head with his hand.

"Ow!" Braden cried again, following Drew out of the room. I heard him grumble from the other side, "Well, how was I supposed to know?"

I stood and dusted off my jeans. "Well, that was embarrassing."

"Why?" Kim asked, standing up as well.

"It's just that... well, you know."

Kim continued to stare, unblinking.

"Never mind!" I said. I could feel my cheeks warming. "Just forget I said anything."

Kim stepped in front of me. "I'd rather not," he answered. "In fact, I'd like it if we could get together later, when this mess has been sorted out. Maybe I could take you to dinner or something. I have things that I would like to say to you."

I pushed a stray hair behind my ear. "Like a date?"

His eyes darted away. "If you will."

I knew I had discussed with Quentin earlier the reasons dating was not a good idea. But now, with Kim standing so close, I couldn't remember any of them.

Luckily, Drew stuck his head in the door before I could answer. "Sorry to interrupt you guys, but someone just showed up looking for Rileigh."

I smiled. "Quentin."

Drew motioned for us to follow but stopped in the doorway. "Oh, and before I forget, Kim, you got a delivery."

Kim frowned. "Odd. It must be the uniforms. I wasn't expecting them until next week."

Kim and I stepped into the dojo where Braden was pacing around a large wooden crate. It was about the size and shape of a small chest. The only marking was a red-stamped "FRAGILE" on the side.

"Where did that come from?" Kim asked.

"The UPS guy." Drew inclined his head toward a brown truck pulling away.

Kim walked closer and inspected the box. "Did they give you a packing order?"

Braden looked around the sides of the box. "No, I don't see one."

Lines deepened on Kim's face. "Braden, go with Rileigh to meet her friend. Drew, grab the crowbar from the closet."

I was about to tell Kim that I didn't need an escort when I felt a strange fluttering sensation as I passed the crate. Weird. My nerves were on the fritz. Not too surprising after a week like mine, though. I should be happy that I could still function enough to eat and get dressed. But at the thought of food my stomach roared to life and I remembered that the only things I'd eaten today were two cups of coffee. Score another point for genius Rileigh.

The second I stepped into the lobby, Quentin wrapped me into a massive bear hug. "I'm ready for our slumber party."

"Can't … breathe … " I gasped.

"Sorry." He released me. "I just can't imagine everything that you've gone through these past couple of days. You must be so freaked. But I don't want you to worry anymore. I'm here now. And I brought supplies for facials, manies, and pedies."

I had to laugh. Only Quentin would think it necessary to bring apricot scrub and nail polish on a hideout. "We can't leave just yet—Michelle's not here to take us to her house. But that's okay." I tugged on his arm. "Now I can introduce you to the guys while we wait for her." Quentin followed me as I pulled him through the door into the main dojo with Braden trailing behind.

Inside, Drew had Kim's crowbar wedged under the wooden lid. He gave the metal bar several good thrusts until the lid finally squeezed open a couple of inches while Kim looked on.

A sudden wave of pain exploded inside of my skull. A gasp escaped my lips as I staggered backward.

"Ri-Ri?" Quentin asked, his eyes concerned.

Braden caught me by my elbow as I wobbled on my heels. "What is it? What's wrong?"

"I—I don't know." I pressed my fingers against the bridge of my nose, but it did nothing to ease the pain. In fact, it seemed to be worsening by the second.

Drew and Kim were so focused on the crate that they hadn't noticed my freak-out. Drew pumped the crowbar, sending a crack through the wood at the same time another jolt of pain ran through my head. I would have fallen to my knees if it weren't for Braden's grip on my arm. After I steadied myself, I could feel it. Through the pain. Inside the crate, coiled and waiting. "Stop!"

Wide-eyed and still holding the crowbar, Drew turned to face me. "What's the—" But I didn't let him finish.

I ran to Drew and ripped the crowbar from his hands. "Get away from it." I held the crowbar up and pointed it at each person in the dojo. "All of you. Stay back." Cool silk slid through my head and melted the pain.

Braden and Quentin remained frozen by the door. Drew joined Kim at the side of the room, looking to him for the answer.

"Rileigh?" Kim's question was laced with concern.

"It's okay. I've got it under control." I glanced into the open crate, and though nothing moved through the shredded packing paper, I could feel its watchful glare. I dropped my voice to a near whisper. "Nobody move." I slowly backed away from the box and sidestepped to the weapon wall. I stopped in front of a katana and felt the first stirrings of the wind inside my center. My hair fluttered gently around my shoulders. Gritting my teeth against the storm in my chest, I curled my fingers around the blade, and the wind erupted.

My hair thrashed my face, forcing me to close my eyes. Even through the roar of my personal cyclone, I could hear the rattles of various weapons shaking against the wall. I was losing control.

"Concentrate!"

I couldn't tell who said it, but I listened. I closed my eyes and breathed in deeply.

The wind is power. YOUR power. Harness it.

I swallowed hard and opened my eyes. Not entirely sure of what I was doing, I lifted my arm and stretched my fingers wide. I felt a pull as the wind gravitated around my hand. Experimenting further, I turned my palm up and curled my fingers, as if to grab on to the power that licked my skin.

It worked. I couldn't fight the grin that spread to my face. As I moved my hand in a slow circle, I could feel the energy shift directions as well. Excited, I looked over at Kim.

He stood against the wall with his arms crossed while everyone else huddled together. My heart skipped and I lost focus. The wind around me picked up speed.

With my cheeks burning, I tore my attention from Kim and concentrated instead on my hand and harnessing the power around it. With a feeling like pushing my fingers through compacted sand, I made a fist and pulled my power back toward my chest. It was as if a hole opened up within me and swallowed the power down. The next thing I knew, everything was calm, but my skin tingled, electrified.

I walked back toward the crate, holding one hand in front of my face with my palm out and flat while the other swung the katana in wide arcs. When I reached the box, I changed my grip on the blade to two hands and readied myself.

Squaring my body with the box, I relaxed my hold on the energy I'd gathered. Before it could stream wildly, I used mental direction to push it forward, then braced myself as the energy slammed into the crate and splintered the side.

The snake's strike seemed to occur in slow motion. As I moved to meet it, I noticed the way its black scales glittered blue against the fluorescent lights and the sparkling drops of venom poised on each of its two hooked fangs.

Its eyes met mine the moment I brought my blade down. The metal in my hand didn't waver as it slid through the giant reptile. The snake fell to the floor in two pieces, twitching several times before becoming still.

A scream rang out through the dojo. I turned from the dead animal to find Q with both hands curled over his open mouth, his bulging eyes looking ready to leap from their sockets.

Kim was at my side, his hands gripping my shoulders.

And I was glad for it, too. The calm left me as quickly as it had come, and my legs gave out under the force of my trembling. The katana slid from my fingers onto the ground, next to the viper's gaping mouth.

"Did you see that?" Quentin squeaked. He stumbled up to Drew and tugged on his shirt. "Did you see that?" The color left his face and he collapsed forward into his arms.

"Oh, geez," Drew grunted, looping his arms around Quentin's chest. "Help! He's heavier than he looks."

Braden rushed to his side and swung Quentin's arm over his shoulder. "Come on, let's get you a glass of water."

Quentin nodded weakly.

Even with Kim bracing my shoulders, I slid to my knees. Kim followed me down to the floor. "Is it completely ridiculous to ask you how you feel right now?" His face was calm but his eyes were electric, like clouds gathering for a storm.

I didn't answer. The hair on my arms stood on end, and it wasn't because of the snake. The man before me was dangerous—maybe not to me, but dangerous all the same. Kim was a warrior, and I never considered what that meant until just now as I watched the tendons in his neck tighten. Some people have looks that kill. Kim had a look that let you know he was about to.

Drew seemed to sense the change in Kim as well and cautiously approached with his own katana. He nudged the half destroyed box with his toe. "Is there anything else in there?"

"No," I answered.

"Are you—"

I cut him off. "I'm sure. But you can jump in there and double check if you want."

Drew frowned as he peered into the packing paper. "I think I'll take your word on it."

Quentin walked out of the break room with Braden.

"How are you feeling?" I asked.

Quentin smiled. "Shaken up. But I'll live." He looked down on the severed snake. "What's going on?"

Kim answered, his voice low and threatening. "I underestimated the threat. And the last time I underestimated someone … " His jaw flexed. "We have a very serious problem here. The Noppera-bō targeting Rileigh knows who we are."

"Well, not only do they know who we are … " Braden stuck his toe at the snake. "It looks like they don't want to be friends."

I staggered a bit as the full weight of the situation hit me. "It's not just me, then. They want to kill *all* of us."

Kim pulled me around to face him. "I will protect you with my life, Rileigh. This threat will not go unanswered." The tone of his voice let me know that his version of answering would have nothing to do with the criminal-justice system.

"What should we do?" Braden asked.

"The crate," Drew offered. "I wonder if there's a clue as to who's behind this." He squatted next to the box and rifled through the shredded paper. Braden walked over and dug in beside him. It wasn't long until Drew found a pink envelope. He turned it over in his hand, paling slightly. He looked at Kim. "It's addressed to Senshi."

Kim took the envelope from Drew and tore it open. He read without breathing. When he was finished, he crumpled the note into a ball and threw it back into the crate. "Change of plan," he said. Fury radiated from him in hot waves. "Where is Michelle? She should be here by now. Braden, call her cell phone. If that doesn't work, try her house."

Braden pulled his phone from his pocket and began dialing. It sounded as if someone picked up, and Braden turned away from us and began talking into the receiver.

"Kim?" I stepped around the box, fingers itching to grab the note within, and stopped at his side. "What did the note say?"

Kim's eyes never left Braden.

"Kim!" My skin prickled as if the mixture of fear and anger were igniting inside my veins like water on a hot frying pan. I was fed up with not getting answers. "What did the note say?"

He looked at me and opened his mouth to answer, but the padded thud of Braden's phone falling onto the mats stopped the words in his throat.

One look at Braden and my stomach dropped to my ankles. His eyes were glossy and unable to focus, which made him teeter on his heels.

Drew raced to secure him by hooking his arm around his waist. Drew then asked the question that was on the tip of my tongue, yet a question I didn't want to hear the answer to. "What happened?"

Braden gasped several times before answering, like he'd been underwater and had just come up for breath. "It's Michelle." He swayed and Drew staggered with him before lowering Braden to the floor as he sank to his knees. "Michelle!" Braden's voice cracked and he buried his face behind his hands, his shoulders heaving.

"Shhh," Drew whispered, running his hand in slow circles along Braden's shoulders. "Tell us what happened, buddy. Then we can fix it."

Braden looked up, his face stained with tears. "That was Michelle's mom on the phone. She told me ... " He paused to suck in a heaving breath. "She told me that Michelle never came home last night."

34

A thousand shards of ice needled into my heart. Michelle was missing?

Kim knelt beside Braden and gripped his shoulders so hard that Kim's fingers turned white. "You listen to me, Braden," he growled. "We will have Michelle back by sunrise tomorrow. I pledge this to you. Do you understand me?"

Braden released a quivering breath and nodded slowly.

"Good." Kim shook him once before releasing him. He stood and moved away from us, so that when he turned, he could address us all. "This is the plan. Drew is coming with me. Our first stop is the company that delivered the crate. From there, we should be able to get some idea of the sender."

I felt a chill go through me when I realized I was standing in the presence of a ghost. The long dead samurai leader Yoshido stood before me issuing orders.

Kim continued. "Braden, I need you to take Rileigh and Q to your house for now."

Braden started to protest, but Kim cut him off with a wave of his hand. "I know you love Michelle, and that's why you can't come. You're too close to this and your emotions will either get you *or* Michelle hurt. Is that a risk you want to take?"

Braden shook his head.

Kim nodded once. "Good. Know that I give you no easy mission. Should Drew and I fail, understand that the enemy will come for Rileigh next. I place her life into your hands."

A knot formed in my throat at the word "fail."

"I understand and accept," Braden answered, rising to his feet.

Kim's smile was brief. "I knew I could count on you. I understand that your father can sometimes be difficult, so I need you to have a solid excuse ready. Then pack your own bags and be ready to relocate tonight if need be."

I watched what little color Braden had left drain from his face and wondered how long it would be before I might be able to see right through him.

"Brother," Drew whispered, "what are we up against?"

Kim stared at the ground, unblinking. "It appears someone from the past has resurfaced."

"Who?" I asked.

He took a deep breath and turned to face me. "A traitor."

The room seemed to grow cold. I looked at the

box, then back at Kim. He raised his chin but made no move to stop me as I stooped down and retrieved the note. I smoothed it out and immediately recognized the scratchy handwriting as the same as in the notes left in my door. Drew, Braden, and Quentin clustered to look over my shoulder.

My Dearest Senshi,
Well, I suppose that is a bit premature,
as I interrupted your coming out party.
I'll make it up to you, though.
Hopefully we will be able to celebrate
your transcending together.
We have a lot of lost time to make up for,
and I am so looking forward to catching up.
I hope you enjoy my gift, and please
give our friends my best regards.
—Sincerely,
Zeami

"Sea-ah-mee." The name left a foul aftertaste on my tongue. "Why do I know that name?"

Kim closed his eyes, Drew turned away, and Braden looked like he was going to be sick.

"Somebody say something!" I crumpled the note and threw it to the ground at my feet.

Kim answered. "Zeami is the man who betrayed all of us. We can attribute our deaths to him."

A knot wound its way inside the pit of my stomach.

I didn't remember Zeami, so why was talking about him affecting me in this way? My eyes stung. Was I going to cry? A memory struggled to push past the curtain in my mind. I saw the gleam of a dagger. And blood, warm and sticky on my fingers. I wiped my hands against my shirt to chase away the phantom sensations. "Did you know he was around?"

Kim shook his head. "He would not be alive if I did."

"That's ridiculous," I said. "You can't go around killing people. It's against the law."

"The only law I am concerned with is the law of the samurai. And Zeami has a debt to pay."

"Besides," Drew added, "if the Network feels someone is a threat, that person vanishes like they never existed."

"The Network sounds like a government agency," I said.

Nobody spoke.

"Oh. Well, if they're an agency, why can't they send in some people to help us?"

"Because," Drew answered, "*we're* the people they'd send in."

Well, crap. This was getting deeper by the minute. "But you're all so young."

"Age is a state of mind," Drew replied. "The three of us are more experienced in battle than half the four-star generals in the military."

"But Michelle knew how to fight, too, and look what—" I bit the words off when I saw Braden's eyes glass over, realizing too late that I'd twisted the dagger buried in his gut. Stupid, Rileigh! But still, I needed some leeway considering the situation. I'd killed a giant viper, Michelle was missing, and a crazy psychopath from the past was out to get me. It was too much to take in. My knees buckled and I sagged to the floor under the weight of it all.

"I'm calling the Network," Kim said, turning on his heels. "They need to be advised of the situation and our next move."

When he was out of the room, Drew turned to Quentin. "You want to give me a hand with this?" He inclined his head toward the dead animal.

"You're kidding, right?"

Drew shrugged and picked up the severed back end of the snake using both of his hands. The tail dragged along the floor as he made his way to the front door. The viper was twice as long as I was tall.

"Thanks for leaving me the half with fangs." Quentin grimaced and carefully wrapped his hands behind the arrow-shaped head before following Drew outside.

Braden hugged himself as he walked over to me. "How are you holding up?"

I shrugged. "I've had better days."

He stared at his lap and nodded. "Me, too."

My careless words from moments ago replayed in my head: *But Michelle knew how to fight.* My cheeks burned and I shifted uncomfortably. "Braden, I'm sorry for what I said earlier. I wasn't thinking. I just can't believe that Michelle's missing. If something happens to her … "

My voice trailed off when my mind refused to consider the possibility.

To my surprise, Braden reached over and patted my knee. "It's going to be okay. Kim gave me his pledge. He'll have Michelle back by sunrise tomorrow."

I nodded, but wasn't so sure.

We both stared at the ceiling for several minutes until Braden broke the silence with a sigh. "I have a confession to make." He cleared his throat and continued. "I used to be so jealous of you."

I didn't know what to make of that, so I waited for him to continue.

"A woman samurai on the battlefield was unheard of. Some even said that it disgraced our village. But Lord Toyotomi knew better. How could someone bestowed with gifts from the warrior spirit be a curse? Warning premonitions and ki manipulations are not learned skills. You are either gifted or you are not. My brother and I were not. We were convinced that since you were in such favor with the warrior spirit, you might have the power to bestow those gifts as well. We vowed to keep training hard so that one day you would find us worthy." His voice dropped to a whisper. "We never got the chance."

"I'm sorry," I told him.

"It wasn't just my brother and me," he continued. "None of us got the opportunity to become what we were meant to. Our destinies were stolen from us. To be killed on the battlefield is one thing ... but to be betrayed! And now that I have a new life, I've found my soul mate, and

I'm happy—but now Zeami's back." He swallowed hard. "Will he take it all away again?"

I balled my hands into fists. He'd been a kid when he died. How was he supposed to deal with such trauma? Adults were put on Prozac for much less. As if it wasn't bad enough that Braden was haunted by the ghosts of his past, now one of the ghosts had become more. A real live monster. It was then, I realized, that the whole time I had been looking to Kim and the others for answers, they needed the same from me. "I won't let that happen," I said.

He nodded and seemed to take comfort in that.

"Braden, were we close? In the past, I mean."

He smiled. "In the last life, Yorimichi and I grew up on a farm, the youngest of five children." His eyes lost their focus as he drifted into his memories. "We were just old enough that our father insisted we start working around the farm, but Yorimichi and I weren't interested. We wanted to be samurai. It was an impossible dream. Our social status wouldn't allow it. That didn't stop us from dreaming about leaving the farm and fighting."

Braden's smile wavered. "You know how they say to be careful what you wish for? During the land wars, our farm was attacked while Yorimichi and I were out in the fields pretending to be samurai. When it grew dark, we arrived home to find our family dead and our home reduced to a pile of ashes. You and Kim saved us. During your pursuit of the invaders, you found us huddled together with our stick swords and brought us to Lord Toyotomi."

I didn't say anything. Braden's story took strength to tell. Soft words would only take away from what he gave.

He took a deep breath and continued. "You went to Lord Toyotomi and requested to personally oversee our samurai training. The request, I'm sure, did little to help improve your standing with the other samurai. If it weren't for you, Rileigh, I don't know where we would have ended up. You, Yoshido, and Seiko were our teachers, our guardians, and ... our family."

I couldn't tell him I was sorry for everything that happened to him in the past. He wasn't looking for sympathy. "I'm glad you told me," I said. "I hope we can be just as close again."

"Me, too," he said. "I wanted to tell you sooner, but I didn't want to scare you. It's not as bad as you would think."

"What's not?"

"Dealing with the past. It's hard at first, with all those old memories feeling like they just happened yesterday. But you'll learn pretty fast how to put the pain behind you."

"Unless it's a pain in the ass," Drew said as he and Kim walked back into the dojo. He pulled a handkerchief out of his back pocket and wiped his hands off. "Especially if that pain in the ass follows you into the next life."

"I alerted the Network," Kim said, "and my request to eliminate the threat was approved. Braden, I need to get Rileigh and Q out of here. Drew, I need you to gather the weapons." He turned to leave, but I stepped into his path. He didn't bother to hide his surprise.

"Wait. This is ridiculous. You can't seriously go after

him." I pointed at the empty crate. "This Zeami guy, he's obviously a nut-job."

He placed a hand on my shoulder and squeezed. "Rileigh, this dojo is just a front. *This* is what we do." He smiled. "Some say that the samurai are cursed to be reborn into every new life as samurai."

"But you don't have to go after him."

His smiled melted. "This is personal. I've waited a lifetime to settle this debt."

"What if something happens to you?"

"Then I die with great honor."

I crossed my arms. "That's stupid."

"You didn't used to think so." A smile tugged on the corners of his mouth. "Would it really matter to you anyway? If I died?"

I opened my mouth to tell him no, but the words wouldn't come. What was it about Kim Gimhae that he could infuriate me at every encounter—yet the thought of losing him twisted fear, like ribbons of barbed wire, around my heart?

Kim laughed when I didn't say anything. "That's what I thought."

"Let me go after Zeami with you!" I said.

He gave me a sad smile. "If you had transcended, I would allow it. You are a gifted fighter, the best I have trained. But you haven't unlocked all of your skills yet. And you haven't trained enough without them. There is no way I can risk it."

"But what if *I* want to risk it?"

He shook his head. "That's not your call to make."

I dropped his hands and balled my fingers into fists, making sure to stand up to every inch of my small frame. "This psycho is after me, and if he hurts Michelle or anyone else who's looking for him, it's going to be my fault. How does all of that make this *your* call?"

Kim cocked an eyebrow. "Rank. More experience. The government. Do you need more?" I opened my mouth to answer, but he cut me off. "Listen to me!" All traces of amusement had left his voice. "I lost you once because I was not prepared. I will not make the same mistake twice!"

All I could do was blink.

"I'm sorry." He turned away, but not before I could see the pain in his expression. "Take whatever you want from the weapon wall. Just please go."

Fine. I wouldn't argue with him, but that didn't mean I had to like it. I tried to storm off, but he caught me by the elbow.

He leaned in and I felt his lips brush against my ear. "Thank you," he whispered.

He stepped in front of me and cupped my face in his hands. "Thank you for trusting me. I swear on my life that I will not let anyone or anything take you from me." He leaned over and his breath, warm on my neck, made me shiver. "I love you, Rileigh."

Without giving me a chance to respond, he turned on his heels, motioning for the guys to follow, and left the dojo.

35

Kim had said he loved me. And now he was gone.

My heart felt like a stone, puncturing organs and twisting nerves as it sank inside of my body, anchoring me to the overstuffed loveseat in Braden's living room. There were too many feelings coursing through me to figure out which were mine and which were Senshi's. My head hurt. I wanted to cry. I wanted to laugh. I wanted to continue sinking down into the cushion until the couch swallowed me whole.

Sitting next to me, Quentin huffed as he played with the chain on his wallet. No one had spoken during the thirty minutes it took us to get to the small, one-story brick ranch in the St. Louis suburb of Webster Groves where Braden lived.

"Well." Braden slapped his hands against his legs as he

sat on the couch opposite us. "No use bringing the bags in, as we might be leaving tonight."

I nodded, not really paying attention. Instead, I thought about Kim. Actually, it was more like worried. Zeami had killed everyone before. If something happened to Kim … No. I wouldn't let myself think about that.

I glanced at Braden and found him staring at the ceiling while chewing on his lower lip. Apparently I wasn't the only one worried. "I'm sure it's going to be fine. Kim will get Michelle back," I told him.

He laughed nervously. "Of course. They're all skilled fighters. It's not like this is the first elimination mission we've gone on."

Quentin's eyes widened, and I couldn't help feeling just as surprised.

His head snapped straight. "I don't think I should have said that."

I shrugged, hoping my face wasn't as pale as it felt. "I'm sorry you're stuck babysitting me."

He rolled his eyes. "I'm not *babysitting* you. Besides, Kim is right—I'd be dangerous on this mission."

"Because you're worried about Michelle?" I asked.

He swallowed and seemed to consider the question. "I'm trying not to be. Drew is an exceptional fighter and Kim is one of the best in the world. But now they're up against Zeami. I can't help but think about how that turned out last time."

I had to change the subject. The thought that something might happen to Michelle, Drew, or Kim twisted my insides. "Do you spend much time with Michelle?"

He smiled. "Every day since she transcended."

"Every day?" Quentin asked.

"Yep. Even though we'd avoid his twenty billion questions, it would almost be a shame to bail before my dad gets home from work. He's always harping on me about how I need to spend time with people other than Michelle. He just doesn't get it and he never will." Braden bit his lip again. "Are you worried about Kim?"

"Yes," Quentin answered before I could. He folded his arms and leaned back in the couch with a smile. "Are you worried about Kim, Ri-Ri?"

I made a face at him. He knew how uncomfortable I got discussing relationships.

"*Are* you worried?" Braden echoed.

I could feel myself sinking deeper into the couch. I didn't know what I was. My emotions were stacked like a game of Jenga, each fighting for the top position, each threatening to bring me to collapse. "I don't know ... maybe a little."

Braden stared at me for a moment before replying. "Maybe it was because I was a child in the last life, but I don't think I remember ever seeing you scared before."

"Not one to wear her heart on her sleeve, our Ri-Ri," Quentin said.

"Unless she's angry," Braden added.

Quentin laughed.

"Hey!" I said. But then I thought about it and

shrugged. He had a point. "That may be, but I don't think I can remember a time when I had so much at stake."

"You have feelings for him." Braden grinned.

I laughed, but it sounded more like a yelp. "Honestly? I'm so mixed up, I don't know how I feel about anything."

He gave me a sympathetic look. "The whole soul mate thing—you just can't fight it." He shrugged. "But who'd want to?"

"Pretty hot, then?" Quentin asked.

"You have no idea." Braden smirked.

"Gotta find *my* soul mate," Quentin mumbled. He shifted in the couch so he could face me. "Would you rather you didn't know?"

"What do you mean?"

"This soul mate thing seems a lot like destiny. Like this is the path you have to take, and this is the person you have to be with. I, for one, would love some hottie to show up on my door and say, 'Guess what, we're soul mates.' But I can imagine how you, Ms. Do-It-My-Way-Or-The-Highway, would have major issues with it."

I frowned at him. "I don't know what you're talking about." When I'd kissed Kim in the bathroom it felt like the rest of the world had dropped away. Even time didn't exist. I could see him as he used to be and as he was now at the same time. If that wasn't possession, what else could it be?

"Love," Quentin answered.

I sat up straight. "*What* did you say?"

"Love," he repeated. "You told me you didn't know what we were talking about so I decided to clue you in."

"Oh." I blinked several times, relieved he hadn't been able to read my thoughts.

Quentin turned back to Braden. "When do you think we'll hear something?"

As if in answer, my cell phone began to ring. Braden and Quentin both leaned forward, straining to glimpse the number on the screen, a number I didn't recognize. I answered anyway. "Hello?"

"Hey, Rileigh. It's Whitley. You are one hard girl to get ahold of."

I widened my eyes at Quentin. "Hi, *Whitley.*" I emphasized his name so the entire room could hear.

Braden narrowed his eyes in confusion, and Quentin walked over and whispered in his ear.

I turned my attention back to the phone. "Sorry about that. My life has been a little crazy lately."

There was a pause on the other end. "That kind of leads me to my next question. Are you in some kind of trouble?"

A lump formed in my throat, and I struggled to swallow around it. "Trouble?" I gave a nervous laugh. "What do you mean by that?"

"I got some weird note delivered to my house. It warned me to stay away from you. You don't have some crazy ex-boyfriend or something, do you?"

"Something like that," I mumbled. I put my hand over the receiver and hissed, "Whitley got a threatening note, too!"

Braden sat forward. "We need that note!"

"We do?"

He nodded. "It might give us a clue to where Zeami is."

"Okay." I removed my hand from the receiver.

"Rileigh, I thought we had a good time the other night and then I don't hear from you," Whitley continued. "First I was bummed. I'd assumed I'd been rejected. But then I get this note and realize there's a lot more going on. I'm worried about you. Is there something I can do to help?"

"Actually, yes," I answered. "I'm staying with a friend in Webster Groves. Is there any way you can bring that note over? It might help."

"Sure thing. What about dinner? Have you eaten yet?"

At the mention of food, my stomach roared to life. In all the excitement, I'd completely forgotten about eating. "That would be great. Could you bring extra for my friends?"

Whitley promised to grab everyone something from a drive-thru. After he took down directions to Braden's house, he hung up.

"Well, this is going to be awkward," I said, setting my phone down.

"Why's that?" Braden asked.

I shrugged. "This whole Whitley thing. He's such a sweet guy, and I had a really good time with him." I shook my head. "Things just got so complicated, and now, with Kim—" I let the sentence hang as I lost the words to explain.

"Just be brutally honest, Ri-Ri," Quentin said. "And

when you leave him wounded and broken," he swung his arms through the air, "I'll be there to pick up the pieces."

"Thanks, Q," I grumbled.

He smiled. "I'm always there for you."

"Well, I'm going to call Kim and let him know what's up," Braden said. He pulled out his phone and dialed a number. After waiting a moment, he touched the screen and ended the call. "Voicemail."

"Is that good or bad?" I asked.

He shrugged, but his eyes couldn't mask his concern. "Neither. Kim probably left his cell phone in the car." He he touched the phone's screen, dialing again. Another moment passed, and again he disconnected. "Drew, too," he mumbled.

The knot in my stomach pulled tighter. "What do we do?"

"The only thing we *can* do," he said. "Wait."

36

Rileigh, wake up. Whitley's here."

I opened my eyes to find Braden crouched in front of me. Startled, I pushed myself up from my slumped position. I'd just wanted to rest a moment. I hadn't expected to fall asleep.

Whitley and his amazing dimples flooded my vision as he knelt down in front of me. "Hey there, Sleeping Beauty." He held up a grease-stained paper bag. "I brought sustenance."

I smiled at him as I stretched. "Thanks. That's really thoughtful."

"No problem." He smiled and smoothed his hands along tied-back hair. He looked even more like a cover model with his chiseled cheekbones exposed. "It's the least I can do. I guess you've had one hell of a week, huh?"

"That's the truth." I took the paper cup he offered me

and sucked a long sip from the straw. I wrinkled my nose. "Is this diet?"

Whitley shook his head. "It shouldn't be. I made sure to ask for regular."

"Mine tasted funny, too," Q said from his perch on the couch next to Braden. "I bet the syrup went flat."

I shrugged and pulled a hamburger from the bag.

Whitley stood up and sat next to me. "Care to tell me what's going on?" He placed a hand on my knee. "I've been really worried about you."

I stopped chewing and stared at his hand. My skin underneath his palm crawled. Weird. I squirmed away, trying to mask the movement by placing my soda on the coffee table. When I sat back, he slid his arm around my shoulder.

Quentin and Braden exchanged a glance.

No longer hungry, I balled up the rest of my burger inside the wrapper. "I guess I have a psycho secret admirer." I stood up and threw the wad into the paper bag on the coffee table. Why was Whitley acting so weird? He was a perfect gentleman on our date, and now he wouldn't keep his hands off of me.

"What makes you think this guy's a psycho?" Whitley asked.

I sat back down next to him, making sure I was just out of groping range. "Well, you should know. You received a note, didn't you?"

He nodded without looking at me. Instead, he reached over and stroked a lock of my hair.

"Whitley!" I jerked back. "What's wrong with you?"

A French fry fell from Quentin's gaping mouth.

Whitley grinned. "What do you mean?"

I stood up, but my world tilted off balance. I immediately sat back down to keep from falling over.

"Oh no, Rileigh."

I glanced over at Braden, who had pressed his fingers against his forehead. Quentin lay draped across his lap. "We've been drugged," he slurred. He slumped backward like a puppet cut free from its strings and braced himself on one arm. "We need . . . " But he never finished. His head flopped back against the couch, unconscious.

I thought I heard Whitley say something, but I was sliding so far inside my body I couldn't hear anything over the beating of my heart. I tried to stand, but only managed to swing my legs uselessly off to the side.

Out of the corner of my eye, I saw Whitley leaning back against the couch, very much enjoying the show. I tried to speak, but my mouth felt like it was stuffed with cotton. Whatever drugs he had used, they worked fast.

I made one last effort to move but only succeeded in slumping over onto my lap. Slowly, my own weight pulled me over and I crumpled into a heap on the floor. The last thing I saw was Whitley's reaching hand.

37

I opened my eyes to black. Was I dreaming? The floor underneath me jumped and I hit my head on something slender and metal. I would have cried out, but my mouth was covered with duct tape. Nope. Definitely not dreaming. Locked in a car trunk. Crap.

Still groggy, I assessed the situation. I tried my arms—they were taped behind my back. My legs—taped too. This just got better and better.

The car slowed, the tires crunching over gravel before coming to a complete stop. The engine died, followed by the slam of a car door. With each footstep in my direction, my heart skipped a beat.

The trunk opened and Whitley loomed over me, framed by a starless sky. "We're home," he sang. His eyes were wide with excitement. He pulled me from the trunk and slung me over his shoulder like a sack. My heart sank as he walked up the short familiar sidewalk to the front door. He was telling the truth—I really *was* home.

Whitley walked right in. The door was unlocked, almost like it was waiting for him. He chuckled. "Bet you never thought I'd carry you across the threshold, huh?" He hummed the wedding march as he pushed the door shut with his back. When the latch clicked, he dropped me onto the floor. Waves of pain danced across my arm as my elbow took the brunt of the fall.

Ignoring my groan, Whitley stepped over me and paced around the room. "Don't have much time. Need to prepare." He paused, looked at me, and then vanished into the kitchen.

Once he was out of sight, I frantically tried to free myself from the duct tape, but only succeeded in tearing my skin. The sounds of my screams were barely audible through my covered mouth.

Whitley returned with a shoebox in his hand. He looked nothing like the guy I had gone to the coffeehouse with. His eyes were tiny black dots surrounded by an ocean of white. When he knelt next to me, I saw little beads of sweat perched on his upper lip. He dug into the box. "I need—I need … Aha!" He pulled out a syringe.

A needle! My heart somersaulted before swan diving into the pit of my stomach. Samurai or not, I simply could not handle needles. With every ounce of strength I could muster, I tried to break free from my bonds.

"Shh." Whitley patted my convulsing body. "You need to relax. That's why I'm giving this to you."

Realizing I was wasting valuable energy, I stilled. As the needle drew closer, I closed my eyes, whimpering when the pointed edge bit into my skin. I inhaled sharply as a low burning sensation followed. The world went fuzzy.

I expected to fall unconscious, but instead I felt myself detach and float away from my body. I could see and hear, but my arms and legs were as useless as the air around me.

"There." Whitley patted my head. "All better, see? Now I'm going to take the tape off of your mouth, so you need to promise to be good, okay? If I leave it on and you vomit, you'll choke and die."

I hoped my look was as dirty as I wanted it to be.

He picked at a corner of the tape, then ripped it violently from my face. Luckily, I was too numb to care. "I've been waiting a long time for this," Whitley said, smiling. "All this time and you were right under my nose." He playfully jabbed my shoulder. "I can't believe I ever thought that *she* could be the one." He looked over his shoulder and I followed his gaze to find a figure, limp on my couch.

Michelle! Despite the drugs working to keep me numb, I felt my veins frost over with fear. A dried ribbon of blood trailed down her arm and stained a deep crimson pool in the tapioca-colored carpet Debbie took two weeks to pick out. I wondered how anyone could lose that much blood and still—no, I couldn't even consider it.

I stared at Michelle, waiting for a sign that she was okay. She didn't move. And each second that passed, I felt an icicle hammer deeper into my heart. Michelle had to be alive. She *had* to. Even though she yammered like a three-year-old on espresso, she was my friend now, and I couldn't let her die.

And then, as if my will alone made it happen, Michelle's pinky finger twitched.

The tightening in my chest relaxed, but a sliver of fear remained. How long could Michelle hang on? I was no doctor, but I knew enough to know that she needed to get to a hospital. And by the looks of it, the sooner the better. I tried focusing all of my energy into my right hand. Seconds later, I was able to curl my index finger.

Whitley shook his head, pulling free from his own thoughts. "I've been looking for Senshi for a long time. When I heard about Michelle, the young martial arts prodigy from St. Louis, I had to come and investigate. But then there was another girl, a ditzy skater girl who fought off three attackers in a mall parking lot. You see my dilemma?" He looked thoughtful. "Two girls and only one can be Senshi. As you can see, though, I've already ruled out Michelle. I wonder what I'll find inside of *you?*"

He pushed me onto my side and unwound the tape from my wrists and ankles. "We have so much to do," he mumbled. "The others are bound to come looking for you once they've figured out what's happened. I bet your little friends are already awake."

Another knot in my stomach loosened. If Braden and Quentin were awake, then they were alive.

"I don't know how long it'll be before they figure out where I've taken you, but by then it won't matter. I'll be more than ready to deal with them." His lips curled into a sinister grin as he discarded the tape over his shoulder. "Yes, we have much to do."

He picked me up and walked into my bedroom where he laid me on the bed on top of Nana's handmade quilt. My throat tightened painfully around the lump of fear wedged there. Still unable to move, I glanced around for anything that might be of help. Shawnee, the stuffed Labrador on my dresser, smiled back. I was on my own.

Whitley knelt down by the bed, folding his arms on the mattress and resting his chin on them. How did I ever find him charming? He smiled and a shiver ran down the length of my spine. I thought about that—I could feel my spine. That had to be a good sign.

"Do you know who I am, Rileigh?"

I glared at him.

"I mean, besides the person you know as Whitley Noble. A long time ago you knew me by another name."

My breath caught in my throat as the realization poured over me like a bucket of ice water.

"Zeami." He exaggerated the name, as if savoring it. "Do you remember me?"

I continued to stare at him, hoping he wouldn't realize that I was now curling and uncurling my index finger.

"No?" he asked in mock surprise. "Well, then, maybe this will help." He ran a finger down the length of a glittering pink birthmark that crossed his left cheek. It was so slight that I had never noticed it before. "You don't recognize that either?" He rose from the floor and perched on the edge of the bed. The skin crawled along my thigh, closest to where he sat. I welcomed the sensation.

"Funny thing about birthmarks," he continued. "They are really scars carried over from past lives. This mark here," he touched his left cheek, "was inflicted by you during the time we spent together in Japan." He smiled. "But don't you go worrying your pretty little head about it. I like it." His eyes narrowed and his voice dripped with sarcasm. "I love waking up every morning and looking in the mirror, only to be reminded of you." He spat through clenched teeth. "Every day. For the rest of my life."

He reached forward and pulled up my tank top, exposing my midriff. I tried to recoil, but only succeeded in tightening my abs. This was also a good sign.

Whitley nodded to himself and circled a finger around a small birthmark to the right of my belly button. I was thankful I couldn't feel his touch.

"This," he said, jabbing the brown discoloration with his finger, "this proves it. Michelle doesn't have a birthmark on her stomach."

That didn't make any sense. How did a blemish prove anything?

He continued to stare, as if mesmerized. "I can't believe I was so off base," he mumbled. "I really should have known, after what you did to Tony during our date."

Tony... Omigod, he meant Devil-boy!

"I paid him to test you, to see if there really was a warrior hiding inside that shallow brain of yours." He laughed. "You always were more trouble than you're worth. I had to pay extra because I promised him you'd be unarmed. How was I to know a homeless woman would pepper spray him?"

I would have given anything to punch him. But then, I would have settled for a good spit, scream, or stomping of his face. All I managed was a grunt.

He shook his head and snapped out of his trance. "You're right." He smiled and pulled my shirt back into place. "There is much to do."

I needed more time. I tried to form words and failed. I tried again and managed a mumble.

"What's that?" Whitley laughed.

"Kim is going to find me." There. It was barely a whisper, but I took satisfaction in the way Whitley startled at the mention of Kim's name.

"Shut your mouth!" He reached back and struck my face with his open hand.

Through the sharp twinges that laced up my face, I felt hope. I was getting sensation back! The problem lay in figuring out what to do with my discovery.

"Kim won't save you," Whitley said. "That fool is following a planted trail to an abandoned warehouse where Tony will be waiting for him. By the time Kim figures it out, either Tony will have killed him or I'll already have my power back and it won't matter."

So that was it. He was a Noppera-bō. But that didn't explain why. Why would he go through so much trouble and hurt so many people for my power? Just so he could kill Kim and the others? The thought ignited the rage in my stomach until it boiled over and bled into my veins. My fingers tingled.

Whitley sucked in a deep breath. "You're distracting me." He got up and walked out of the room. Moments later, I heard water running from the bathtub faucet. After several minutes, Whitley reappeared next to my bed. "There." He dusted his hands together. "I've placed the herbs in the bath for your cleansing. You see, you stink of Kim, and his essence could contaminate the ceremony." He grunted as he hoisted me over his shoulder. "You'd think after five hundred years the guy could wear a different cologne."

As he carried me down the hall, I tried to ignore the razor-edged knot of fear rolling around inside of my stomach and instead focused on my anger. That above all else seemed to help me overcome the effects of the drugs. I could now clench my hands into loose fists. If I could stall Whitley long enough to gain control of my body, I might be able to fight back. First I had to get through whatever he had planned next.

Whitley stepped into the bathroom. Under other circumstances, the scene that awaited me might have looked inviting. The calming scent of lavender wafted from the flickering candles positioned around the tub and sink, bathing the dark room in an orange glow. Whitley left the lights off as he took me to the edge of the tub, where I could see an assortment of colored flower petals and leaves floating in the dark water. He leaned over and, despite my attempt not to, I flinched. Whitley hesitated and I held my breath, hoping he wouldn't decide to inject me with any more drugs. He dumped me, fully clothed, into the scalding water.

My scream was mangled from the water that scoured my throat.

"Okay, now the directions say we need to rinse and repeat." Whitley laughed. "But seriously, we need to submerge you." I barely had time to suck in a breath before he knotted a fist into the back of my hair and yanked me underwater.

The heat seared my face, but I managed to remain still. I tested my strength by making another fist underwater. It was stronger, but I still needed more time.

Whitley pulled me out of the water and I resurfaced with a gasp. "Such a pain in the ass, these rituals," he mumbled. "Now I'm going to get all wet." He sighed dramatically as he lifted me from the tub. Dripping water as he went, he carried me back into my room and dropped me on my bed. "Wait here," he said with another laugh. "I need to grab some things from the other room."

Alone, I decided it was a good time to take inventory of my physical capabilities. I balled my hand into a tight fist. That was good. I leaned forward and propped myself up on my elbows. That was better. As I heard his footsteps returning to my room, I quickly laid back in my original position. I just needed a few more minutes.

"It's almost time," Whitley sang from outside my door. He appeared moments later and sat down next to me on my sopping bedspread. "Soon we'll invoke your transcending." He stroked my wet hair, and my muscles resisted the urge to squirm under his hand. "You're just as lovely in this life as you were in the past." He stopped playing with my hair and ran his thumb down the length of my cheek. "It's almost romantic, don't you think? Finally the two of us will be together, joined as one for all eternity." He shrugged. "Your death is really such a small price to pay for all of that."

My eyes widened as I considered this new twist. Joined together?

Whitley hushed me like he was soothing a small child. "Don't be afraid. Only your body will die. You will continue to live inside of me. Your transcending will join us forever, from this life until the next." His eyes glittered with excitement. "You will be mine forever. I will have your power and you will have my love."

38

That did it. I was already teetering on the edge of hysteria, but the thought of living through this psychopath, even the smallest part of me—well, I'd rather die. I brought my legs into my chest and thrust them forward, savoring the look of shock on Whitley's face as he collided against my dresser. The toaster that started this whole thing leaned on its side before it crashed against his skull.

"Son of a . . . " Whitley rubbed the top of his head as he struggled to get up. "Okay, have it your way. We'll dance before you die."

"I'll lead," I growled. I pushed myself off the bed and onto my feet, careful not to fall as the room tilted through my staggering vision.

Whitley smiled. "You never fail to disappoint." He slipped his polo shirt over his head and discarded it on the floor. It was the first time I'd seen him without a shirt collar, and I couldn't help but notice a faint pink line that stretched across the length of his neck. Whitley smiled at my startled expression. "My neck? Would you like to know what happened?"

"Not really." I narrowed my eyes and lifted my fisted hands up in a defensive stance.

Whitley ignored me. "I was given power. Great power." His eyes flashed. "It was payment. All I had to do was provide ninja access to Toyotomi's mansion, kill you, and deliver Yoshido to my benefactor." His smile was cruel. "Of course, that's not what happened. Oh no. The noble Yoshido took the death blow that was meant for you. My benefactor was infuriated, blaming me for his death." The smile fell from his face. "I was beheaded. Did you know that when you are beheaded, you don't die instantly? No, it's not that easy. Instead, you slowly watch the world swim away as you gasp for breath that never comes." He lashed out with his hand and sent the picture of Quentin and me hurtling against the wall, where it shattered. "Your chest burns, as if on fire. But of course your chest isn't really there. It's maddening!"

He was insane! My vision swam, and I shook my head to clear it. If I didn't get over the effects of the drugs, I was dead for sure.

Whitley held up his hands and closed his eyes. When he opened them again, he smiled. "Never mind that. The past is the past." He held a hand out to me. "Now, I believe you offered me a dance."

On many levels I knew that fighting Whitley was not

a good idea. First, the drugs were not completely out of my system. Second, Whitley was a psycho. Third, I hadn't transcended yet and was not really in any condition to be fighting an experienced samurai. But if I didn't at least try, my future held certain death.

He grinned as if he could read the doubts floating through my mind. "What's the matter, my love?" He stretched his arms in front of him, then settled back into a fighting stance. "Do you not remember the steps? Don't worry. I'll remind you."

His speed surprised me. Or maybe the drugs were affecting my reaction time. Either way, he was upon me before I realized he had moved.

As I stumbled backward, a pair of discarded sweatpants ensnared my foot, pulling me down onto my knees at the exact moment Whitley's fist went soaring over my head. Thank God I'd missed a few things during my cleanup. I scrambled forward on my hands, only to have Whitley grab the waist of my jeans. I twisted in his bony grip and kicked out, making contact with the knee he used to block his groin.

Whitley laughed. "You're nothing of the warrior I remember."

My fear mixed with the drugs left my throat parched. "Maybe that's because you drugged me!" I croaked.

He reached forward and snatched my hair, pulling me roughly to my feet. He wrenched my head back and hissed into my ear. "Even so. I always thought that Toyotomi made too much of a fuss over you and Yoshido."

"Kim is twice the warrior you'll ever be." I thrust my elbow back, making contact with his gut.

He released me as he doubled over. "Bitch!" He lifted his head and glared at me with watery eyes. "Don't you dare speak that name in my presence again." He launched forward and grabbed my wrist, spinning me so that my back was against his chest. He slipped his right arm under my arm and across my shoulders, pinning my neck in a painful downward angle. He pulled tighter, forcing a grimace to my lips. "We will soon be one, and together *we* will be twice the warrior. And this time, Kim will not be able to save you." He thrust me to the floor.

My knee took the impact, sending needles of pain up and down my leg. "Even if he doesn't save me, Kim will still kill you."

"Not if we kill him first."

I kicked out, but Whitley caught my shoe between his hands before I could strike. He twisted it sharply, and I found myself balanced against the floor on my outstretched hands.

"When will you learn?" Whitley snarled before he brought his foot down on my back, knocking my chest against the floor and the air from my lungs.

I lay there for a moment, breathing heavily and trying to figure out how I was going to escape.

He chuckled from behind me. "Why do you insist on fighting me? It's our destiny to be together. Why don't you see that?"

"I'd rather die."

"That *is* the point."

I reached under my bed and grabbed the first thing I could find: one of Debbie's boots that I'd worn on our date. Perfect. I twisted onto my back and threw it at him.

He stumbled back when the pointed heel cracked against his forehead. "Son of a bitch!" he screamed, rubbing furiously at the red welt.

I pulled myself to my feet using the side of my bed and planted a right hook into his temple.

He blinked several times before slowly turning his gaze back to me. Rage burned like wildfire in his eyes. "This is getting old," he whispered. He grabbed the front of my shirt and pulled me into him. I braced myself for impact, but it never came. Instead, he fisted his other hand through my hair and shoved his lips against mine.

With a muffled scream, I struggled in his grip, but it only made him pull me that much closer. When I felt his narrow tongue pry against my clenched teeth, I promptly bit down on the tip until I could taste his blood, sweet and metallic, on my tongue.

He slapped me hard enough to make my vision swim in colorful dots. Dizzy, I fell back to the floor.

"You little tease." He smiled, licking his lips. A small line of blood had trailed down his chin, and he wiped it away with the back of his hand, inspecting the smeared blood on his fingers. "It feels just like old times." Whitley leaned over and twisted his fist into the front of my shirt. With a rough tug, he jerked me back to my feet.

Still dizzy, I teetered to the side and onto the bed, where he let me fall.

"No more distractions." He looked around the room, a slow smile curling onto his lips when he spotted what he was looking for. "Aha! This will do nicely." He walked over to my open closet and plucked my leather belt off the floor. He walked back over to me, snapping the leather together with a crack. "This should hold you."

Icy waves of panic flooded my veins. I couldn't let myself be tied up. With the little strength I had left, I pushed myself from my bed only to meet the back end of Whitley's striking hand. My vision swam in waves of black as I desperately tried to remain conscious.

"This would be so much easier on the both of us if you would just stop fighting!"

He twisted my arms behind me and secured them with my belt. He looped the leather around my wrists so tightly that I could feel it biting into my skin. Finally, when my head felt like it had stopped spinning and I found I was able to move again, I could do little more than struggle in place and scream out in frustration.

"Shh," Whitley whispered in my ear as I thrashed. I did manage to roll over and fall off the bed, landing hard onto my already-sore shoulder. Whitley shrugged as he turned and walked out of the room. He returned moments later with the same cardboard box he had taken the syringe from.

My stomach did a cartwheel.

Whitley caught sight of my expression and laughed.

"Don't worry, I'm not getting out any more needles. A lot of good that did me, anyway." He rummaged through the box. "Let's see, next we need the herbs. Ah, here it is!" He pulled out a small glass jar filled with an oily brown paste. He opened the jar and grabbed a small basting brush from the box. "This mixture will help open your chakras," he said, "and ease the transfer of power."

As he drew closer, I squirmed back. "You're disgusting and I want nothing more than to rip those putrid dimples off your face."

Whitley shrugged. "We're going to be spending a lot of time together, so you better get over that attitude." He dipped the brush into the brown sludge and dangled it over my face, as if deciding where to begin. As it lingered inches above my nose, I detected strong scents of lavender and mint emanating from the ooze. He pressed the stiff-bristled brush against my forehead, and a slight breeze pushed out from my skin, rustling the hairs that had escaped Whitley's ponytail.

He sat back and smiled. "It's working already."

He was right. My head suddenly cleared and my vision sharpened. All traces of the drug were erased, as well as the dizziness caused by his repeated slaps.

Whitley continued to work his way down my body, pausing to smear the herb mixture on the middle of my forehead, neck, chest, and both hands. I lay quietly as he worked. When I had released my power at the dojo, it had stemmed from my chest, but this time, the power surged down the entire length of my body from each point that had been smeared with paste. The wind wasn't nearly as wild as it had been in the dojo. The swaying bedroom curtains were the only proof that it was there at all.

Whitley placed the jar on the ground and held his arms out wide. "All the years I had to wait—now it will be all mine!" He clenched his hands into fists and threw his head back as he smiled. "Finally!" He lifted his eyes to meet mine, and all traces of humanity were gone. He crawled across the floor until he was positioned over me. "Perfect." His voice was barely a whisper. "Absolutely perfect."

I fought against the shudders that threatened to wrack my body. I didn't want to give him the satisfaction of seeing me squirm.

Whitley leaned down, bringing his face inches from my own. I smelled the sourness of blood on his breath. I kept my eyes locked on his. If he wanted me so badly, I would make sure he got the part of me that was consumed with hate for him.

"You know," he said, lifting a hand to tuck a piece of my hair behind my ear, "there was another before Michelle. A tragic mistake."

I narrowed my eyes. "What are you talking about?"

He shrugged. "Some girl in California. She made the news because she fought off a cougar that attacked her while she was hiking. I thought for sure it was the great Senshi. But when I got ahold of her, it was pretty apparent she lacked your spirit and grace. She broke so easy. Not like you." He touched his finger to my nose.

"Burn in hell."

He laughed. "See! That's exactly what I'm talking about. The Senshi fire. Here you are, faced with death, and instead of begging for your life, you're mouthing off." He clapped his hands together. "It's just like old times!"

"You're pathetic." I reared back and spit on his face. Until that moment, I didn't realize there was a stronger emotion than hate, but there was, and it was consuming my insides in its black fire.

I understood then what Kim meant when he said he was a samurai for life. Wielding death was not a curse but a gift. By extinguishing evil, we could make the world a better and safer place to inhabit. Gone were the days of guarding nobility. A samurai's duty was to serve the world.

Whitley ignored me, absently wiping his cheek with his palm. "I almost forgot the candles." He stood up and retrieved the cardboard box from the bed and pulled out a clear bag of short red candles. After dumping the bag over onto my bed, he went about my room, placing the candles in various locations and lighting them.

The swirling wind stopped.

"You feel that?" Whitley smiled. "We've contained your power to this room. There is only one thing left to do." He turned on his heel and walked out into the hallway.

Frantic, I struggled to pull my hands free. The leather burned into my skin, but I ignored the pain. I could feel my wrists growing slick with sweat, or possibly blood—I couldn't be sure. It didn't matter. Whatever it was lubricated my palms enough to allow them to slide slowly forward.

Whitley appeared moments later holding a katana. He held it for me so see, turning it so the sapphire embedded in its hilt winked in the candlelight. "Do you recognize this?"

I forgot all about freeing myself as my heart began to pound like a jackhammer. "My katana!"

"I can't believe I actually thought it would be a challenge to get it," Whitley said. "The decoy was an annoying surprise, but with Kim out searching the city for me, it was no trouble to break into his apartment and steal the real one. Can you believe he actually kept it in plain sight on his wall? This whole thing's been too easy." Whitley sighed. "I was hoping for more of a challenge. I'm almost sad that this will all be over soon."

I didn't like the sound of that. I went back to working my hands free. I had to bite my lip to keep from crying out. I could feel my skin tear as I pulled.

"My own transcending was a disappointment." Whitley made a show of polishing the blade with the hem of his shirt. "I had my memories back and my fighting skills, but no powers!" He shook his head. "It wasn't until later that I figured out that because the power wasn't mine to begin with, it wouldn't stay with me. It's more than a little irritating that I've had to go through all of this just to get it back." He held the sword above his head and examined it in the light. "But it's so worth it."

I could barely hear him over the pounding of my pulse

inside of my head. My katana—the very thing that could save or end me—was wrapped inside Whitley's long, pale fingers. I could almost remember how it felt to curl my own fingers around the handle, and how it always felt so right in my hands. I closed my eyes and clenched my teeth against the burning of my wrists. The sword Whitley held was mine, and I was going to get it back.

He held the sword back like he was taunting a child. "I'm not just going to hand it over to you. This works a bit different."

"So do it already!" I screamed. "Or maybe you'd like to sit around and talk about it for another hour."

He looked thoughtful. "You know, my dear, for once we agree. The time is now." He gripped the handle with both of his hands and swung the sword high above his head. With a feral yell, he brought it down.

I only had one shot. I rolled over and tore my hands free from the belt just as the metal blade cracked into the hardwood floor. I bared my teeth at him, screaming as I pushed myself off the floor. I spun on one foot and landed a back kick squarely into his stomach.

Whitley doubled over, but kept his hold on the blade.

I brought my knee up toward his head, but instead of it meeting his skull, Whitley ensnared my thigh with his arms and twisted me sharply to the side, releasing me onto the bed. I turned myself around just in time to see him bearing my sword down upon me.

I gasped in surprise as the blade cut through my shoulder. Being stabbed didn't feel like I expected. A heaviness pulled at my chest and filled my lungs. I turned my head to the side, startled by the sight of my own glassy eyes staring back at me from the metal piercing my shoulder.

Now that I had seen the wound, a slow burning ache began to build from it. I trembled, suddenly very cold despite the warm liquid I felt running up my throat and dribbling down my chin. I tried to take a breath, but my lungs had turned to stone.

Whitley let go of the handle and took a step back, looking around the room. "Nothing is happening," he hissed angrily.

He was right. I felt no return of memories or wind of power sweeping through the room. There was nothing except me impaled on my bed and dying.

Whitley's face appeared above mine, his eyes bulging. "Are you or are you not Senshi?"

I opened my mouth to speak, but all I could do was cough.

He screamed and grabbed a fistful of my hair. "Answer me!"

I coughed, and he recoiled from the blood that I spattered across his face.

In truth, I was just as disappointed as Whitley. Kim had been wrong; I wasn't Senshi, I wasn't a samurai, and I wasn't his soul mate. The sense of loss that overcame me was crippling, and I would have gladly exchanged it for another sword in the shoulder. I was nothing at all.

I was going to die, alone with a madman, as just Rileigh.

39

Japan, 1493

Senshi ran to Yoshido but kept her arm twisted against her chest. She refused to touch him, afraid to confirm her worst nightmare. Surely the heartbeat that lulled her to sleep at night wasn't still. Impossible. Senshi dug her nails into her arms, the pain a reminder that she was still very much alive. And alone.

"Well, that was unfortunate," Zeami grumbled from behind her.

The voice startled Senshi. She turned and narrowed her eyes on the man responsible for Yoshido's death. "What have you done?"

Zeami's eyes flew wide open. "Do not blame me. *You* are the one who is supposed to be dead. I was under strict orders to bring Yoshido back alive." He shrugged. "No matter. I cannot say that his death brings me any great sorrow."

"I will bring you something much worse than sorrow," Senshi growled.

Zeami smiled. "Oh no, my dear, it is I who have plans for you." He clapped his hands and more than twenty ninja crawled over the stone fence that enclosed the garden. "I have waited a long time to have you, Senshi—a very long time." He untied his silk robe, baring his chest as he stalked toward her. "And when I am through with you, I have promised whatever is left to my men to do with as they see fit."

Senshi felt a shift among the ninja and took her gaze off Zeami long enough to see what they were doing. The men clad in black had quietly surrounded her and laced their bows with arrows. Their eyes, the only visible part of them, bore down on her.

"Do not worry, Senshi," Zeami laughed. "They are not aiming to kill. Now throw down your sword and play nice."

Senshi glanced around the deadly circle and assessed her situation. She laughed quietly and shook her head. It would all be over soon and she would be with Yoshido again. She found strength in that.

Zeami hesitated. "What is funny?"

Senshi continued to smile as she plucked her sword from the ground. She had enough strength left to finish this. With a gentle push, she released her last bit of energy and pushed it into the katana. She wavered a bit, but managed to drive the pulsating blade into the ground before she collapsed behind it, gasping.

Zeami called out to the ninja, and Senshi lifted her

eyes in time to see a wave of arrows raining down upon her. She crept back a little and laid her head against Yoshido's chest, trying to ignore the scent of burnt flesh as she watched the arrows bounce harmlessly away from the small shield of energy she had raised with her sword.

She sighed, reaching her hand up and stroking Yoshido's now coarse and brittle hair. "This is how it ends for us, my love," she whispered. "The honorable death you always wanted." She was surprised by the tear that trailed down her cheek and quickly wiped it away with the back of her hand.

"Senshi!" Zeami's voice sounded from far away. "You cannot hide in there forever!"

She sucked in a sharp breath. He was right—she only delayed the inevitable. She rolled over slowly and pushed herself up on shaking arms. Once on her feet, she reached out and touched the thin blue field, rippling it like a pebble tossed into a pond. It would only last a few minutes longer.

The ninja, as if sensing this, ceased their fire and watched her like waiting lions.

Zeami laughed as he strode toward her, stopping when only a few feet remained between them. "Are you blind? There is no escape."

Senshi slid her hand inside of her robe and felt for the crooked dagger tucked into her sash, a dagger she had never used before. She pulled the dagger out of her robe and held it out in front of her, smiling.

"What are you doing?" Startled, Zeami took several steps backward.

"Do you not know?" She held the blade against her palm, admiring it. "Samurai do not allow themselves to be taken captive. I will die with honor."

Realization flashed through his wide eyes. "No! You fool!" He turned to the ninja. "Stop her!"

The ninja charged forward like a black wave.

Senshi watched them come through the small holes that were stretching through her shield. She was out of time.

"Yoshido, I am coming," she whispered, squeezing the handle of the dagger as tight as her sweat-drenched hands would allow. She sucked in a deep breath and screamed so loudly that she thought her eardrums might burst. Loudly enough, she hoped, that Yoshido would be able to hear her from the beyond and find her. When she had used the last of her breath, she thrust the cold steel into her belly.

Pain, like a roaring tsunami, crashed against her, taking her breath away and driving her to her knees. In training, Yoshido had instructed her to pull the blade up, saying death would come so much faster that way, but Senshi lacked the strength to even breathe. Blackness crawled along the edge of her vision. She found herself face-to-face with Yoshido without realizing she had fallen.

His face was beautiful even in death. A silent angel at peace.

Soon, she thought amidst her agony, *soon I will be at peace as well.* The shield was gone, but no one dared approach her. Her vision narrowed further, and she blinked her eyes furiously. His face alone was the only thing keeping the pain from driving her insane.

Please, she silently begged, *please no more.*

As if in answer, a hand slid through the darkness and wrapped around hers. That touch alone stilled her agony, and she fell into peace.

40

The first stirrings of wind fluttered through my hair, reminding me that I was still very much alive and still pinned to my bed with a sword through my shoulder. In the next instant, a tornado slammed my closet and bedroom door shut and ripped my curtains free from their rods. I flung my arm over my face to shield myself from the debris flying around my room. The wind came from nowhere and everywhere all at once, twisting and turning, whipping my hair across my face and pelting my head with dirty socks. I twisted my head and cupped my hand over my eyes to see Whitley huddled against my door, struggling to remain standing.

The wooden windows rattled in their sills as my room grew thick with power. The pressure crushed down upon me until I thought I would be smashed flat. I opened my mouth, but the wind pushed my scream aside as it forced its way down my throat. Suddenly, the room around me became still as the power that had threatened to tear it down poured inside of me. My body bucked and jerked as the power searched for a way out. It stretched and pushed until I thought my skin would shatter like glass.

And then it found an opening.

The katana burst from my shoulder as the wind streamed from my wound, giving me seconds to roll across my bed to keep from being stabbed a second time when the blade came back down. I rolled to the ground on my knees, panting as I leaned my head against my mattress.

My room had become the eye of a cyclone again. I thought I heard Whitley screaming, but I couldn't tell where the sound was coming from. I could no longer see anything. The energy had grown so strong that it had become a visible force of white streamers. I ducked as unidentifiable objects soared overhead only to become wedged into the drywall.

Ignoring the pain in my shoulder, I flattened myself to the floor and crawled forward, hoping to reach the door. I didn't make it far. As if sensing my intentions, the wind bore down on me again, pelting me repeatedly with everything from underwear to books. I curled myself into a ball, keeping my arms protectively over my head. I felt an internal snap and the first piece of me break away.

I didn't have time to react. In the next second there was a shake, followed by a pop, and then an earsplitting crack. Shortly after, I found myself somewhere near the ceiling, staring down at my crumpled body on the floor.

Terrified, I tried to make my way back to my body, but it was like swimming in quicksand. The harder I struggled, the farther I felt myself being carried until I was through my ceiling and outside of my house.

At first, as I watched my house shrink to nothing more than a blue speck, I was filled with terror. But the higher I flew, the more a growing sense of awe and wonder filled me until my fears were completely pushed aside. My suburb shrank and soon the entire city lay beneath me. The buildings and cars shimmered like gems on a bed of black velvet. The Arch reflected in the Mississippi River like a million glittering diamonds.

I wanted to stay forever and stare down at the city of jewels, but the wind carried me higher still, pushing me through a blanket of clouds that I couldn't see through. I thought this should make me feel nervous, but then I realized that I didn't feel anything. I was the air around me and the wind blowing through me. I was everything, and yet, I was nothing that could be.

Just above the gray night clouds, my flight came to a halt. The air holding me ripped, giving me a moment to admire the black hole that lay underneath before it swallowed me.

At the rate of speed I fell, everything should have been a blur. Instead, I saw it all with crystal clarity. The image of a smiling young woman with raven hair and almond eyes appeared before me. She held out her hand, and, even though I had no form, I took it, letting her join with me and lead me down to the life that was.

The memories flickered past like images from a movie projector, but the emotions they stirred stayed with me, embedding themselves into my being.

I was a toddler, playing alone with a broken doll on a bamboo floor.

I was a child, braiding my mother's hair as she stared at her reflection in a mirror.

I was a scared young girl with a torn robe and a knife, refusing to give my body away without a price.

Then I saw *him.* A braid of jet-black hair swung past his knees as he stepped forward and held out his hand.

I reached back only to find that he had vanished, leaving behind a crooked blood-stained dagger. Unable to stop myself, I picked up the dagger and, without hesitating, plunged the blade deep into my flesh.

Screaming, I opened my eyes and found myself back on the floor of my bedroom. I inhaled the thick smell of smoke, but a twisting pain in my stomach made me gasp. I sat up and hugged my sides, my fingers running across something warm and sticky that soaked into my tank top. I slowly lifted my shirt and found that the small birthmark to the right of my belly button had split open, spilling fresh blood down my waist.

"What did you do?" Whitley screamed. I looked up as he gripped my shoulders. His hair had fallen completely out of its ponytail and knotted into a halo around his face. He shook me hard enough that my head flopped against my shoulders like a rag doll. "My power is not back! How did you keep it from me?"

Smiling, I put my hand on top of his, and he stopped shaking me. His eyes filled with disbelief. Suddenly it was all so clear. I knew what had happened. I could feel it in my center and coursing through my blood.

"Your ceremony trapped energy into this room," I whispered.

Uncertainty flashed in his eyes. "I trapped your energy so I could take it when you died."

"You forget," I hissed, "that I have the ability to manipulate ki. But the only problem when using life force energy is that it's like a battery. The more you use, the weaker you become. And if you use all your ki before time and rest can restore it, you die."

"So why aren't you dead?"

"Because of you." I smiled. "When you contained my ki to my bedroom, you made it a battery charger. You trapped the energy you tried to take and gave me an endless supply of power."

Whitley paled as he stumbled back away from me. "No!"

I could feel the power flowing inside of me. Like a warm river, it mixed with the blood flowing through my veins, energizing me. As it worked through my body, I noticed a tingling sensation in my shoulder and stomach. Carefully, I pulled my torn and bloody tank top past my shoulder to find that my stab wound was no bigger than the size of a dime, and it appeared to be shrinking before my eyes. I lifted up the bottom hem of my shirt and wiped away the smeared blood with my hand, discovering nothing but smooth skin underneath.

I stood up.

Whitley scrambled backward, tripping over one of my shoes and falling onto his back. With a yelp, he crab-crawled in reverse until his back hit my door. With a shaking hand, he pulled three palm-sized metal squares from his back jeans pocket. The tips gleamed where they had been filed to a point. "Don't take one step closer!" he screamed.

"You're actually threatening me with shuriken?" I asked, remembering the weapons fleeing ninja used to discourage pursuers. "Really, Whitely, isn't that a tad cliché?"

"Why change something that works?" He looked like he was about to say more, but snapped his mouth shut as his eyes wandered over my head. "Look!" He inclined his head to point behind me. "Fire!"

I rolled my eyes. "Please, how dumb do—" But my words trailed in the air as I spotted orange flames licking out from under my closet door. One of the candles must have fallen and rolled into my closet during the wind storm!

I froze. Michelle lay dying on my couch, my house was on fire, and I was alone in my room with a homicidal maniac. Which problem did I address first?

A scream from behind me forced my decision. I looked up seconds before three flying shuriken hit me.

Reflexively I lifted my arm to protect my face and felt a disturbance in the air made by my swinging arm. When I opened my eyes, Whitley's right shoulder had been pierced through to the wall with one sharpened square, a second pinned his left forearm in place, and the third wedged firmly into the middle of his thigh. He howled as he pulled against the metal that gouged him. I watched, mesmerized, as the blood stain crawled down Whitley's thigh until most of his left pant leg turned a brilliant red.

Unable to move his arms, he shifted his shoulders and looked up at me with desperate eyes. "The fire!"

I looked behind me to see that the flames had spread from the closet to the entire back wall. Thick black smoke collected on the ceiling and pressed down by the second.

I snatched my katana from the bed and paused briefly in front of Whitley. A thousand emotions passed through me in a second. He had tried to kill me and, rightly, deserved no mercy. But I wasn't sure I had the strength to walk away and deal with the stain his blood would leave on my conscience.

Whitley quit struggling and fell limp against the wall. "You can't leave me here," he pleaded. "I'll die."

"You deserve to." My voice sounded hoarse as I struggled to breathe through the thick air.

"But I'm the only one who can get us out of here."

I narrowed my eyes. "You would say anything to save yourself."

The smoke had now descended to waist-level and Whitley coughed several times before he was able to continue. "I'm telling the truth! Transcending should have drained you of your power, but I have contained it to this room. Once you break the barrier, you'll lose all of your energy. But if you let me go, I give you my word that I will get you and Michelle out of the house safely."

I took a moment to consider that. "So my choice is to let you go or lose all of my energy?"

Whitley nodded and smiled. The expression was identical to the smile worn by Zeami the night he killed Yoshido.

"You know what? I think I'll take my chances with the fire."

His face crumpled. "No! You can't do this!"

I paused in the doorway and gave him one last look over my shoulder. "As much fun as it's been, consider this our last date."

I left the room without looking back.

41

Whitley had told the truth about one thing. The moment I stepped from my bedroom, my energy slipped away like sand through my fingertips. The smoke was already thick and rolling down the hallway when I stumbled to the floor.

I heard Whitley's wordless screams, but after a loud crash followed by a slight tremor in the floor, he fell eerily silent.

I couldn't help but taste the irony, cold and bitter on my tongue. I had survived an attempted sacrifice as well as my transcending, but now I was going to be burned alive in a house fire before I could pull my friend to safety. Just my luck.

I tightened my grip on the katana and shimmied forward down the hallway on my elbows. When I could no longer see out of my watery and burning eyes, I buried my head against my arm, coughing up the thick air that cut like razors down my throat. After rubbing the tears from my eyes with my shoulders, I lifted my head back up. The wave of heat that pressed against my face surprised me. The fire had beaten me down the hall and was making headway into the living room where Michelle lay helpless, and there was nothing I could do to save her.

I was too exhausted to be afraid. A violent series of coughs wracked my body, and when it was over, I collapsed my head onto the floor and stared at the shadows cast by the orange flames dancing against the wall. I couldn't look away.

A loud crack sounded to my right, followed by something white-hot searing into the skin above my left elbow. I shuddered but was helpless to do more.

As the burning sensation spread, I tried to keep the panic threatening to overtake me at bay. Quentin had given me tips for dealing with anxiety once. He suggested that reciting the alphabet backwards would keep my mind too busy to succumb to an anxiety attack. It seemed silly, but I had to do something while I waited to die.

Z, Y, X, W, V…

A memory of my mother popped into my mind. I had just turned thirteen and was sitting on the couch watching a movie when I heard soft sobbing coming from my mother's room.

Startled, I turned the TV off, tiptoed down the hall, and eased her bedroom door open. "Mom?"

"Oh, Rileigh!" Debbie quickly wiped away her tears

with the back of her hand before burying her face in her pillow. Her voice was muffled, but I could still understand her when she said, "I didn't want you to see me like this."

I crept to the edge of the bed, careful to not step on the dozens of crumpled and ripped pictures of my mom from her modeling days that littered the floor.

I could remember the strangeness of cradling my mother in my arms. When her sobbing stopped and her heaving chest stilled, I got the nerve to ask the question I'd always wanted to ask. "Do you regret keeping me?"

She sucked in a breath and held it for the longest seconds of my life. Finally, she let it whoosh out before pulling herself up and locking her puffy red eyes onto my own. "Never. Not even for a second."

I blinked back the tears clinging to my lashes, afraid that if I spoke my voice would betray the emotion flooding through me.

"You're so strong." She cupped my face with her hand. "I know I haven't been the best mother."

"Mom, you—"

"No." She squished my cheeks with her fingers. "Let me finish. I've made mistakes, Rileigh. Stupid, immature mistakes that ruined my reputation and ended my career. But somehow, amidst all that, I managed to do one thing right."

"What?" I asked with my fish lips.

She shrugged and released her hold on my face. "I have no idea, because despite it all, here you are—the most amazing person I know."

U, T, S, R, Q…

I remembered dancing with my best friend a month ago at my junior prom.

"Rileigh, will we always be friends?" Quentin asked.

I looked up from his shoulder. "Always."

He smiled and spun me in a circle. "Even if I get into a car accident and my face looks like this?" He rolled his eyes into the back of his head and stuck out his tongue.

I smiled. "Without a doubt."

He pulled me against him and lowered me into a dip. "Will you still be friends with me when I steal all the high-tipping salon clients?"

He pulled me up and I shrugged. "Sure. But keep in mind I'll put Nair in your shampoo."

"Understood." He nodded. "Would you still be friends with me if I left you alone for a minute so I can ask Brad Stevens to dance?"

I laughed. "I knew there was a point to this." I dropped my hand from his shoulder. "Go. Dance. Be merry."

He gave me a quick kiss. "Love ya!" He turned to leave, but hesitated.

"What's up, Q?"

He smiled and pulled me into a tight hug. "You know I *do* love you, right?"

"Of course." I hugged him back.

"Like a sister," he whispered in my ear.

"Like a sister," I agreed.

P, O, N, M, uh, L…

I was having more difficulty concentrating on the

letters as my mind wanted to bring into view the one person I couldn't bear to think about.

K

Kim. The name raked like nails across my heart, filling me with more pain than the smoke burning through my lungs. What I thought was a spirit trying to take me over had really been the voice of my heart. And I'd refused to listen.

Now it was too late.

I sobbed with the knowledge that I would never see his almond eyes or smell the sandalwood that infused everything he touched. He had said he loved me, and in return, I had said nothing. Now I would die and he would never know that I remembered.

That I loved him still.

Yoshido, my soul mate, lost to me again. The tears running down my cheeks felt as hot as the flames drawing nearer.

I heard another crack above me and braced for the impact that would follow. Instead, my vision swam in black. I wondered if I had passed out, but I could feel strong hands sliding underneath me and picking me up. Was I dreaming? Surely if I was, I wouldn't be able to feel the thick film of sweat that coated my skin and ran in streams down my neck.

My body jerked forward and something soft brushed past my face. A blanket? Seconds later, I shivered as the cool night air melted against the sweat on my skin. A golden hand pulled the heavy wool away from my face and the chocolate eyes that stared down projected a mixture of fury and terror.

I smiled up at him. Kim. My Kim.

He pulled me tighter against him. "Oh, thank God. Rileigh, I—"

But I could no longer hear him. Unconsciousness pulled at me, and I sank away. I had seen his face and been held in his arms. I couldn't ask for anything more.

42

I wasn't dead. The aches and pains of my body that seeped into my dreams assured me of that. Groaning, I tried to sit up, but two strong arms tightened their hold around my waist. I glanced down to find Kim's face drawn into tight lines even as he slept. His upper body draped awkwardly over my lap while his lower half sat half-spilled in a chair pulled up to the side of my bed. Gradually, his face relaxed and his arms loosened their grip. I shifted my body and let my hands rest on his head, curled in his hair.

My first thought was that I was in a hospital, but glancing around, I decided this was like no hospital I'd ever been to before. It looked more like the medical ward on an episode of *Star Trek.* My room had no windows, yet was eye-flinchingly bright. It was almost impossible to tell where the white walls ended and the floor began. Several flat-screen monitors hanging on the far wall displayed a rainbow grid of lines and numbers. To the side of me, blinking instruments and tools unlike anything I'd ever seen sat on stainless steel shelves.

"Where am I?" I murmured.

"I wish I knew."

Startled, I looked up and found Quentin staring at me from an additional chair tucked off to the side. I sucked in an excited breath and felt a great ease in the pressure that had built in my chest. Quentin was okay.

He leaned forward, and the blanket that had been pulled up to his chin fell against his waist. "I think we're in a secret government infirmary or something. They took you and Michelle here after they pulled you from the fire. You looked so bad with the blood and … I, well, all of us were freaked," Quentin whispered. "But he," Q inclined his head toward Kim, "went absolutely crazy. He hasn't let anyone within five feet of you."

As if in response, Kim mumbled something incoherent and pulled me tighter.

"Michelle's here too?" I asked. "Is she okay?"

"She's going to be. Drew found her in the nick of time." Quentin paused. "But what about you? Are *you* okay?"

I wasn't sure. While he watched, I stretched and flexed various muscles, careful to make my movements as minimal as possible so as not to disturb the sleeping guy who held me. Aside from stiff joints, sore muscles, a burn on the back of my arm, and several swollen bruises, everything seemed to be in working order. "I'm okay," I answered.

Quentin smiled and relaxed back against the chair.

"How is everyone else?" I tried to sit up, but quickly abandoned the idea when Kim's arms tightened.

Quentin rolled his eyes and waved his hand. "You don't need to be worrying about anything right now. Braden, Drew, me—we're all fine. Everyone is fine ... well, except that guy with the horn tattoos. Drew told me that Kim beat him within an inch of his life. That's how they got him to spill where you were."

I couldn't say I felt too bad for him. "And my house?"

Quentin looked away.

"It's gone, isn't it?"

He nodded. "Your mom knows. She's a little hysterical, but that's to be expected."

"Where is she? Can I see her?"

Quentin chewed on his lip. "Um, she doesn't know you're *here* exactly. She thinks that while we were at my house your place had an electrical fire. She's staying in a local hotel."

That didn't make sense. "I thought she was out of town."

"Yeah." Quentin darted his eyes around the room like a bird preparing for flight. "They didn't make it. There's something you should know about your mom's boyfriend ... "

My stomach clenched tightly. "I knew it! He's bad news, isn't he? What is he? Another Noppera-bō?"

"Um, not exactly." Quentin looked like he was going

to say something, but his eyes moved past me and he was suddenly standing. "I think I'll get us some lunch."

"Lunch?" I gripped the side of my bed ail. "You're not going anywhere until you tell me what's going on!"

"Gotta go! I'll be back soon." He tossed the blanket across the chair and practically ran out the door.

"Q!" I yelled after him. When I realized he wasn't coming back, I settled against the bed with an angry growl and found myself staring down into Kim's quiet eyes.

"Rileigh, I—" Kim swallowed hard. "How are you feeling?"

"So much better," I whispered, smiling at the face I never thought I'd see again. It felt like a lifetime had passed since the last time we were in a hospital room together, and in a way, it had.

Kim gently pushed off of me and stood up. "Show me."

I didn't bother to hide the hurt in my eyes as I stared at him from the bed. "What?"

He motioned me up with his fingers. "Please show me that you are okay."

I pushed the blanket off and dropped my bare feet onto the cold tile, trying to swallow the hot anger that tightened my throat. We had come so close to losing each other. I wanted nothing more than to cling to him, and he wanted me to touch my toes?

I moved slowly, trying to ignore my screaming muscles as I worked through the various stretches that Kim directed. When he gave me a final nod, I straightened my back and put my hands on my hips. "Satisfied?"

"Not entirely." His jaw flexed and I watched a strange battle between anger and fear play through his eyes.

I dropped my hands to my sides. "Kim, what's wrong?"

He nodded to my shoulder. "What is that from?"

I looked down at the dried blood crusted underneath the neck opening of my hospital gown. I pulled it down my shoulder to reveal a faint pink scar.

"And that?"

I followed Kim's line of sight, to the crimson discoloration on my abdomen.

Just because I was mad and proving a point, I lifted the hem of the gown past my navel, exposing my pink, heart-covered underwear so he could see that no wound lay underneath, only smooth, unharmed, blood-stained skin.

Kim paled as he balled his trembling hands into fists. "What did he do to you?"

I dropped the gown back in place and tried my best to smooth it out with my hands. "I'm fine."

He growled, turning and punching his hand straight through the drywall behind him. Kim's shoulders heaved as he slowly removed his bloodied hand. I tentatively placed my hand on his back, but he refused to turn around. "I failed you again," he whispered. "I am unworthy."

"What?" I slid my hand along his shoulder and gave it a tug, but I might have had better luck pulling on a brick wall. "Kim, how can you say that?"

He turned around but kept his eyes locked on the floor. "I am no good for you. Twice, under my protection, harm has befallen you. Surely you would want better for yourself."

"Kim!" I struggled with his name, trying to keep the panic from rising to my voice. "I don't understand what you're saying."

The tendons in his jaw flexed as he ground his teeth together. "It would be better for us both if you just left. And spare me your pity. I don't need your soft words."

I staggered back, his words seared across my heart like hot wire. "Don't you—don't you love me?"

Kim's eyes widened and he closed the distance between us in two long strides. "Oh no, Rileigh, please never think that."

I threw my hands in the air. "What am I supposed to think? You just told me to go!"

Kim fell to his knees and wrapped his arms around my waist, pressing his forehead against my waist. "No, no, no." He shook his head back and forth. "I would rather die a thousand times than have you think for one moment that I don't love you." He pulled away and I could see the unshed tears that hung from his lashes. "It is because I love you that I want you to have so much more than I can give."

I sank to my knees and slid my hands on both sides of his face, forcing him to look at me. "You gave up your life for me. Who could possibly be more deserving of my love than you, Yoshido?"

His head jerked up. "You—you remember?"

I smiled. "Everything."

His eyes widened. "And you forgive me for failing you?"

I slid my hands over his shoulders and laced them behind his neck. "Let go, Kim," I whispered. "Let responsibility lie where it falls. Zeami was the sole person responsible for our deaths."

Kim's eyes fell to the floor.

I ducked to meet his gaze. "Would you like to know what you are responsible for?"

He waited.

"You, Kim, are responsible for the way my breath catches in my throat when you walk into the room."

His face softened.

I continued. "You are responsible for the way my pulse races when I watch you smile. You are responsible for the heat that burns through my skin when you touch it, and you are responsible for the ache in my heart when you're not around."

He smiled and ran his hands gently through my hair. "If I have already given you my heart, what more would you have from me?"

I pressed my face against the curve of his neck, inhaling the warm scent of him. "I would like to keep you, Kim Gimhae."

His arms pressed me closer until I could no longer tell where I ended and he began. "Then I'm yours, Rileigh Martin. From this life into the next."

A voice cleared behind us and I reluctantly pulled back

from Kim's arms to find Dr. Wendell dressed in a lab coat and clutching a clipboard.

"You!" I cried, sliding my legs back into ready position and bringing my arms up to fight. "You better have a good explanation for being here!"

Dr. Wendell's eyes grew large as he took a step back. "Kim, a little help?"

Kim slid an arm around my waist, anchoring me in place. "Relax, Rileigh."

"Relax?" I thrashed against him until he was forced to secure his other arm around me as well. "How can I relax, Kim? This guy is a Noppera-bō!"

"Noppera-bō?" Dr. Wendell smiled. "I'm afraid you have it all wrong, Rileigh. I work for the Network."

I looked to Kim for confirmation and he nodded, letting his arms slide free of my waist. "Why didn't you tell me?" I asked Kim.

"I didn't know until we arrived here with you," he answered.

I felt sick to my stomach. If Dr. Wendell worked for the Network, then what did that mean for my mom? Was he even interested? Or were the dinners and flowers just an excuse to get closer to me?

"I'm sorry I couldn't tell you sooner," Dr. Wendell said. "My objective was classified until we flushed the Noppera-bō out."

"Your *objective?*" I said.

He smiled. "As your handler. I've been assigned to train you in your new position with the Network."

I narrowed my eyes. "I don't remember *accepting* a position with the Network."

"Er, well . . . " Dr. Wendell dropped his gaze to his clipboard. "Of course you'll want to join. The Network is an elite organization. Only the best of the best are employed." When I remained silent his voice took on a pleading quality. "With your skills, think of all the evil you can stop."

"Right now I'm only thinking about making sure my mom is okay, finding a place to stay, and finishing my senior year." I folded my arms.

Dr. Wendell looked to Kim. "Talk some sense into her. You were her superior once—*order* her if you have to."

Kim snorted. "I led our band of samurai with trust and respect. If my troops are so unwilling to do something that I am forced to use orders, then I have failed as a leader."

"This is ridiculous." Dr. Wendell turned back to me. "You can't be seriously considering turning down a position with us."

Kim chuckled. "Rileigh is *always* serious."

Dr. Wendell threw his arms in the air. "You know what? Let's not worry about the Network right now. You've been through quite an ordeal, so let's do a quick examination to make sure everything checks out."

"Sure thing." I thought about how happy my mom seemed lately. If Dr. Wendell was only using her, well, I'd make his life miserable—starting now. "As long as you don't touch me."

Dr. Wendell tossed his clipboard into the air and left

the room with his shoulders hunched, muttering obscenities under his breath.

Even after getting rejected, the Network was kind enough to provide me with new jeans, a plain white T-shirt, and tennis shoes for my departure, which was a good thing considering all of my clothes were ash. My emotions were stretched in a game of tug-of-war where part of me wanted to mourn the loss of my shoe collection while the other half thought the idea of crying over footwear was ridiculous. Clearly, even after transcending, I had some issues to work out.

Quentin's parents agreed to let me stay with them until Debbie and I found a new place to live. I'd spoken to her briefly on Quentin's cell phone and he was right: she was a mess of sobs and shrieks. Debbie may never be in the running for mother of the year, but she was all I had, and I loved her. Her hotel was my next destination after I made one final stop.

I nudged open the door, which led into another futuristic hospital room, identical to the one I left. Michelle looked up from talking with Braden and met my eyes. Her smile illuminated the already painfully vivid room. "Rileigh!" Her voice sounded like a cat had clawed its way up her throat.

Braden stood from the chair by her bed. "Hey, Rileigh." His smile was etched with pain. I understood. You could never be truly happy when the person you loved lay in a hospital, especially a secret underground government hospital. "I think I'll grab a soda. Be right back."

I nodded as he passed me by on his way out the door.

"I'm so glad you're okay," Michelle said. "Is it true? Did you really transcend?"

"Let's see." I walked over to her side and sat in Braden's abandoned chair. "Yorimichi." I opened my eyes and looked at her. "You composed haiku on parchment you kept under your sleeping mat."

Her eyes widened. "You knew about that?"

"Braden—who used to be Kiyomori—had a scar on his right shoulder from the time Lord Toyotomi's monkey bit him."

Michelle giggled. "He hated that monkey. He's got a birthmark on his arm where it happened."

"And then there's Drew, otherwise known as Seiko." I smiled. "He would celebrate each victory with sake."

Michelle clapped her hands together. "He still does!" She leaned her head against her pillow as if drained from her burst of excitement, bringing back the image to my mind of her lying motionless on my couch.

I shivered and tried to mask the movement by reaching for her hand. It felt cool and sticky, like a lump of sushi rolled in seaweed. "How are you feeling?"

Michelle frowned and closed her eyes. "Well, they say I lost a lot of blood, but I'm still alive, so that's saying something." She gave my hand a weak squeeze before sliding it under the sheets. "I don't… it's just hard to talk about, you know?"

I nodded, even though her eyes stayed closed.

Michelle cracked open an eye. "Is everything all right with you? You seem… I don't know, quiet."

I shrugged and stood up. "I guess. I just thought that when I transcended, I wouldn't still feel at conflict with myself. I thought I'd either be taken over completely by Senshi or I'd get rid of her all together. But instead, the old me has been thrown together with the new me and they're not mixing so well, you know? Like oil and water."

Michelle opened both eyes and smiled. "We've all been there. I can only tell you that it'll get easier."

I sighed. "That's a relief. It's not easy having two conflicting thoughts going on in my head at the same time. So how does it happen? Do I just have to give it time?"

"No." She yawned and sank back into her pillow, closing her eyes. "You have to choose."

"Choose what?"

"Who you want to be."

I grunted. "Choose who I want to be? I'm seventeen. Even if I didn't have the memories of a past life, I still wouldn't know that."

Michelle answered, and the words were long and low, pulled down by the sleep sucking her in. "I never said it would be easy."

"It never is," I murmured back, knowing she was too far gone to hear. I gave her a quick hug before leaving the room. I knew it would be difficult figuring out how to balance my senior year with my life as a samurai. But it wasn't impossible. Between homework assignments and past-life memories, dojos and skate parks, swords and lip gloss, I would find myself. As Lord Toyotomi always said, "A journey is just a walk without a destination in mind."

I smiled as I followed the neon exit signs through a maze of white corridors. It amazed me how easily the memories now came. How they sprouted like seeds inside my mind, growing into something I could almost brush my fingers across.

I turned another corner and stopped when I saw Kim waiting at the end of the hall. It still felt like a dream. He grinned and my pulse fluttered, reminding me that it wasn't. I walked up to him and slid my hand inside of his waiting one. It felt like I'd been gone forever and I'd finally made it home. It didn't matter that my house was burned, that my things were ash. What mattered most was that we were together, even if it did take a lifetime.

Kim raised an eyebrow, as if trying to read my thoughts. "Ready to go?"

"Lead the way."

He pushed the steel door open with his shoulder, but waited for me to go first. I kept hold of his hand as I crossed in front of him and stepped outside—where my new life waited.

The End.

Photo by Kyle Weber

About the Author

When Cole Gibsen isn't writing she can be found shaking her booty in a zumba class, picking off her nail polish, or drinking straight from the jug (when no one is looking). Cole currently resides in the Greater St. Louis area with her husband, daughter, and one very cranky border collie.